DUTCH RIVER

A WALTER HUDSON MYSTERY

CHARLES AYER

outskirtspress

DENVER, COLORADO

Dutch River
A Walter Hudson Mystery
All Rights Reserved.

Outskirts Press, Inc.
http://www.outskirtspress.com

ISBN: 978-1-4787-4054-4

Library of Congress Control Number: 2016910693

Outskirts Press and the "OP" logo are trademarks belonging to Outskirts Press, Inc.

PRINTED IN THE UNITED STATES OF AMERICA

ACKNOWLEDGMENTS

I spent almost forty years of my life in the rough and tumble world of corporate finance, and I thought that anything I pursued after that would be a relative piece of cake. That's what I get for thinking.

Publishing a book, no matter how you go about it, and regardless of what its ultimate rewards may or may not be, can be a brutal experience. I've needed a lot of help along the way.

First, I'd like to thank the entire team at Outskirts Press. I don't know most of their names, but everyone, from the pre-production team to the cover design artists and the layout specialists, has been professional, helpful, and supportive. In particular, I'd like to thank the long-suffering Lisa Jones, without whom I would have been reduced to a warm puddle of unpublished anxiety long ago. Thanks again, Lisa.

As usual, I'd like to thank my sisters, Becky Lennahan and Susan Ayer, my brother, John, and his wife Jan, and my dear friends Dave and Barbara Grigg for their continued advice and support.

Finally, I'd like to thank the person to whom this book is dedicated: my wife Claudia. My decision to abandon the corporate world, and my thick-skulled determination to turn myself into a novelist, a dubious undertaking at best, affected her life as profoundly as it did mine. She never complained, although there were times she should have, and she has steadfastly stood by me as I walked down a lonely road in the uncertain light of evening. So, no matter what else this book is, it will always be...

For Claudia

ALSO BY CHARLES AYER

Placid Hollow
A Deadly Light

PROLOGUE

H E FELT LIKE A HEEL LYING TO HER, but, sadly, there was
nothing to be done about it. And the Hotel Grenadier in Midtown
Manhattan was as good a place as any for dishonesty, he thought distract-
edly, as he regarded the woman who had slipped silently into the room
and taken a seat opposite him on the edge of the large bed that dominated
the small, dowdy room on the third floor.

"The usual deluxe accommodations, I see," she said, casting her eyes
around the room. Many would call her attractive; most men would doubt-
lessly call her desirable; but few would call her beautiful. She was dressed
modestly in a raw silk blouse and gabardine slacks.

The Grenadier had, in fact, seen better days, though it still maintained a certain toothless allure, its windows looking out over Seventh
Avenue with the jaundiced aspect of the world-weary septuagenarian that
it was, winking warily at the lower class of clientele that nowadays sought
its hospitality.

But allure wasn't what the woman had come here for, and neither had
the man, who was sitting in one of the room's two chairs. He was dressed
casually in a pink cotton shirt and a pair of Levis, holding the day's edition
of the *New York Post* in his hands. He was clearly older than the woman,
but he took good care of himself, and his hair was still thick and dark.

"And good afternoon to you, too, Estralita," said the man to the woman, putting down the newspaper on the table beside the chair.

"Why do you always call me that when you know I hate it?"

"Because it's a beautiful name. Don't you like being called a little
star?"

"Not so much," she said. "And how do you find these places, anyway?"

"Oh, it's not that difficult in this city. The Hotel Grenadier was actually once a fine hotel. Sadly, these days its only virtues are its devotion to
its guests' privacy and its willingness to accept cash."

"And luckily you have plenty of cash, don't you, Marty."

"Yes, yes I do."

"I trust your trip down from Boston was uneventful," said Estralita as she handed him a set of car keys and a valet parking ticket. The man had, according to long habit, driven down to New York that morning.

"It's hard for that trip to be anything but uneventful," said the man, in turn handing the woman a set of keys and a valet ticket for a car of the exact same make, model, year, and color as the one whose keys the woman had just handed him. "But the foliage this time of year is beautiful, so I can't complain."

"You stopped for your usual lunch, I assume."

"Of course I did. A corned beef and Swiss cheese sandwich and a full sour pickle at Rein's Deli is the only thing worth stopping for in Connecticut. I love their mustard. And Vernon's not a bad little town, as little towns go."

"You're so funny. You never stay at the same hotel, but you always eat at the same place."

"There's nothing funny about it. People who work at hotels remember faces; waiters at crowded restaurants don't. They're all friendly and competent, but it's always busy, and the only thing they're concentrating on is fast service and getting the next customers seated. And besides, I only stop at Rein's twice a year. I'm not a regular."

"If you say so."

"Don't worry about it; I know what I'm doing."

"Let's hope so. I take it that, as usual, you don't want to check the contents I've delivered?"

"No need," said Marty, sitting forward slightly. "I know what I'm getting. You folks have always been honest, and this has all worked out well enough for everyone, hasn't it? It's never been in anyone's interest to cheat anyone else."

"I guess you're right," said the woman. "Why kill the goose that lays the golden eggs, right?"

"That's right," said Marty. He paused and then said, "I was sorry to hear the news from your end."

"We were all sorry," said Estralita, "but we don't see any reason why that should change anything."

"That's good to hear."

"Don't worry. You have nothing to worry about."

"Good," said the man. "Now, I've arranged for dinner and a show this evening. I hope you won't be too tired to enjoy it."

"Oh, Marty, that sounds great," said Estralita, after hearing where they'd be dining and the show they'd be going to see. "You know how much I enjoy our evenings out." By necessity, the restaurant was unrenowned and in a less-than-trendy neighborhood, and the show was Off-Off-Broadway, but still, this was New York City.

"And we both know how much I enjoy our afternoons in," said the man, an expectant smile lighting up his face, making him look almost boyish.

"How could I forget?" said the woman, smiling back. She rose and slowly began to unbutton her blouse. "You're not too tired, right?"

"I always make sure I'm well rested for our visits, Estralita," said the man, unbuttoning his shirt even as the inevitable spasm of guilt clutched him. He loved his wife deeply and had never been even remotely unfaithful, not even an innocent flirtation, with any other woman. Except this one. He puzzled over it constantly, but he concluded that nothing about these once-a-year meetings had anything to do with who he really was, so he let go of the thought and directed his attention to the young woman.

"I always wondered, Marty, if you had to choose, would you give up our little time together or your lunches at Rein's?" said the woman as her brassiere fell to the floor. She had a voluptuous body, and she let herself enjoy the man's hungry gaze.

"Maybe it's better for both of us if we never have to find out," said the man, as he tossed his slacks on the chair.

The woman laughed throatily. "Perhaps you're right," she said as she fell on the bed beside him. "Perhaps you're right."

She felt like a heel lying to him, especially while they both had their clothes off, but, sadly, there was nothing to be done about it.

1

"I NEVER HEARD OF THE PLACE," said NYPD Detective Lieutenant Walter Hudson to his wife, Sarah, as they stood in the small kitchen of their modest home in Fresh Meadows, Queens. Sarah was holding a torn envelope in one hand and a typewritten letter in the other.

"It's upstate," said Sarah.

"What does that mean, Westchester County?" said Walter. Geography had never been one of his strong suits in school and, like most New York City natives, he vaguely understood that the world came to an end somewhere just north of Yonkers.

"Idiot," said Sarah. She was dwarfed by her six-foot-four husband and weighed less than half his 240 pounds, but she hadn't for a moment in her life been intimidated by the big cop. "It's a lot farther north than that."

"How much farther?" asked Walter, a grin beginning to spread across his broad face as he combed an enormous hand through his thick, unruly dark hair.

"You know, a lot farther," said Sarah, her olive complexion reddening.

"I'm glad we straightened that out," said Walter, his grin widening as he headed out of the kitchen.

"Where are you going?" said Sarah, following him.

"Well, since we've now established that neither of us knows a blessed thing about New York State geography, I'm going to look this place up on the computer. What's it called again?"

"It's called 'Dutch River,' wise guy."

"Okay, let's see what we can find out," said Walter as he sat down at their PC and started punching keys. His work required him to do a lot of typing, and his thick fingers tapped swiftly on the keys.

They both stared at the screen, wide-eyed, as a map of New York State appeared.

"I guess I'd forgotten how big this state was," said Sarah, as she pulled her shoulder-length brunette hair away from her face with one hand.

"I'm not sure I ever knew."

"So, where's Dutch River?"

"Right here," said Walter, "where this red dot is, just south of Albany and east of the river."

"Is that the Dutch River?"

"It's the Hudson River, Sarah. Come on, you've got to keep up here."

"It is not. You're just saying that to see if you can fool me."

"It is, too. Look," said Walter as he punched a key and the image zoomed in. "See, it says right there, 'Hudson River.'"

"Okay, so just this once you're right," said Sarah as she leaned in closer to the screen. Walter turned his head and gave her a quick kiss on the cheek. Sarah smacked him playfully on the back of his head and said, "Cut it out, you."

"You want to fool around before the girls get home from school?"

"No, I certainly do not want to 'fool around.' You make it sound like we're still in high school."

"You haven't changed a bit since then, you know," said Walter as his arm encircled her small waist.

"You're just saying that to get me out of my clothes."

"Of course I am," he said, nuzzling her neck.

"Well, it's not going to work," said Sarah, making a halfhearted effort to get away from him, "and besides, Daniel's going to wake up any minute."

"No he's not," said Walter, standing up from his seat at the computer. "I just checked on him, and he's sound asleep."

"Walter, this is serious. We really need to spend some time looking into it," said Sarah, casting a helpless glance back at the computer.

"You're damn right it's serious," he said as he picked her up in his arms as if she weighed nothing. "I'm working the night shift tonight, and I'm not sure you're going to be able to bear the wait until I get home. I don't want you to suffer any deprivation, you know."

"You're a fool," said Sarah, but her mouth was already searching for his.

"What was the name of that place again?" said Walter as they collapsed together on the bed.

"What place?" said Sarah, reaching for a button on her big husband's shirt.

2

"I DON'T GET IT," said Walter. "It's the Hudson River that runs by it, right?"

"That's right, but don't forget that the entire Hudson River valley was settled by the Dutch," said Leviticus Welles between bites of his pastrami and Swiss cheese sandwich. He and Walter had met for lunch along with Sarah and Levi's wife, Julie Remy, at the Ninth Avenue Deli, which was just around the block from the Midtown South precinct house where Walter worked. Levi was an unprepossessing looking man of about fifty, with a slight build and thinning gray hair cropped close, but he had a razor-sharp mind and a rare gift for languages. He worked for the NYPD's Intelligence Division, and he and Walter had developed a close personal and professional bond after working together to solve two major cases. Although he'd worked for the NYPD for less than two years and had previously been an unemployed salesman, it was already rumored that it was only a matter of time before he ran the division.

"But wasn't Henry Hudson English?" said Walter, as he polished off his Reuben and started on his fries and half-sour pickle.

"Yes, but he sailed for the Dutch, and the Dutch controlled this entire area until the English squeezed them out," said Levi. "Many of the famous Hudson River Valley families, like the Roosevelts and the Vanderbilts, were of Dutch extraction."

"President Martin Van Buren was from upstate New York, wasn't he?" said Sarah.

"Yes, he was," said Levi. "He was born in a little town called Kinderhook, which is actually just down the road from Dutch River. He was the only U.S. president who was a non-native English speaker. His native language was Dutch, and he spoke English with a heavy accent."

"Smarty-pants," said Walter, grinning at Sarah.

"So, anyway," said Julie, as she polished off her grilled pastrami on rye, "tell us more about this house that you've inherited." Julie, like Sarah, was a small woman. She was in her mid-forties, but she didn't look it, with a pale complexion and thick, curly, strawberry-blond hair that belied her North African *pied-noir* heritage. She also had an enormous appetite for a woman so small, and she easily finished her thick sandwich as Levi struggled with his.

"It's an old farmhouse on fifty acres of land in Columbia County, which is right near Albany, the state capital," said Sarah as she looked out onto busy Ninth Avenue and tried to imagine what fifty acres of land looked like. She was a city girl, and she understood spaces in square feet, not acres.

"Were you close to this great-uncle who left it to you?" said Levi.

"Not at all. He was my father's uncle on his mother's side. I only met him once when he came down for a family wedding. I think I was maybe seven years old, and I barely remember him. He was a bachelor and pretty much of a recluse, and he almost never left his farm."

"So why did he leave it to you?" said Julie.

"It's hard to tell. He never wanted to leave it while he was alive, so he never sold it, and I'm one of his few living relatives."

"But your father's still alive, isn't he?" said Levi.

"Yes, he is," said Sarah, "which makes this all a little puzzling, although you'd have to stick a rifle in my father's back and threaten to shoot to get him out of Queens. He considers the Bronx a foreign country."

"It isn't?" said Walter.

"Idiot."

"Did he say anything in his will about his reasons?" said Julie.

"I don't think so," said Sarah. "I got a letter from his attorney inviting me to the reading of the will next Tuesday, but as far as I can tell, all the will says is that the farmhouse, the outbuildings, the surrounding land, and 'all the property and belongings on the property, whether or not they are known at the time of the reading of the will,' all belong to me. And of course there's the letter from my uncle that I mentioned to you."

"Do you have the letter with you?" said Levi.

"Yes, I have it right here," said Sarah, reaching into her purse. "Do you want me to read it to you?"

"Sure."

"OK, here it is. It's dated about three months ago."

"That's interesting," said Levi. "I wonder if he knew he was dying."

"I don't know if we're ever going to find that out," said Sarah. "Anyway, it's handwritten so this may go slowly. It says,"

Dear Sarah,

I haven't seen you since you were a little girl, and if you remember me at all it's probably only a vague recollection, so it has probably come as a surprise to you to be informed that you have inherited my farm.

Being a city girl, particularly one who is married to an NYPD detective, I'm sure that your first inclination will be to sell the place. It is now your property to do with as you please, and I won't blame you if you do. You will probably be surprised to find out how much it's worth, and I'm sure you will put the proceeds from the sale to good use, especially as I understand that you now have three children. Being a bachelor, I have no direct knowledge of such matters, but I have been told on good authority that parenthood is an expensive undertaking these days.

However, I do hope that you will not do so, at least not right away. I believe that you and your husband, who, I have been told, is a fine detective, will find spending some time on the farm and getting to know it a fascinating and rewarding experience. I'm willing to bet you've never seen the inside of a barn before!

Whatever you choose to do, I wish you and your family good fortune and all of God's blessings.

Your great-uncle,
Armin August Jaeger

"'Yay,' not 'Jay,'" said Levi.

"What?" said Sarah.

"Germans pronounce a 'j' like a 'y,' so his name is pronounced 'Yayger.' It means 'hunter' in German, and it's a very common name. And whoever gave him his given names had a sense of humor."

"What do you mean?" said Walter, never tiring of Levi's tidbits of trivia.

"'Armin,' who is known in history by his Latinized name, 'Arminius,' was the German general who routed Augustus Caesar's Legions in the Teutoburg Forest about the time Christ was born. That defeat preserved a distinct Germanic culture and changed European history forever."

"So he was German, not Dutch?" said Walter.

"Yes," said Sarah, "I knew at least that much. You know that I'm half Sicilian from my mother's side, but my father's side is a little more complicated. But my grandmother, Dad's mother, was German. I at least knew that."

"When did that part of your family come to America?" said Julie.

"I think they're the only part of my family that's been here a long time. They've been here since before the Revolution. But I remember Grandma telling me that they all still spoke German at home. Grandma always had a little bit of a German accent when she talked."

"Wow," said Julie. "So how long has your family owned the farm?"

"I never really knew, but the lawyer who called me said it's been in the family since the 1700s, and that they used to own a lot more land, maybe 500 acres."

"I didn't know you were descended from landed gentry," said Walter.

"Do I *look* like landed gentry?" said Sarah.

"No, you look too—" said Walter, cutting himself off as Sarah glared at him and Levi and Julie smiled from across the table.

"So, are you going up there next week for the reading of the will?" said Levi.

"I guess I should," said Sarah. "Walter can't get the time off, but I think I can get there and back in a day as long as things wrap up early, and as long as the car doesn't break down along the way." Walter and Sarah had recently bought a used car to replace the one that had finally broken down completely, but their budget was limited, and they were already having trouble with it.

"Would you like some company?" said Julie. "I've been looking for a reason to get away from the consulate for a couple of days. It might be a nice break for me, and we could take my car. I never drive it, and it could probably use a good, long trip." Julie worked at the United Nations embassy of a small but wealthy Arabian Gulf state, where her fluent Arabic and French, along with her diplomatic gifts, were highly valued.

"That would be terrific," said Sarah, without a second's hesitation. "The idea of making that long trip to a strange place by myself has been giving me the willies."

"And you'll be able to ride in a late-model Mercedes instead of our ten-year-old Saturn," said Walter. Julie had been left independently wealthy by a former employer, an Arab sheikh whose family she had saved from disgrace.

"OK, then," said Julie, as she finished off the last of her fries, "it's a plan. What time do you want me to swing by your house to pick you up on Tuesday morning?"

"It'll be a lot easier if I take the Seven Train into Grand Central and you can pick me up there, say about eight? The reading of the will isn't until one o'clock, but I have no idea how long it's going to take to get there."

"Sounds perfect," said Julie, "Tuesday at eight it is."

3

"And this is good old Boston
The home of the bean and the cod,
Where the Lowells talk only to Cabots
And the Cabots talk only to God."

A ND THE SEWALLS EXPECT GOD TO SPEAK WHEN SPO-
KEN TO, thought Charles Martin Sewall, the early autumn sun
shining down on him like a blessing as he left Rein's deli the next day and
climbed into the nondescript Mercedes-Benz E-Class he had exchanged
for its identical twin in New York. He was the current scion of the Boston
Brahmin family whose earliest American descendant, Ebenezer Sewall,
was the first Pilgrim to set foot on Plymouth Rock, no matter what the
history books said. The Sewalls were the arbiters of their own history.

Martin, as he was known to his family and a few privileged friends, lived
with his wife, Abby, also a Mayflower descendant, in the Beacon Hill town
house the Sewalls had called "home" for three hundred years; and one day
their son, currently attending Harvard Law School as had generations of
Sewalls before him, would occupy it and raise his own family there, an out-
come as predictable as the tides of Boston Harbor. It was a comfortable life.

Comfortable now, perhaps, thought Martin, but he had been obliged to con-
front uncomfortable challenges his forebears had never had to face. Irresponsible
investments by the family's financial managers and, he was ashamed to admit,
his own carelessness, had left the family nearly destitute in the wake of the Great
Recession, a fact known only to Martin and the family attorney.

So Martin had taken action, action that his ancestors would have considered unthinkable. But the only thing that was unthinkable to Martin would
have been for the Sewall family to lose not only its fortune, but something far
more important than money: its place in Boston Society. He owed it to his
wife, his children, his ancestors, and his descendants not to let that happen.

At first he had been frightened and ashamed, but those feelings had
faded and been rapidly replaced by satisfaction, even pride, as the family

balance sheet had been restored to its rightful prosperity. He had done his duty: no more, no less.

But he had not stopped there. Why should he? The world was a different place now, and the family's once impressive multimillion-dollar fortune had seemed paltry compared to those being accumulated by people who hadn't even rid themselves of their foreign accents, people with no breeding, who had no place in proper society. It was just wrong, and Martin had seen no reason not to right that wrong.

Abby had been too thrilled to concern herself with the source of this newfound wealth. She was now not just a member of one of Boston's Great Families; she was a Great Benefactress, a woman without whose attendance no fundraising banquet or ball was considered a complete success. She had hired a full-time social secretary and her own personal driver. She gave intimate dinners at the Beacon Hill town house that were the most sought after invitations in Boston. This, she knew, had been her destiny, her birthright, and how she had suddenly achieved that destiny was part of God's greater plan and not for her to worry about.

Martin truly loved his wife. She was a remarkable, attractive woman. Their marriage was the foundation of everything that was important in his life, and with the exception of his annual infidelity with Estralita, he had been completely, happily faithful to her during their long and successful life partnership. By nature he didn't have a wandering eye, and he had to admit that he didn't find Estralita all that attractive or interesting, especially compared to Abby; but he also knew that it had little to do with her. These trips to New York, these isolated twenty-four hours out of the long year, were the fleeting moments in his life when he allowed himself to escape the burden of being the scion of the Sewall family, the brief emotional holiday when he shrugged the heavy mantle of his family's history from his shoulders and basked naked in the sunshine of boyish irresponsibility. But it wasn't really who he was, and he knew it. Besides, he liked who he was. It was good to be a Sewall.

So Martin looked forward to getting home. His work would be completed in a few short days, in time for Abby to announce their gift to Massachusetts General Hospital to fund the construction of the new Women's Health Wing, now to be named the Abby Sewall Institute for Women. Yes, life was good, he thought, as he pulled back on to Route 84.

He felt the first tingling in the tips of his toes as he crossed the border into Massachusetts.

4

"**I** HATE TO ASK YOU THIS, BUT DO YOU THINK YOU COULD DRIVE?" said Julie as Sarah opened the passenger-side door of Julie's metallic black Mercedes-Benz 550SL two-door roadster. It was sleek and low and looked like it was going 100 sitting still. "I'm not sure I can handle this little monster."

"Sure," said Sarah, walking around to the other side of the car, "no problem." Sarah had seen Julie come lurching down Forty-second Street, barely missing two other cars and at least one pedestrian, and she had begun to wonder how they were ever going to make it to Dutch River in one piece. In addition, Sarah loved driving fast cars, a trait she had inherited from her father. She was an excellent driver, but after her fourth speeding ticket on the Southern State Parkway in her father's vintage GTO before she turned twenty-one, he had taken her keys from her, and she'd had little opportunity to drive since then. Having the unexpected opportunity to drive a car like this one made her heart beat a little faster.

She made herself comfortable in the exquisitely contoured black leather driver's seat that made her feel like Walter had his hand on her behind and took a few seconds to check out the controls while Julie fiddled with the GPS system.

"OK," said Julie, "this thing says that the fastest way to Dutch River is on the Thruway, but that the most scenic route is the Taconic Parkway."

"Then we'll take the Taconic."

"Why? I thought you'd be in a hurry to get there."

"I am, but 'scenic' usually means a lot of hills and dips and curves, and this little puppy looks like it wants to go for a run. I'm pretty sure we'll get there in plenty of time. You got your seat belt on?"

"Yes."

"Good."

"JESUS," said Julie, "I feel like I need a cigarette. I think that's the most fun I've ever had in my life besides sex."

"I know," said Sarah, laughing. "After this, Walter's going to have to up his game."

They'd made the trip in two hours flat, despite the usual delays getting off Manhattan Island. Sarah knew she could have done better, but she didn't want to ruin her time, and her bank account, by getting a speeding ticket, though she had hit a couple of curves at 95. The foliage along the Taconic had been stunning, but neither if them had really noticed it.

They'd parked the car on Main Street, apparently the only major thoroughfare in Dutch River. The street was lined for three blocks on both sides with brick buildings, all of them three or four stories tall. About a third of them looked empty.

"Where's the lawyer's office?" said Julie.

"I don't know," said Sarah, peering out the window, "but I'm willing to bet it's a couple of blocks either way from here. Anyway, it's only a little after ten, and the reading isn't until one, so let's poke around a little, then find someplace to have a cup of coffee and maybe something to eat."

"Sounds like a good idea."

The little town didn't have a lot to offer a couple of city girls, but they were surprised to find a tastefully stocked women's apparel store named "Margie's Essentials" where Julie bought a blouse and Sarah purchased a scarf. The proprietor of the store, the eponymous Margie, was friendly in a way that they initially found disconcerting; Manhattan store managers kept their distance until they saw money on the counter.

Margie, a small, middle-aged woman with a thin but not unfriendly face, told them that Dutch River had once been a thriving depot town where barges from New York City on their way to Buffalo along the Erie Canal had docked and unloaded farm equipment and dry goods for the local farms, which were numerous and prosperous.

"Now, of course, things have changed," she said, as she busied herself with rearranging items on the shelves for no apparent reason. "There aren't that many working farms left, and the ones still operating are just hanging on by a thread. The children who would have inherited them are all leaving. A lot of the old farms have been converted to Bed & Breakfast places, but now there are too many of them and half of them have gone broke."

"We couldn't help noticing a lot of empty storefronts along Main Street," said Sarah.

"It's sad, isn't it?" said Margie. "Things were bad enough before the Recession, and then they just got worse. But for most of us, this is the only place we've ever called home, so we keep trying to hang on."

"No new industries are interested in coming to this area?" said Julie. "It's such a lovely place."

"New industries don't come looking at places like Dutch River. Mostly we rely on folks like you, who are passing through on their way somewhere else and stop here to find a bite to eat. And sometimes they poke their heads into the stores looking for antiques. We're a little busier in the summer, but not much. Where are you folks headed? It's a little late for the racing season at Saratoga, isn't it?"

"We're actually headed right here," said Sarah. "It seems that I inherited my great-uncle's farm, and we're up here for the reading of the will this afternoon. But from the sound of it, I won't be owning it for too long."

"Which farm would that be?" said Margie.

"My great-uncle was Armin Jaeger," said Sarah.

"Oh dear," said Margie, "you won't have any trouble selling that place."

"Well, that's good news, but why do you think that? After what you've told us, I would have guessed that I'd have a terrible time selling it."

"Oh, it's just an awfully nice piece of property, that's all. If any place is going to sell quickly around here, it'll be the Jaeger farm. But I have to say it'll be a sad day for our little town if you do sell it. The Jaegers were one of the founding families, and Dutch River will never be the same once the family is finally gone."

"Did you know my great-uncle?"

"Not really," said Margie. "He taught Sunday school when I was a child, but I've only met him a couple of times since then. He almost never left the farm. But nobody ever took it as unfriendliness, and we were all heartbroken to hear of his passing."

"I know that he was pretty old when he died," said Sarah. "Are there many people left in town who might have known him?"

"Not that I know of. Like I said, it wasn't that he was old as much as he pretty much kept to himself."

"Was he always like that?" said Sarah. She didn't really know why she was asking. She'd never known the man in his lifetime, and the farm that she'd inherited from him was beginning to feel more like an albatross around her neck than a gift. She was starting to worry that just unloading the place would be, at best, a breakeven proposition.

"Oh, probably. Farmers are like that, and Armin was a farmer to the bone," said Margie. "All I know is nobody thought that he'd ever die. He was just always going to be here, you know?"

"Look, I know this was difficult," said Sarah, "but thanks for talking to us about him. It helps me feel like I know him, at least a little bit, now."

"You're welcome," said Margie. "I do hope you folks don't sell the farm too soon. It'd be nice to get to know you a little bit."

"Well, we'd like to get to know you better, too, but we're not exactly farm people."

"Oh, I understand. It's nice to see some new faces, is all."

"Just one last favor," said Julie, "do you think you could direct us to a place where we could grab a quick lunch? We should probably eat before we go to the reading of the will."

"Sure," said Margie, "just turn right when you leave the store. There's a little place called Avery's right down the block. You can't miss it."

They had obviously been able to miss it once, since that was just about where they'd parked the car, but all the storefronts were so nondescript that Sarah didn't find that at all surprising. They paid for their purchases, thanking Margie as they walked out the door.

"That was kind of sad," said Julie as soon as they were out on the sidewalk.

"Yeah, it was," said Sarah, "but it was at least nice to know that my great-uncle was well-liked."

"But it doesn't sound like it's going to change your mind about selling the farm."

"Oh, Julie," said Sarah, "I know my great-uncle wanted us to hold on to it, at least for a little while, and perhaps I should honor the gift by respecting his wishes, but what are Walter and I ever going to do with a farm, for heaven's sake? Neither of us knows the back end of a cow from the front end of a taxicab."

"Well, either way, you shouldn't make a big decision like that on an empty stomach," said Julie as they arrived at the entrance to Avery's. "I don't know what this place has to offer, but I don't see anything else nearby, and it's not like either one of us is a picky eater."

5

AVERY'S WAS LAID OUT IN CLASSIC DINER FASHION: a counter with stools on the right as they entered and booths on the left. It looked clean and well kept although, just as at Margie's boutique, they were the only patrons. The booths were well upholstered with a heavy cotton fabric, not the cracked plastic that they had expected to find, and they looked hardly used. They took a booth about halfway down, and a man who looked to be in his thirties with thick blond hair that made his head look too big for his slight frame immediately arrived to offer them menus and asked them if they would like something to drink.

"We have a fully stocked bar," he said, pointing to rows of alcoholic beverage bottles lining the wall behind the counter, "but we only serve alcoholic beverages accompanied by a meal order. We're a restaurant, not a bar."

"I think we'll both stick with iced tea," said Sarah, with Julie nodding her agreement, "but thank you anyway."

"No problem," said the waiter. "I'll be back in a few minutes with your drinks and to take your orders. You'll see that we have an extensive menu. By the way, my name is Adam, and I'm the chef and owner. And today, I'll also be your waiter."

"So are you Adam Avery, then?" said Julie.

"Yes, I am, ma'am, but the restaurant isn't named after me; it's named after my grandfather. He started the place when he got back from the war, and it's been in the family ever since."

"Would that have been World War II?" said Julie.

"Yes, ma'am. He fought with General Patton in Germany."

"So he must have been about the same age as my great-uncle, Armin Jaeger," said Sarah. "Do you know if they were friendly?"

"Oh, so you're relatives of old Armin, then."

"Well, I am," said Sarah. "By the way, my name is Sarah Hudson, and this is my friend, Julie Remy."

"It's a pleasure to meet you both," said Adam with a smile. "Armin's passing was a big loss for us here, but I really wouldn't know if the two men ever knew each other all that well. Your great-uncle pretty much stayed on the farm, and Granddad's been in a nursing home for quite a few years now. I'm afraid I don't visit him as much as I should. I hate to admit it, but I never really knew him that well. I'll be right back with your drinks, okay?"

Adam headed back to the kitchen and Julie and Sarah perused the menu. In addition to the standard diner fare, they were surprised to see a wide variety of fresh salads, homemade soups, and even locally caught seafood and wild game offerings.

"You know," said Julie, "I was going to order a burger and fries, but I think I'm going to try the trout meunière."

"And I'm going to try the breast of chicken in white wine sauce."

"We may live to regret this, you know."

"What's life without regrets?"

"I guess I'd like to know," said Julie, a bit ruefully.

Adam returned and smiled as he took their orders. "May I suggest a cup of our fresh tomato bisque as an appetizer?" he said. "I made it from tomatoes I bought from a local farmer just this morning, and I top it with a dollop of fresh sour cream that I buy from a local dairy."

"That sounds great," said both women in unison.

"And I don't mean to be pushy, but I have a wonderful bottle of '05 Pouilly-Fuissé already chilled that would nicely complement the meals you've ordered." Julie was surprised to hear Adam pronounce the difficult French vowels perfectly.

Sarah stared at Julie, a puzzled expression on her face.

"It's a very nice white wine from northern France," said Julie, "and Adam is right, it would go beautifully with both our meals."

"I'm not sure that we could drink a whole bottle by ourselves," said Sarah.

"But won't it be fun to try?" said Julie, a mischievous smile lighting her face as she turned to Adam and said, "That sounds wonderful."

The meals arrived shortly, and the women were astonished at the expert preparation that went into them. And Sarah, whose experience with wine was limited to the jug wines at the local pizzeria, was amazed at the subtle yet deep flavor of the Pouilly-Fuissé.

"Adam," said Sarah when he returned to their table to clear the dishes, "please don't take this the wrong way, but that food was not what we expected. Where did you learn to cook like that?"

"No offense taken," said Adam. "Most people who stop in here don't expect to find much more than a typical greasy spoon. I'm glad you enjoyed my cooking. I went to the Culinary Institute of America down in Poughkeepsie, and I graduated near the top of my class. I got a lot of offers from some very prestigious Manhattan restaurants when I graduated, but this place would have closed down if I hadn't come back to run it, and that would have broken my parents' hearts."

"That was a wonderful thing to do," said Julie, emboldened by the wine, "but it was also a pretty big sacrifice. Do you ever regret it?"

"Not for a minute, to be perfectly honest. I was born and raised a country boy, and I wasn't looking forward to moving to a city like New York. Besides, my wife is from the next town over, and we're both content to be here. And it's a wonderful place to raise our two kids. My wife, Beth, volunteers at the local nursery school and sits on the town council as well as being a full-time mom and homemaker. We both keep pretty busy."

"Sounds nice," said Sarah.

"I really couldn't imagine living anywhere else."

The wine had put Sarah and Julie in good humor, and they engaged in friendly banter with Adam as they settled their bill. They were just standing up to leave when a police car with "Dutch River Police" emblazoned on its doors and all its lights flashing pulled up in front of the restaurant. A police officer emerged from the car and entered the restaurant, loudly banging the door behind him. He was short and decidedly chubby, with a jowly face and a pink complexion that made him look like a piglet well on its way to becoming a crucial component of someone's breakfast. Sarah guessed him to be about the same age as Adam. He looked slightly ridiculous, like a fat Barney Fife, in his full uniform, replete with cap and sidearm and a nameplate that said "Steffus," but he was clearly angry about something. He looked around the restaurant and gave a slight nod to Adam, who noticeably winced.

"Morning, Bert," he said. "Is there anything I can help you with before you scare all my customers away?"

"You can tell me who's illegally parked outside your restaurant is what you can do," said Officer Steffus. "And don't start giving me any trouble, Adam."

"Is it the black Mercedes, Officer?" said Sarah, trying to avoid a nasty confrontation between the two men.

"Yes, it is," said Officer Steffus. "Why is it that rich people with fancy cars always feel like they can park wherever they want in this town?"

"Aw, c'mon, Bert," said Adam, "what are you talking about?"

"I'm talking about the fact that the vehicle is occupying two parking spaces, *that's* what I'm talking about!" said Steffus, his jowls swelling, and his face turning even pinker.

"Are you talking about the fact," said Adam, looking out the window and starting to sound angry, "that one of the tires is sitting on top of the parking line and not inside it?"

"That's exactly what I'm talking about! Regulations are regulations!"

"For Chrissake, Bert, it's the only parked car on the whole damn block. Who gives a shit?"

"Adam, this has nothing to do with you! Now, unless you want to make things even worse for these ladies, you'll butt out, do you hear me?"

"Please, please," said Sarah, "let's not make this into more than what it is. I understand the importance of regulations, Officer Steffus. My husband is an NYPD policeman, and so is my friend's husband."

"Well, they must be paying policemen awfully well in New York City if the two of you are buzzing around up here in the sticks showing yourselves off in that thing."

"Please, Officer, it's not like that," said Julie.

"I don't care what it is, and if you think that I'm impressed just because your husbands are big-city policemen, think again. They have no jurisdiction here, and you gals better be careful or you'll be getting more than a parking ticket. I can put you in jail for attempting to unduly influence an officer of the law."

"Dammit, Bert, that's enough," said Adam, suddenly pounding his fist on the counter. "You are going to let these ladies go on their way, and you and I are going to discuss this with Stan if that's what you want. Otherwise, you can just leave. I've had it, do you hear me?" At the mention of the name "Stan," Officer Steffus noticeably quailed. "Well, which one is it?"

"I'm not scared of going to see Stan, you know. I'm just doing my job. There's nothing wrong with that."

"'Doing your job' does not entail terrorizing the few tourists who stumble into our town and are willing to stay for a while and help out the local businesses, including mine. This is a conversation we've already had and you do not want to have it again, at least not if you want to keep your badge."

Steffus's mouth opened and closed a couple of times, like a hooked fish struggling for oxygen. "We'll see about that," he finally said, and abruptly walked out, slamming the door once more behind him.

"I'm so very sorry about that, ladies," said Adam.

"Please, it wasn't your fault," said Sarah. "Thanks for the help."

"It sounds like this isn't your first encounter with Officer Steffus," said Julie.

"Not by a long shot," said Adam. "He and I have been going at it since grade school, and it just keeps going from bad to worse. And it's not like he gets along with anyone else any better."

"How big is your police department here?" said Sarah.

"You just saw all of it," said Adam. "We shouldn't even have one. Most of the other small towns around here depend on the county sheriff's department and the state police. But Bert's a local boy whose family has lived here for generations, and he'd always dreamed of being a police officer, ever since he was a little kid. As you can probably imagine, he couldn't qualify for the state police or the sheriff's department, so the town bought him a uniform and a car, and he spends all his time making a general nuisance of himself."

"I'm surprised he's allowed to carry a gun," said Sarah.

"It's never loaded, and he's not allowed to carry any ammunition. And, yes, a lot of people call him 'Barney' behind his back."

"So who's Stan?" said Julie.

"Stan Barry. He's a sergeant in the county sheriff's department who supervises Bert. He generally keeps him under control, but Bert's like a beagle puppy, you know? The minute you let him out of your sight, there's no telling what kind of trouble he'll get himself into. I'm sorry he ruined your lunch."

"Nothing could have ruined that lunch, Adam," said Julie.

"Thanks for that. It means a lot."

"Now, we have about ten minutes to get to the law office of Maas and Maas," said Sarah. "Do you think you could direct us there?"

"Well, that's not too tough," said Adam, walking back to the front window and pointing directly across the street. "It's on the second floor right over there. You'll be there with eight minutes to spare."

6

OFFICER BERTRAM STEFFUS fumed as he left the restaurant and walked over to his patrol car. He'd been hoping to get through the day without yet another humiliating encounter, but he'd come to know better.

Officer Steffus was not unaware of the fact that he was an object of ridicule, and like many people suffering that affliction, he tended to view himself from a tragic perspective.

He generally avoided looking at himself in the mirror when he got out of the shower in the morning because the sight inevitably left him with an urge to weep. He had always been overweight. No. He had trained himself not to use that self-serving euphemism. He had always been fat, fat from his jowls right down to his feet. If he'd been fat but big and strong like some of the farm kids who were All-County linemen at Columbia Regional High, or a state champion heavyweight wrestler like his cousin Harvey Steffus, it wouldn't have been so bad. But he was short and awkward and surprisingly frail; and his rebellious body had resisted all efforts to strengthen it. His intermittent attempts at weight training in the high school gym had left him with nothing to show for his efforts but strained tendons, aching joints, enormous bruises that seemed never to go away, only change color from day to day, and a chronic limp. He finally gave up when he was called into the guidance counselor's office one day and asked if he was being abused at home.

He even could have learned to live with being fat and physically untalented: Presidents Taft and Cleveland had been fat men, as had the famous financier Diamond Jim Brady, and he had been a ladies' man! But his personality had been as malformed as his body, leaving him prone to impulsive behavior, fits of temper, and a reputation for immaturity and unreliability.

When he had finally donned a police officer's uniform, he had hoped that, like some lost character in *The Wizard of Oz*, he would somehow be imbued with the quality he so coveted: the ability to command respect without asking for it. But that was not to be, not now and perhaps not ever, as people found the sight of him squeezed, sausage like, into a uniform, hilarious. Herm Montag over at Herman's Fine Men's Wear should have known that and cut the uniform with some more room. But he was probably in on the joke. Or maybe he'd just gained a few pounds since he'd been fitted for the uniform. He didn't want to think about it.

But beneath the blubber and the bluster, there was one quality that Bert Steffus knew he possessed, even if no one else recognized it: He was smart. People could think what they wanted. He actually preferred it that people were so oblivious to his intelligence and his powers of observation that they weren't careful about what they said and did in his presence. His mother knew, and she used to try to warn people that "little pitchers have big ears," but they'd just laughed and ignored her. Good.

And in Dutch River, there were things to be seen and things to be figured out. They were complex things, and he hadn't worked everything out yet, but someday he would. And then he'd show them.

He tripped over a crack in the pavement as he reached for his car door, and he felt a painful twinge as his ankle, the weak one, of course, twisted painfully.

"Ouch," he said out loud.

7

THE LAW OFFICES OF MAAS AND MAAS took up the second floor of a four-story building that a plaque beside the entrance announced to be "The Maas Building." The other floors appeared to be, at least from the street, unoccupied.

The second floor comprised a large reception area, two modestly sized offices with one desk outside for a secretary, and a conference room looking out on Main Street furnished with what appeared to be an old dining-room table with eight chairs, which matched neither the table nor each other. The secretary's desk was occupied by a thirtyish-looking woman with long dark hair, heavy makeup, and a tight blouse that generously displayed an abundant bosom barely restrained by a bra not up to the task. Sarah suspected that the desk was mercifully hiding an equally tight skirt of an immodest length, since immodesty seemed to be the hallmark of everything about the woman, whom the nameplate on the desk announced to be "Dot Ferguson, Legal Assistant." The nameplate outside the office on the right said, "Peter Maas, Managing Partner"; the one on the left said, "Jill Maas, Senior Partner."

"Good afternoon, ladies," said Dot with a wide smile that displayed unnaturally white teeth and a wad of gum in her cheek, "how may we help you this afternoon?"

"My name is Sarah Hudson, and this is Julie Remy. We have a one o'clock appointment with Mr. Peter Maas for the reading of my great-uncle's will. His name was Mr. Armin Jaeger."

"Well, let me see, then," said Dot as she pulled out an appointment calendar and opened it to the current date. Sarah couldn't help noticing that the calendar for the remainder of the day, as well as the next, was empty. "Yes, here you are. We were expecting only you, Mrs. Hudson, but I'm sure we can accommodate your friend. Mr. Maas just got back from a town council meeting, and he's running a little late, but I'm sure he'll be with you momentarily. In the meantime, I can make you comfortable in the conference room. Can I get you ladies something to drink? Coffee? Soda?"

"Coffee would be great," said Sarah and Julie in unison. After the heavy lunch, they both needed the caffeine.

"You said he just came back from a town council meeting?" said Sarah.

"Oh, yes. He's been the mayor of Dutch River for, like, forever."

"He must be a busy man, then."

"Well, being the mayor of Dutch River doesn't exactly force you to break a sweat, you know? Anyway, would you like cream or sugar? Our cream is fresh from one of our local dairies, and we also have Splenda if you prefer, although you two don't look as though you have to struggle with your weight the way I do."

"Cream would be wonderful, no sugar," said Julie, and Sarah nodded her assent.

"You gals are so smart. I have such a sweet tooth! And it goes straight to my hips, let me tell you. You go right in and make yourselves comfortable, and I'll bring the coffee."

Dot returned momentarily with a tray bearing two steaming mugs of coffee and a creamer. Her skirt was indeed short and tight, displaying plump thighs and the kind of hips that had made the inventor of Spanx rich, but that a lot of men likely found irresistible. Following behind her was a man, probably in his late fifties, Sarah guessed, of medium height with a thick head of red hair going to gray, wearing what looked to be a remarkably well-tailored, charcoal-gray Brooks Brothers suit with a heavily starched white shirt and a burgundy tie. He was, in turn, followed by a woman who looked to be in her mid-thirties, taller than the man, with a head of equally red hair and wearing the female version of the man's suit.

"Good afternoon! Good afternoon!" said the man, shaking both their hands vigorously. "I'm Peter Maas, and this is my daughter and, more importantly, my law partner, Jill."

"Pleased to meet you both," said Sarah. "I'm Sarah Hudson, and this is my friend Julie Remy."

"Sit you down! Sit you down!" said Peter. "I hope Dot here has treated you well."

"Yes, she has," said Sarah, "thank you."

"Wonderful! Wonderful! Now, what can I do for you ladies?"

Sarah and Julie exchanged puzzled glances before Sarah replied, "We're here for the reading of my great-uncle Armin Jaeger's will. You wrote me and said that it would take place at one o'clock today."

"Of course! Of course! You know, in these modern days of multi-tasking, I sometimes get a bit bewildered, is all. Actually, there is one other beneficiary that I was expecting to be present, so if you don't mind we'll wait just a few minutes."

"There was only one other beneficiary?" said Sarah.

"Yes, that's all. Your great-uncle kept to himself, you know. Nothing wrong with that! Nothing wrong with that!"

"Who is the other beneficiary?"

"Fred Benecke, of course. I say 'of course,' but how should you know? How should you know?"

"Was he a friend of my great-uncle's?"

"Friend? Friend? I wouldn't know that. Probably the closest thing he had to a friend, though, now that I think about it that way. He's the farmer who owns the place next to Armin's. From what I'm told, Armin stopped doing any farming himself years ago, and he rented the land out for free to Fred and let Fred keep any profit he made from farming it. He didn't want the land to run wild, you know."

"I guess I never would have thought of that."

"Why would you? Why would you? Fred also helped your great-uncle maintain the house. You probably haven't seen it yet, but it's a big old place. Beautiful, but big, and it got to be too much for old Armin."

Their conversation was interrupted by the appearance of a tall, ruddy man with an unruly mane of iron-gray hair that stood up from his head like the comb of a rooster. He stood in the doorway, clenching a gray fedora in his enormous, large-boned hands like a small child clinging to a security blanket, even though his shoulders were approximately the width of the doorway. Sarah guessed him to be seventy, but figured she could be off ten years either way; and she had no doubt that he had the strength and stamina of most men half his age.

"Come on in and sit down, Fred," said Jill Maas. "I'd like to introduce you to Sarah Hudson and Julie Remy. Ms. Hudson has inherited the Jaeger farm." They were the first words the woman had spoken. She possessed a strong, authoritative voice, pitched closer to tenor than alto, which matched her physical appearance. She was at least five foot ten and Sarah guessed that she must have weighed 150 pounds, although she was not at all fat and, if Sarah had to guess, there was a spectacular body lurking beneath the somber business suit.

"Yes, ma'am," said Fred in a gravelly voice that made Sarah suspect that he was, or at least had been, a smoker. She winced as he plopped himself down in one of the chairs with a thud and, as if to confirm her suspicion, pulled a large meerschaum pipe out of his pocket. He made no attempt to fill or light it, but just stroked it with a calloused thumb like it was a pet mouse. He nodded curtly to the women.

Jill Maas handed out two sheets of paper apiece to Sarah, Julie, and Fred, keeping a set for herself. Her father sat at the table with nothing in front of him, but he seemed neither to notice nor to mind.

"It's only two pages long, plainly written, and you can all read for yourselves, so I won't bother to read it aloud," said Jill. "As you can see, you, Sarah, inherit all the property, including the furniture, the art on the walls, and the farm equipment. You also inherit all of your great-uncle's financial assets except the amount that he left to Fred, which as you will note is two-hundred and fifty thousand dollars."

"Two-hundred and fifty thousand dollars?" said Fred, looking up with a stunned expression on his face. "I've never cleared more than twenty-five thousand cash money in a single year of my life. What am I supposed to do with it?"

"Whatever you want, Fred. Whatever you want," said Peter Maas.

"Should Fred assume," said Jill, turning to Sarah, "that you will want him to continue to farm the land and maintain the house and the outbuildings pending your sale of the property?"

"Of course," said Sarah.

"Now," said Jill, "after the payout to Fred, there remains approximately $275,000 in his bank account at the Columbia Bank and Trust. Would you like the funds to remain there for now, or would you like them transferred to your personal account? The will has been properly probated, so the funds are available to do as you want with them."

Sarah stared mutely at Julie, who said, "Why don't you leave everything where it is right now."

"Okay."

"Good," said Jill, passing a single page document over to her. "By signing this, you will become the owner and signatory of the account."

"Is that all?" said Sarah as she signed the document and passed it back. She felt more nervous than she ever had in her life, and all she wanted to do was leave the office and go home. The only thing that was keeping her upright at this point, she felt, was Julie's comforting presence next to her. Julie had long practice in dealing with large sums of money.

"Actually, we have two more important topics to cover," said Jill. "The first one is your great-uncle's art collection."

"He was an art collector?" said Sarah.

"Yes, he was. When he returned from Europe after the war, he began to collect art of the Hudson River School. It was relatively unknown at the time, and he made some artistically important and financially shrewd acquisitions."

"How many paintings did he own?"

"Thirty-seven in all."

"And where are they?"

"Hanging on the walls of the farmhouse, protected by state-of-the-art climate control and security systems, which Fred has kept well-maintained and constantly updated with the most current technology."

"I guess I pictured a run-down old farmhouse in the middle of nowhere," said Sarah, looking at Fred with a new respect. Fred stared back bashfully.

"If you're all finished with me here," he said, "I'll leave now if you don't mind. I don't think the rest of this is any of my business."

"Mr. Benecke," said Julie, "would it be possible for Ms. Hudson and me to visit the house this afternoon? Perhaps you can show us around and we can finalize any arrangements we need to make."

"No problem, ma'am," said Fred, once again twisting his fedora nervously. "I'll be there the rest of the afternoon doing some chores. It's fit for you to stay the night there if you please. The beds are all made and the pantry's stocked."

"Thank you so much, Mr. Benecke," said Sarah, "but we'll probably be heading home tonight."

"That's up to you, ma'am," said Fred. He abruptly turned and left.

"Well," said Jill, "perhaps we should move on here, especially if you plan to return to New York City this evening."

"Have the paintings ever been appraised?" said Julie. It was a question Sarah wouldn't have thought to ask. The only art that adorned the walls of her and Walter's home in Queens were drawings the girls had made in art class.

"Of course," said Jill. "We had an appraisal made by Sotheby's during the probate process."

"*Sotheby's?*" said Julie.

"What does that mean?" said Sarah.

"You're about to find out," said Julie. "Please go on, Ms. Maas."

"The current estimate of all the paintings at auction is $35 million, but, of course, that will be subject to estate taxes and brokerage fees should you decide to sell. Even so, I would estimate that you will net in excess of $15 million from a sale."

Sarah's face lost all color, and she clutched Julie's arm, looking as though she might faint. "I . . . I don't understand," she said, looking at Julie.

"Who knew? Who knew?" said Peter Maas more to himself than anyone else, a bemused smile on his face.

"Don't think about it right now," said Julie, recalling her own shock at learning that she was suddenly a wealthy woman. She turned to Jill and said, "You said that there was one other matter. I assume you were referring to the house itself."

"Yes, I was," said Jill, now staring warily at Julie. "The house and property, net of the art and any other contents, has been appraised at $1.1 million."

"I find that surprising," said Julie. "From what we've heard, people are practically giving away farm properties in this area."

"Mr. Jaeger's property has been highly sought after for years. It's prime farmland and also well suited for residential development. And just to show you that it's a valid appraisal, I have here an offer for the immediate purchase of the property for that exact amount." She withdrew several documents from a folder. Julie recognized a deed, an engineer's report, and a document bearing the letterhead "Rensselaer Partners" among others. "I anticipated that Ms. Hudson would not be interested in occupying the house. We can effect the sale right now, if you please, if you would just sign these few documents, Ms. Hudson. I will either have a cashier's check prepared or I will have that amount deposited electronically in the bank account of your choice." She pushed the documents toward Sarah, carefully avoiding eye contact with Julie.

"No."

All eyes swung to Julie, who was staring hard at Jill Maas.

"Ms. Remy," said Jill, "I hardly think that this is your decision to make."

"I agree with Julie," said Sarah, rapidly regaining her composure.

"Ms. Hudson, I am sure that $1.1 million is more money than you ever imagined you would find in your bank account. The offer can be withdrawn at any time . . ."

"I don't mean to insult anyone, but I'm beginning to feel like I'm being rushed into a very big decision, and it's making me very uncomfortable."

"That's the last thing anyone intended, Ms. Hudson," said Jill, pulling the documents back.

"I think that Ms. Remy and I will be spending the night at the farm after all. I'd like to get to know the place before I make any decisions." She turned to Julie and said, "Is that okay?"

"That's fine with me," said Julie, smiling.

"Who knew? Who knew?" said Peter Maas.

8

B Y THE TIME HE REACHED THE MASSACHUSETTS TURN-
PIKE, Martin Sewall was becoming alarmed. He could barely feel his
feet and driving was becoming difficult. He decided to pull off at the first
rest stop, just a mile or so from the entrance to the highway, and stretch
his legs. He was getting older, he thought, and his circulation just wasn't
what it used to be. Perhaps he'd pick up a cup of coffee.

But when he opened the door and tried to get out of the car, he
realized that the numbness was spreading up his calves, and he fell back
heavily onto the car seat. He finally got himself upright, but he was not
at all sure that he could make it into the pavilion housing the restaurants
and rest rooms. He sat back down and pulled the door shut. He thought
of calling home, but decided that he didn't want to alarm Abby needlessly,
and, besides, she was probably out anyway. He'd just rest a while until the
discomfort passed, which it surely would.

But a half hour passed and if anything, the numbness seemed to be
spreading, past his knees and up his thighs. He thought of calling 911,
but he simply couldn't convince himself that he was in any kind of serious trouble. This was definitely disturbing, and he would make sure
to mention it to his personal physician at his next appointment, but it
would doubtless pass if he just waited a little longer. Sewalls don't panic,
he reminded himself; he hadn't panicked under worse circumstances than
this, and he wasn't going to panic now. Fifteen more minutes had gone by
when he experienced a strange sensation in his groin and was appalled to
look down and realize that he'd wet his pants. His first thought was that
he couldn't allow himself to be seen in such undignified circumstances,
but that thought was replaced by sheer panic as his breathing now became
labored.

What was happening? Simply taking a breath now required conscious
effort. He was forced to admit to himself that he had to do something, but
oxygen deprivation was beginning to prevent him from thinking clearly.
Phone Abby, he thought. That's right. Abby was a very practical woman,

and she'd know just what to do. His hand was still able to grasp the phone, but once it was in his hand, he couldn't remember why he had picked it up. He stared at it for a few minutes, and then decided he should punch some numbers, any numbers, but his numb fingers kept missing their targets. And then the phone slipped out of his hand on onto the floor of the car.

And then he couldn't remember what the problem was. Everything seemed bright, and colors became remarkably vivid. A wave of peace overcame him as he realized that everything was going to be all right after all. Of course it was. Abby would take care of everything. She always did.

It was so good to be a Sewall.

9

"**O**H MY GOD, IT'S A ONE-HORSE OPEN SLEIGH," said Sarah as she stared at the contraption sitting on its wooden runners off in a corner of the large, airy barn. In addition to the floor where they were standing, the cavernous structure had a loft accessible by a ladder, and a lower level accessed from the inside by a hatch in the floor and from the outside, because the land under the barn sloped, by a large double door at the rear of the barn. Fred informed them that the loft was, indeed, a hayloft, and that the lower level was used to house livestock. She walked over to the sleigh and stroked the gleaming horsehair upholstery and the supple leather reins. "It looks like new."

"That sleigh is older than I am," said Fred Benecke, "but I've tried to take good care of it."

"Does anyone ever use it?" said Julie.

"Sure," said Fred, "what with the winters around here, sometimes it's the most reliable way to get to town. At Christmastime, I give the local kids rides up and down Main Street."

"That must make Officer Steffus crazy," said Sarah.

"Funny thing, nobody loved riding in that sleigh more than Bert when he was a little kid, and he's really good with the horses. He's good with all animals, actually. He can't sit in a saddle worth a darn, but he drives that little sleigh like a pro, and the horses always seem to know when he's around, and they respond to him."

"How many horses do you have?" said Sarah.

"Oh, I've only got two left, and besides taking turns pulling the sleigh in the winter, they just loaf around and eat hay. Not a bad life. I probably would've gotten rid of them, but old Armin just loved them. He paid me to keep them, and of course I don't mind. When I was a kid we had a dozen horses, all of them working."

"It must have been a nice life," said Julie.

"It was a hard life, is what it was. Not a lot to get nostalgic about, let me tell you, except the big family and the horses."

"How many people live on your farm now?" said Sarah.

"Just me. I had three older brothers, but they're all dead now, and I've got a sister in Albany. My wife and I had four kids, but they weren't interested in the farm and moved away, and I lost my wife five years ago. I probably would have sold the place off years ago, but I've been able to keep my head above water with the extra income from the Jaeger place, and I don't know what else I'd do. Farming's all I've ever known, and the farm is the only home I've ever had." They left the barn and strolled back to the house.

The house itself was a revelation. It was set back about fifty yards from the road, which, when the house was built in 1790, had obviously been nothing more than a horse path. The exterior sparkled with a fresh coat of paint, and the lawn and the shrubs were well tended.

"Did you paint the house recently?" said Sarah.

"No, Armin did that, just this past spring."

"Oh, I would have thought that at his age a job like that would have been beyond him."

"Armin? Nah. He may have been ninety, but that man still had the strength and stamina of a plow horse. He'd still put in twelve-hour days with me working the farm in the summertime. Anyone who tells you he was old and frail didn't know the man."

They reached the front door, and Fred showed them how to punch in the code to the security system.

The door led them directly into the kitchen, which gleamed with modern appliances, though the flooring was made of solid maple planks that, to Julie's eye, looked to be original. The far door of the kitchen led them into the living and dining rooms, which were sparsely, but expensively, furnished. The center of the kitchen was dominated by an enormous table of simple design and construction.

"Oh, Sarah, look," said Julie. "These tables and chairs are Shaker, and they're antiques."

"Julie," said Sarah, "I'm in way over my head here. I do all my furniture shopping at garage sales."

"It seems that a lot of the valuable art in this house isn't just hanging on the walls. You can't find this furniture anymore, and you couldn't afford it even if you did. Your great-uncle has been eating his meals on a priceless museum piece." She turned to Fred. "Is the rest of the house like this?"

"Pretty much, I guess, although I wouldn't really know for sure. I'm more like your friend here. Furniture is just sticks to me. But Armin, he was a funny guy, and he was awful particular about the stuff he bought."

"And look at these carpets," said Julie as they walked into the living room. She knelt down to touch them.

"What about them?" said Sarah.

"They're Persian, they're silk, and they're antique. Just the carpets in this house are worth hundreds of thousands of dollars. Your great-uncle must have bought them for a song before everybody in the United States discovered them."

"Like I said," said Fred, "Armin was a funny guy."

"And just look at these paintings. My God! This one's a Bierstadt. And this one's a Frederic Church. Sarah, you have to go to the Metropolitan Museum of Art in New York or the Wadsworth Atheneum in Hartford, Connecticut, to see paintings like this. And some of these contemporary works are fabulous. If anything, I bet Sotheby's was being conservative."

"And the house itself is so lovely," said Sarah, gazing. "I'm not sure what I expected a farmhouse to look like, but I certainly didn't expect it to look like this. I can't imagine the amount of work that must have gone into the upkeep."

"Well, like I said," said Fred, "you can credit your great-uncle with that. He wasn't much on modern technology, so I managed all the climate control and security systems, but the house itself, inside and outside, that was his work, right up to the very end."

"He never had any help besides you?" said Sarah.

"Nope. He did all his own cooking and cleaning, too. He was a man who treasured his privacy, and there was never anything wrong with him, physically or mentally, right up until the day he died. I never knew him to have as much as a sniffle or a pulled muscle."

"It's funny. The impression I got was that he was a frail old man who depended on you to do everything." Fred's only reply was something resembling a snort.

Like many houses of its vintage, the farmhouse had two staircases that led to the second floor, one in the front and one in the rear. Just for the novelty, they used the back staircase to reach the second floor, where they found five bedrooms and two large full bathrooms, each with a capacious tub and separate shower. They also found another staircase that led to the attic.

"There used to be seven bedrooms up here," said Fred, "but, of course, when this house was built, there was no indoor plumbing, so adjustments had to be made. Armin did all that when he came home from the war." Fred showed them the two bedrooms that he thought might be most agreeable to them, although any would have done.

"Which room was Armin's?" said Sarah.

"This one right down the hall," said Fred, leading them down to it. "I made up the bed after he died, but other than that, nothing's been touched."

Sarah and Julie were surprised to find that it was the smallest of the five, but as with the others, it was exquisitely furnished and exuded comfort and warmth. There was a modest double bed situated between the two windows that looked out the back of the house, a desk opposite the bed, a chair, a small table in one corner, and a large bookcase on the wall to the left of the bed. A heavy book rested on the table with a leather bookmark about halfway through the text. There was no television, no computer, and no telephone.

"Did he spend much time in here?" said Sarah.

"I don't really know, since I didn't spend much time in the house, except when I was working on the security system, but I always had the impression that this was his favorite room in the house. He drank his morning and evening coffee in here, and he also had his afternoon cocktail here before he went downstairs for his dinner."

"Was he much of a drinker?" said Julie.

"No, he wasn't, but he cherished his afternoon cocktail, and he never missed it. It was the same drink every night: bourbon and bitters. He bought some fancy bourbon that was still plugged with a cork, not sealed with a screw cap. I never saw him buy anything else. It was plenty expensive and, boy, did it pack a wallop. He only had one a night, but he wasn't shy when he poured. He asked me in to share a drink every once in a while after we'd been out working, and I have to tell you, I could barely make it back to my place afterward. But that wasn't often. As I've said, Armin treasured his privacy."

"Did he have any hobbies?" said Sarah.

"Not really," said Fred. "He worked seven days a week, and he put in long days. Farmers don't have a lot of time for hobbies. He loved to read, though."

Julie walked over to the large bookcase and perused its contents. Her eyes immediately came to rest on some large volumes on art history, which didn't surprise her, except that they mostly focused on European, not American, art. But then again, she thought, judging from the collection hanging on the walls, he was the arbiter of his own taste, and he probably could have written a book on the subject himself. There were three Bibles: a King James, an annotated NIV, and a German language version. A complete set of Will and Ariel Durant's *Story of Civilization* took up most of the bottom shelf. One of the books, the second in the series, was missing from its spot, and Julie guessed that it was the book lying on the table. There were also a great many works of modern fiction, including Herman Wouk's *The Winds of War* and *War and Remembrance*; and an entire shelf devoted to works of German literature, a collection of Goethe's poetry the only one she could recognize. They all looked well used.

She walked back over to the table beside the chair and picked up the book lying on it. As she had surmised, it was the missing Durant book, *The Life of Greece*. She picked it up and opened to the bookmark. Apparently Armin August Jaeger had been reading about Socrates just before he died. Not your average farmer, she thought, feeling immediately guilty. She'd never met an actual farmer in her life before she'd met Fred Benecke, so who was she to judge?

"I almost hate to ask," said Julie, "but is this where Armin died?"

"Yes, ma'am, it is."

"Did he die alone?"

"No, he didn't, but only by a couple of minutes."

"Who was with him?"

"I was."

"Oh," said Sarah. She hesitated for a moment, and then gave in to her curiosity. "Would you mind telling us about it?"

"I don't mind at all," said Fred. "It's about time someone asked me about it."

"Someone must have interviewed you. The police? A doctor?"

"Not really. The only thing they seemed to care about was that I was here when he passed. I think that meant that they didn't have to go to the time and the expense of performing an autopsy. He was a ninety-year-old man with no family who died of natural causes. That was the end of the story as far as they were concerned."

"Did you have any reason to believe that he didn't die of natural causes?" said Sarah.

"Oh, I don't know. They were probably right. How should I know anything different? It just bugged me, is all. It just seemed like they didn't give the guy the time of day, you know?"

"So what happened?" said Julie.

"Well, it was one of those occasional days that I'd told you about. We'd put in a long day mending a fence where a cow had gotten loose. We had to waste an entire day just getting her back. So, anyway, Armin invited me in to share a drink with him. When he invited me over, we'd sit out on the porch in the back. It was a warm evening, as I recall. Anyway, I was getting up to leave, and he was heading in to make his supper when all of a sudden he said, 'You know, Fred, I suddenly don't feel so well.' It was the first time I'd ever heard him say anything like that, and I told him so. And then I said, 'You know, Armin, you're ninety. Maybe those cocktails are finally starting to get the better of you.'"

"What did he say?" said Sarah.

"He used a word I usually don't use in polite company, and then he said that he'd get over it. I told him I'd see him in the morning, and I left."

"So how was it that you were here when he died?"

"I know Armin was a tough old cuss, but he really didn't look good when I left. So about nine o'clock, just before I went to bed, I decided to give him a call. There's no answering machine on his phone, so it just rang and rang. I must've let it ring twenty times. I told myself he'd probably just gone to bed and didn't feel like coming downstairs to answer, but, I don't know, it just bothered me. So I decided to come over. I knocked on the door, but there was no answer. I went to punch the code in to the security system and found out that he'd never set it. That started to make me really worried because he never, ever, forgot to set that system. He was religious about it. I called for him, and he didn't reply, so I went upstairs. I found him in his bed, but he hadn't even managed to get out of his clothes or get under the covers."

"Did he say anything to you?"

"Not really. He was mumbling something, but I think it was in German, which I don't speak. He was saying something over and over again. And then suddenly he went quiet. I ran downstairs to call an ambulance. When I got back upstairs I think he was still alive, but he never said anything else. I just held his hand until the ambulance got here, but he was dead by then."

"I'm sorry, Fred," said Sarah, "it must have been awful."

"Well, I've seen a lot of death, and I've had plenty of losses in my lifetime, but I won't lie to you. Losing Armin hurt. I know it's silly for an old man like me to say it, but he was like a second father to me. I guess that's why it riled me so much that they didn't treat his passing with a little more, you know, deference. He was a fine man, and he deserved better."

"Did they ever say anything besides that he died of natural causes?" said Julie.

"Oh, they told me it sounded like heart failure or something they called, 'general system failure due to old age,' whatever that means. I told them how could that happen to a man who'd just spent twelve hours repairing forty feet of fence? They just said all the exertion was probably what brought it on."

Suddenly, they heard the sound of a phone ringing from somewhere in the house.

"That'll be for you, I imagine," said Fred.

"Where are the phones?" said Sarah.

"There's only one, and it's in the kitchen."

Sarah ran downstairs and picked up the phone after the fifth ring. "Hello?" she said, tentatively.

"Hello, Sarah. This is Adam. Adam Avery from the restaurant?"

"Sure, Adam, how could we forget?"

"Well, thanks for that. I'm calling because I heard that you and your friend Julie decided to stay the night at the farm."

"Oh, you did?"

"Don't worry. I wasn't being nosy or anything, but, you know, this is a small town and news travels fast. I guess you're not used to that where you come from."

"Not really, but that's okay. What's up?"

"I just thought you'd like to know that every Tuesday night I close down the restaurant to the public, which there isn't usually much of anyway, and serve a meal for all the local merchants and anyone else from the community who feels like wandering in. Everybody brings in local produce and their own wine and beer, and I just whip up whatever strikes my fancy once I get a look at the ingredients that everyone brought in. I thought you might like to stop by. It would be a good chance for everybody to get to know you and for you to get to know them."

"That sounds wonderful, Adam. Thank you so much. We'll definitely be there. What time?"

"How does six o'clock sound? I know that's awfully early for city folks, but most people around here are up with the sun."

"That sounds perfect. We'll be starved by then, especially knowing that we're going to be getting some more of your cooking. And Adam?"

"Yes?"

"We weren't expecting to spend the night here, so we both could really use some toiletries and perhaps, you know, some other stuff?"

"No problem. Annemarie Jacobs and her husband, Henry, run the local drugstore, and I'm sure Margie, who you've already met, could help with the other stuff, if I'm guessing right."

"That's great. How late are they open?"

"Oh, don't worry about that. They'll be here for dinner, and they'll just open up so you can get what you need when you get here."

"That's great, Adam. Thanks so much. We'll see you at six."

"Six it is."

10

"**Y**OU SAID THIS GUY WAS RICH?" said Detective Lieutenant Walter Hudson. He was sitting in his cubicle in the Midtown South Precinct's detective's squad room with his feet up on his desk, his phone cradled to his ear.

"Yeah," said Massachusetts State Police Sergeant David Mayhew, sitting at his desk in the Sturbridge State Police Barracks in much the same manner. He was a big guy, like Walter, but about five years younger though his hairline was already rapidly receding. "Why do you sound surprised?"

"The Hotel Grenadier isn't exactly a high-class hotel, that's all, and there are a lot of hotels within a few blocks that are more the type that I'd expect a guy like that to stay in."

"All I can tell you is that the GPS system in the car had him leaving that address at about ten o'clock yesterday morning."

"And he died where?"

"At the Charlton rest stop on the Massachusetts Turnpike just after you cross the Connecticut border."

"Do you have a cause of death yet?"

"No. All I know is that there were no signs of violence. The only reason we found him at all is that a guy parked beside him and noticed that he was still sitting there when he was getting in his car to leave. He rapped on the window, and when he got no response he called 911 from his cell phone. There's a state police barracks almost next door to the rest stop, so we got there right away."

"Is that your home base?" said Walter. It was really none of his business and hardly relevant to the discussion, but he was a natural interrogator, and he couldn't help himself.

"My home base is the Sturbridge Barracks," said Sergeant Mayhew, not at all put off by the questioning. Unlike so many frosty New Englanders, he was a friendly sort. "My family and I live right in town. Maybe you've heard of it. I grew up there and so did my wife."

"Sturbridge? Oh yeah. That's the place with the colonial village, right?"

"That's right, Old Sturbridge Village. I worked summers in the blacksmith's shop there when I was in high school and college. Best job I ever had. You really ought to come and visit it sometime. If you have kids they'll love it."

"Actually, my wife has mentioned that."

"Well, stop by and say 'hi' if you ever get up this way."

"I will. You're not a Red Sox fan, are you?"

"Aw, please don't tell me you're a Yankees fan. I was just starting to like you."

"Nah, don't worry. I'm a Mets fan to the bone."

"My condolences."

"Yeah, well, don't forget '86." Both men laughed.

"So, anyway," said Mayhew after a brief pause, "his wife said that he was in perfect health, and the ME said he could see no signs of any heart trauma when he gave him a quick postmortem examination at the scene, so we're treating it as suspicious right now. We were hoping you guys could swing by the hotel and see if you can find out anything. The newspapers are going to be all over this, and we'd like to stay ahead of it."

"So this guy was a big shot, huh?"

"He belonged to one of the oldest families in Boston, and so does his wife. They were also major philanthropists and very high profile. You were always seeing their pictures in the Sunday magazines and stuff like that."

"Got it. I'll see what I can do. If you hear anything about the cause of death, give me a heads-up, okay?"

"Will do. Thanks for your help, Lieutenant."

Walter had just hung up the phone when Leviticus Welles walked into his office.

"Levi! How are you? Are you stopping by to tell me the girls got arrested or something?"

"Actually, it sounds like they almost did get arrested, but it's nothing to worry about. They had a pretty eventful day, though, and when Julie called to tell me about it she said that Sarah had been trying to call you but you were apparently stuck on a very long call, so I told her I'd swing by and give you the news."

"So what's going on?"

"Quite a bit, actually. But first, Julie told me that they'd decided to stay the night at the farm in Dutch River."

"Are they okay?"

"They're fine, but Sarah wanted you to know that she'd already arranged for babysitting for Daniel for tomorrow, and she also convinced the babysitter to stay until you got home tonight and make dinner for the kids."

"Jeez, this is going to start getting expensive."

"Walter?"

"Yeah?"

"I don't think you have to sweat the 'expensive' part."

"What do you mean?"

"Well, I'll let Sarah explain all that to you, but it seems you're married to landed gentry after all."

"That sounds interesting," said Walter, not knowing exactly what to make of what Levi was telling him. "I'll give her a call right away."

"Actually, they're out at a dinner with a group of new friends right now. Sarah said that she'd call you later tonight as soon as she got back to the farm."

"I guess that'll be an interesting conversation."

"Oh, yes."

11

"MY GOD, ADAM, HOW DO YOU DO IT?" said Julie as she polished off a fried chicken leg and a raised biscuit slathered in cream gravy, washing it all down with what was left of her third glass of locally produced white Riesling wine.

"When you get to work with the world's freshest food, all locally produced, it's pretty easy," said Adam, but smiling proudly just the same. "That chicken you just polished off was wandering around Ed James's yard just this morning. All free range and no hormones or antibiotics. We've all forgotten what a real, humanely raised chicken tastes like. And the same goes for the steer that donated that steak you just finished, Ms. Hudson. Raised on an open pasture farm, grass fed, and slaughtered humanely right on the farm. It's been dry aging in the back of my restaurant for a month. You didn't even need a knife, did you?"

"It was the tastiest piece of beef I've ever eaten," said Sarah, "and that salad you whipped up was marvelous. Thank you so much. And you've got to start calling me 'Sarah.'"

"The nice part about it is it isn't work for me. These are my friends, and cooking is what I love to do. And having a restaurant kitchen with all the best appliances, especially a commercial grade dishwasher, really makes it all easy."

"And all these people are so nice," said Julie, "but I've met so many people all at once that I'm never going to remember all their names."

"Well, I hope you at least hang around long enough to get to know everybody. I know you never intended to stay here more than a couple of hours, but if you give it a chance the place will grow on you."

"It already has," said Sarah. "I'm a city girl to the bone, but I have to say, people here are friendly in a way that city people just aren't. It's not that city people are unfriendly or anything, but they tend to keep to themselves."

They had already met Adam's wife, Sally, and their two children, but with the exception of Margie, all the other faces were unfamiliar.

"Tell me again," said Julie, "who's that couple over there?" She pointed to a couple in their late thirties or perhaps early forties.

"Oh, that's Doctor Melvin Williams and his wife, Evelyn. They're relative newcomers around here. They came here seven years ago after he finished his residency. He went to medical school at Johns Hopkins in Baltimore, and then did his residency at Bellevue in New York City. We were lucky to get him."

"And what does his wife do?" said Sarah.

"She's a registered nurse who also has an MBA from Columbia. She manages his practice for him."

"How did you ever get him to come here?" said Julie. "I'm sorry, I guess that came out wrong."

"No need to apologize," said Adam. "We were down to zero doctors within a ten-mile radius after old Dr. Miller died. Mel and Ev had come up to the Culinary Institute for dinner and a tour while I was still training there. I was asked to show them around, and we wound up having a nice conversation. So when we decided that we really needed to recruit a doctor, I gave him a call to see if he could recommend anyone, and he wound up recommending himself."

"He must have had a lucrative Manhattan practice waiting for him. And heaven knows his wife could have had any number of great jobs in health-care administration with her background. You must be quite a salesman," said Sarah.

"I know I'm partial, but I like to think that the area sold itself. They were impressed with the people and the beauty of the area when they came up for a visit. But I think what swung it was that, as I said, we really needed a family doctor around here, and we made Mel a really good offer. A modern office with state-of-the-art equipment, and we also guaranteed him an income."

"How did that work?" said Julie.

"We said that if his fees, net of all his expenses, didn't hit a certain level, the town would make up the difference for him. And the kicker was that we would pay his malpractice insurance premiums for him."

"In short," said Sarah, "as my Sicilian relatives would say, you made them an offer they couldn't refuse."

"Something like that," said Adam, smiling. "Like I said, we really needed a doctor. We were afraid the town might finally die completely if we didn't have one, so we dug deep."

"I couldn't help noticing that Officer Steffus isn't here," said Julie. "He must be the only person in town who isn't."

"He never comes," said Adam. "Despite all our difficulties I always go out of my way to invite him, but he always declines. He claims he has to make sure that he maintains his official objectivity as a police officer, and he knows we all drink wine and beer while we're here. But I think it's just an excuse."

"What do you think his real reason is?" said Julie.

"I wish I could tell you," said Adam, but he'd barely finished his sentence when there was a ruckus near the door. Then the room went quiet as everyone stared at a man, clearly unconscious, lying facedown on the floor. A red-faced Margie stood over him.

"Who's that?" said Sarah in a low whisper.

"That's Mike Hunter, Margie's husband. This happens more often than not, I'm sorry to say."

"Is he an alcoholic?" said Sarah.

"I'm no expert, but I don't think so. He's a CPA, and he had a good job with a local accounting firm until a few years ago, but the firm folded. He tried to start his own firm, but there just wasn't enough of a client base for him and it failed pretty quickly. He's basically been unemployed for the past three years. I never knew him to get even a little tipsy when he had a job."

"That's so sad," said Sarah.

"Yes, it is," said Adam. "Margie's got her shop, and they get by financially, but it's not the money. It's his pride. People like to feel useful, you know?"

"Oh, I know," said Julie. She and Levi had met after they'd both gone through prolonged periods of unemployment during the Great Recession. "Perhaps we should leave now. This is probably embarrassing enough for Margie without a couple of complete strangers looking on."

"Oh, please stay," said Adam. "I flash froze some fresh strawberries that I bought from one of the local farmers at the height of the season. I've got shortcakes just coming out of the oven and I'm going to whip up some fresh cream. I thought it would make a really nice end-of-summer dessert. And besides, I think it would be more embarrassing for Margie if you left right now than if you stayed. She'll get him up; she always does, and we'll get some hot coffee in him. And as usual, we'll all kind of pretend nothing happened."

Julie and Sarah looked at each other, then Sarah turned to Adam and said, "Okay, you've got us convinced."

"I was hoping you'd say that," said Adam. "How would you like to come and help me whip up the cream?"

"That sounds wonderful," said Sarah, as they headed off toward the kitchen.

———

Officer Bert Steffus sat in his patrol car a block down from Avery's Restaurant with the lights off and the engine idling quietly, the chilly evening air matching his mood.

He had been asked repeatedly over the years by Adam to attend their Tuesday night get-togethers, and he had never had any doubt that the invitations were sincere. These were, after all, the people he'd grown up with, gone to school with, and whose weddings he had attended. The fact that most of them thought him a buffoon didn't change the basic bonds that connected them all.

He was pretty sure that Adam thought he wouldn't attend because of the drinking that went on, and the driving afterward. To some extent that was true, but not because he disapproved, which was easy to assume because he was a teetotaler. His abstinence, however, was not grounded in any sense of moral disapproval; it was simply a practical matter. He just found it much easier to turn down a beer than a fourth slice of pizza, and any opportunity to avoid additional calories had to be seized upon.

No, he didn't attend because he grew more convinced with each passing year, and lately with each passing month, that one day, he would have to arrest one of them, and maybe more than one. That day would be painful enough as it was, and he was not about to make it any more painful by allowing himself to be drawn into that circle of friends and acquaintances any more closely than he already was.

So let them think what they want. He had a job to do. He pulled away from the curb quietly. He didn't turn on his headlights until he was well away from Main Street.

12

"I'M NOT SURE I'M READY TO BELIEVE ANY OF THIS YET," said Walter Hudson, taking a sip of the red wine that Leviticus had ordered. He wasn't much of a wine drinker, but this evening he wasn't really tasting much of anything anyway. The four of them, Walter, Sarah, Levi and Julie, were sitting at a small table in a crowded bistro just a block away from Julie's town house in Soho in Lower Manhattan where she and Levi lived. Julie loved to cook, and normally they would have invited Walter and Sarah over for a home-cooked meal, but she and Sarah had just gotten back to town after leaving Dutch River in the middle of the afternoon, and they were both tired.

They had both slept late after the festivities of the night before, but had been pleasantly surprised to discover freshly made coffee in the kitchen when they'd stumbled downstairs, undoubtedly compliments of Fred Benecke. As they sat at the ancient Shaker table and drank their coffee, the mild early autumn sun pouring in the window like Joni Mitchell's butterscotch, Sarah couldn't help feeling a sense of comfort, a sense of home here in this isolated house, on this remote farm, that she had rarely felt in her life.

There had been enough food in the pantry for a hearty breakfast, but they'd decided instead to stop in at Avery's for a late brunch prior to meeting with Maas & Maas before departing, a meeting that Jill Maas had arranged over dessert the night before. Adam had served them up a classic farm breakfast of eggs, sausages, and toast, along with coffee and apple juice. "We don't grow oranges up here," he'd explained.

"It gets more believable to me every minute," said Sarah, as she recounted to Walter and Levi their meeting with the lawyers prior to their departure. "I never thought I'd have people try so hard to throw so much money at me."

"So they were still trying to get you to sell the house right away?" said Walter.

"'Trying' doesn't begin to describe it," said Julie. "They were practically shoving the papers at her. And it wasn't just for the sale of the house. They'd also been in touch with Sotheby's to set up a preliminary date for an auction of all the artwork, including the carpets and the furniture. Talk about a bum's rush."

"Thank God Julie was there," said Sarah. "I was completely overwhelmed, but Julie was a real tiger. I don't know what I would have done without her."

"Well, don't forget, I've had to negotiate with Arab terrorists in the past. You haven't had the benefit of that experience. But just so you know, negotiating with the Maases wasn't a whole lot different."

"I don't get it," said Walter. "Why are they in such an almighty hurry to get rid of you? You'd think that they'd have welcomed having a relative at least willing to consider holding on to the place."

"I know," said Sarah, "but they kept trying to tell me that since we have no ready cash on hand it would be tough to hang on to it and, besides, they never stopped reminding me that we have no clue how to run a farm."

"That's ridiculous," said Levi. "It's true that you're going to have to sell off some of the artwork to pay the estate taxes, but a good accountant along with an independent appraiser can help you select some of the paintings to raise the cash for the taxes and support the farm, and make sure that you're able to keep most of the pieces you really want to keep. Or, if you're not interested in the art, they can simply sell off the collection for you. You won't just be able to keep the farm; you'll be rich. The farm can become a vacation getaway for you and the kids. And in the meantime, don't forget that you've got $275,000 in the bank, which will keep you going for quite a while. And I'm sure Fred Benecke will be more than willing to help with the farm."

Walter looked at Sarah inquisitively, an amused smile on his face.

"What?" she said.

"You tell me," said Walter, his smile broadening. "I'm just starting to suspect that the idea of being landed gentry is starting to appeal to you. You know, 'let them eat cake,' and all that."

"Oh, give me a break."

"But . . ."

"But what?"

"It's just that I've been sitting here listening to you describe that farm, and I think you're starting to like it, that's all."

"Oh, Walter, I don't know. On one hand, the Maases are right: What business do a couple of city rats like you and me have owning a farm, for crying out loud?"

"But on the other hand . . ."

"OK. All right. Yes, I do like it. Don't ask me why, because I don't know. All I know is that I feel very much at peace there. It's like this fantasy getaway island where all the cares in the world disappear. And it's *ours*, Walter. Can you believe it? I don't know, maybe in the end, the whole idea is ridiculous, but I want some time to think about it. And I also want you to see it before you dig your heels in."

"Sarah, I'm busy at work. And what about the kids?"

"You know," said Levi, "this coming Monday is Rosh Hashanah."

"What?" said Walter.

"Oh my God, that's right!" said Sarah. "I forgot all about it with all the craziness about the farmhouse. The schools are closed on Monday and Tuesday. We have a four-day weekend!"

"Aw, Sarah, I've . . ." but one look at the expression on his wife's face made him realize that this was no longer a negotiation. "Okay," he said, resignedly.

"Oh, thank you!" said Sarah, leaning over to give her husband a kiss. "And you guys could come too!" she said, looking across the table at Levi and Julie. "The place has five bedrooms, for crying out loud. Let's use some of them, at least just this once."

"I should check on my workload before we commit one way or another," said Levi, looking at Julie doubtfully. "I've been up to my neck lately."

"You know," said Julie, giving Levi a look that she usually didn't give him in polite company, "I bet you've never had an actual roll in the hay, have you?"

Levi stared back at his wife, for once speechless, his face reddening.

"All I'm saying, Levi," she said, her expression now smoldering, "is that maybe you should give that some thought before you go making up your mind, you know, one way or another."

13

"CAN YOU BELIEVE IT?" said Walter. "Levi and I are going to be helping Fred bale some hay this morning. That's not something I ever thought I'd hear myself say."

"That's fine," said Julie, patting Levi on the back, "we're through with it."

"Oh my God!" said Sarah, hooting. "I thought you were joking!"

"I don't kid about rolls in the hay," said Julie. "You guys should try it. It's a whole new kind of naked."

"Julie, shhhh," said Levi, "the kids might hear."

"The kids are out picking apples in the orchard," said Sarah. "They're having the time of their lives, and they're well out of earshot. I don't think it ever occurred to them before this weekend where apples came from. This is such a wonderful experience for them."

"What makes you think *I* knew where apples came from?" said Walter.

"Go ahead and joke, but just think . . . Since we've gotten here, the kids have gathered the eggs they ate for breakfast, they've milked a cow, and they've baked bread in a brick oven. And all on their own farm."

It was Monday morning, and they were sitting at the long Shaker table in the kitchen, having wolfed down omelets, bacon, and toast made from fresh baked bread. Since arriving on Friday night, they'd learned a lot about the farm, and farming. The milking cows in the barn and the chickens out back belonged to Fred, but he'd been able to expand his operation by utilizing Armin Jaeger's barn and grazing land. It was not a large operation by commercial farming standards, but it was an enormous undertaking for one man, especially a man of Fred Benecke's age, and it was no wonder that he had continued to rely on Armin's help right up to the end of his life.

The house, too, continued to be a revelation. All the bedrooms had been furnished with valuable antiques, and there were many more collectibles in the enormous attic, which even Walter could walk through without ducking his head. Julie had told Sarah that she could raise thousands of dollars in cash just by selling off some of the stored furniture, though Sarah already had ideas about how some of it would fit into their small house in Queens, or perhaps a larger home in Queens, which they would now be able to afford.

But the biggest revelation had been the effect on the four of them. In just two days, they had worked harder physically than they ever had done in their lives. Their skin was already browning, and their spirits were high. They ate vast quantities of food and fell into bed exhausted before ten o'clock. Even bookish Levi had demonstrated a capacity for hard labor that had astonished not only him but his wife as well. "And that's just the stuff he's been doing while he's had his clothes on," she'd joked.

"I feel like a character out of one of those early utopian novels by Nathaniel Hawthorne," Levi had said over Sunday night dinner.

"Yeah, that's just what I was thinking," said Walter.

"I never read a Nathaniel Hawthorne novel," said Sarah, "at least not on purpose, but I know what you mean. I love the city life; it's the only life I've ever known, but I feel wonderful. I know a lot of it is the novelty of the whole experience, and I'm not sure that I could live like this year-round, but I love the idea of knowing that this place is here."

"And all the people we've met are so friendly and nice," said Julie.

"Well, people are people, I guess," said Walter, "but I can't argue with you."

"I knew you'd love it once you got here," said Sarah.

"Please, let's not get ahead of ourselves," said Walter. "I still can't convince myself that there isn't some hidden flaw lurking somewhere."

"I'll try not to," said Sarah, "but it's getting harder by the minute. We'll have a chance to reassess everything after we've had our meeting with the Maases this afternoon."

"In the meantime, you should probably chase down the kids, and Levi and I need to bale some hay, whatever that involves."

They all worked together to clean up the kitchen, and after that Sarah and Julie went upstairs to clean up. Walter and Levi had learned that taking a morning shower made no sense on the farm, so they just headed outside. The door had barely closed behind them when Walter's work cell phone, which he hadn't been able to convince himself to leave behind, rang. He didn't immediately recognize the 508 area code, but once he did his eyes widened.

"Lieutenant Hudson speaking."

"Hello, Lieutenant, this is Sergeant David Mayhew, you know, from the Massachusetts State Police?"

"Hello, Sergeant Mayhew, how are you? I was thinking of you last night when I noticed that the Red Sox lost yesterday. I'm not so great with numbers, but doesn't that make them mathematically eliminated from playoff contention?"

"I can understand how that would be difficult for you to figure out, Lieutenant, seeing that it's been ten years since the Mets were ever mathematically *in* contention."

"Wise guy. Anyway, what's up?"

"I just wanted to give you an update on the Charles Martin Sewall death. Have you been able to find out anything on your end?"

"No, I'm sorry, I haven't. I was called out of town unexpectedly, and I guess I was waiting to hear from you whether there was actually anything to investigate. So what's up?"

"It looks like you're going to have something to investigate, is what's up."

"What's going on?"

"It appears that Mr. Sewall died anything but a natural death. An autopsy revealed large amounts of a substance called conium maculatum in his body."

"Never heard of it. What is it?"

"Hey, the only thing I remember about chemistry is that I flunked it in high school. It's just some poison, I guess, but it appears that he ingested it with a midday meal."

"So do you think it was a suicide? Did he buy some food at the rest stop and chase it down with the poison?"

"We don't think so. The contents of his stomach didn't reveal any food that was available at the rest stop. It looks like he'd recently eaten a corned beef sandwich and a dill pickle. And anyway, I'm told that this particular poison is not fast acting, so he could have ingested it a couple of hours, even more depending on the dosage, before it killed him or he even noticed that something was wrong. My guess is he stopped at Rein's Deli in Connecticut."

"Why do you say that?"

"Because that's where everybody stops on their way from New York to Boston, and they serve terrific corned beef sandwiches."

"Let's keep that in mind," said Walter, as Levi started to look on curiously. "Look, I'm heading back to the city tomorrow night and I'll pay a call to the Hotel Grenadier right away. Could you please fax me a picture of the guy?"

"No problem. I really appreciate your help on a case that's not in your jurisdiction. And, oh, by the way, speaking of things out of your jurisdiction, another odd thing came up."

"What was that?"

"Well, we did a more thorough examination of the GPS and the E-ZPass activity for the car that he'd been driving, the Mercedes Benz E-Class. Funny how those things didn't even exist a few years ago, now people won't go anywhere without using them. Anyway, we confirmed the car left the Hotel Grenadier in New York City that morning, but the funny thing is, the car didn't come from Boston the day before."

"Where did it come from?"

"It drove down to New York City the previous day from a place I've never heard of. It's in upstate New York."

"Tell me where and I'll see if I can coordinate with the New York State Police if you want me to."

"That would be really helpful."

"So what's this place called?"

"It's called 'Dutch River.'"

⚓

"So what did he say the name of the poison was?" said Levi, as he and Walter hiked over to the field where they had agreed to meet Fred.

"Oh, I don't know. I lasted about a week in chemistry in high school before I dropped it, and I didn't have my notepad with me so I didn't write it down."

"Well, I didn't last much longer, but I learned a lot about poisons when I was in Army Intelligence when I was younger, and you'd be surprised at how much poison people attempt to smuggle into New York City. The next time you talk to the guy, try to think to ask him."

"I will. So, Levi, have you ever heard of this Sewall family? Sergeant Mayhew said that they were kind of a big deal in Boston."

"My mother was from New Orleans, and my father was from New York. I think I've visited Boston maybe twice in my life for sales calls, but that's about it. So, no, I've never heard of them. I do know that Boston is a much smaller city than New York, but it seems that their elite society is a lot like New York's, kind of a combination of old money with old names and the new superrich. I've heard, though, that their old money crowd is even snobbier than New York's."

"Didn't Julie live in Boston once?"

"She did. After her parents left France they moved to Boston and that's where she went to high school. But they weren't rich, and they definitely weren't a part of the elite society crowd. Julie skedaddled to New York for college and never left."

"So I guess the question is," said Walter, looking out at the vast countryside surrounding them, "what would a guy like that be doing in a place like this?"

14

S ERGEANT DAVID MAYHEW may have been from Massachusetts, but he knew nothing about Boston, and he liked it less by the minute as he made his fourth attempt to find the Beacon Hill neighborhood where the Sewall family resided. He was mildly irritated that people from outside the region knew little about his home state except that Boston was its capital and that the Red Sox played there. He made it a personal point of pride to go there as little as possible, limiting his visits to his annual pilgrimages with his brother-in-law to Fenway Park to see the Red Sox play. But his brother-in-law always drove, and he hadn't even recognized Fenway Park as he drove past it on I-90, so hard was he concentrating on the road signs. He missed his exit anyway, got off at the wrong one, and proceeded to get forced down a series of one-way streets, all going in the wrong direction. Boston is an old city, at least by American standards, and its bewildering street layout has to be learned, preferably when one still possesses the optimism of youth, by long, painful, direct experience, which Mayhew neither had nor desired to have.

He finally found himself in the right general vicinity and located a parking spot blocking an alleyway on Chestnut Street. A shop owner came out of his store across the street and looked on, annoyed, but he knew complaining about a Massachusetts State Police car illegally parked would get him nowhere and went back inside. Mayhew checked his map, wandered over to River Street and up to Mount Vernon Street, then started the climb into the warren of small, pre-Revolution lanes that comprised Beacon Hill.

Sergeant Mayhew was unfamiliar with wealth, but he knew it when he smelled it, and the aroma was overwhelming as he stood in the foyer of the Sewall town house on polished oak floors that had borne footsteps for centuries and would undoubtedly do so for centuries more. Nothing was ostentatious and nothing was outsized or gaudy, but everything looked like it had been just this way forever. He was not a sophisticated man, and he couldn't place a name or a vintage on anything, but everything from the paintings on the walls to the furnishings looked old and original, and subtly conveyed a sense of value not just of the objects, but also of the family that lived within. Somewhere down the hall a clock ticked. Somewhere upstairs a bell tinkled.

A young Hispanic maid had answered the ring of the doorbell, looking like she'd wanted to bolt at the sight of his uniform. But she had managed to maintain her composure, asking him to take a seat, please, while she announced his arrival to Mrs. Sewall. The foyer contained many chairs, but upon inspection an intimidated Mayhew chose to remain standing.

The maid returned and asked him to follow her. They climbed into a small elevator in the hallway and after a brief ride he was shown into a small but elegantly furnished room on the third floor that looked like a combination of a private office and a sitting room. Looking out the windows he could catch a glimpse of the Boston Common and the golden dome of the Massachusetts State House. He guessed things didn't get much more exclusive than this.

A woman was seated at a small escritoire situated by a window, wearing a sky-blue silk blouse and oatmeal-colored linen slacks. The maid announced him and inquired about refreshments. The woman turned from her desk and said that coffee would do, the time being that awkward interlude between breakfast and lunch. The maid left quietly.

If Sergeant Mayhew had any preconceived notions about Abby Peabody Sewall's appearance, or the woman herself, they were shattered on first sight. The photos he'd seen of her in the Society sections of the local press had seemed to give her a hard sheen, an unapproachable, almost imperious image. But this woman in front of him was nothing of the sort. She exuded warmth, kindness, and sincerity, all now cloaked in a spectral mantel of profound grief. She had plainly loved her husband.

No one would have said that she was beautiful, except perhaps her husband. In elite society, the quip that a woman can never be too rich or too thin was received gospel, and her small, fragile-looking body was too thin and her face too gaunt from years of relentless dieting. Her nose was slightly crooked, her mouth a little too small, and the striking blue eyes just a little too close together. Her rich, honey-colored hair was carelessly tied back in a ponytail. But the overall impression was startlingly attractive, unmistakably feminine, and disconcertingly alluring. This grieving woman was at least fifteen years older than he was, but Mayhew felt a shocking, unprofessional, almost overwhelming desire to take her in his arms as she walked toward him with an outstretched hand.

"Good morning, Sergeant Mayhew," she said in a soft but rich voice that conveyed a hint of intimacy, locking his eyes with a direct gaze that left him with the uneasy sense that she knew exactly what had been going through his mind. Her hand felt warm, dry, and firm in his big paw, and he regretted having to let it go. No wonder, he thought, that this woman was such a successful philanthropist: Who could say no?

"Good morning, ma'am," said Mayhew, managing to sound in control of himself, "and thank you for seeing me on such short notice and at such a difficult time."

"Please, Sergeant, think nothing of it," she said as she led him to a corner containing two chairs and a small table. The maid returned and placed the coffee tray on the table. "Thank you, Maria, that will be all," said Abby, "and please tell Anna that I will not be receiving any calls while I am with Sergeant Mayhew." She spoke with an unaffected but distinct Boston accent that reminded him of the Kennedys.

"Yes, ma'am," said Maria, and left.

"Cream or sugar, Sergeant?" said Abby as she poured the coffee.

"No, thank you, ma'am. Black will be just fine."

"Then we have something in common, Sergeant," she said. The coffee tasted fresh and rich, without a trace of bitterness. Abby must have noticed the look of surprised pleasure on his face.

"I'm glad you like it. It comes from Indonesia."

"Indonesia?"

"Why do you think they call it 'Java,' Sergeant?"

"I don't know," he said, then, seeing the smile on her face said, "Oh."

"Now, how can I help you?" she said, having put him completely at ease.

"Ma'am, as I believe you've been told, your husband died not of natural causes but from ingesting a large quantity of poison, conium maculatum."

"I understand that, Sergeant, and I presume that your first task must be to determine whether my husband committed suicide, was murdered, or if this was all just some tragic accident."

"Well, yes, ma'am."

"Let me tell you directly, Sergeant, that it was simply not possible for my husband to have committed suicide."

"Ma'am?"

"Sergeant, my husband was a Sewall, a family that traces its origins back to well before the settling of this continent. One of his ancestors fought alongside Henry V at Agincourt. I'm not saying this out of any sense of superiority or pride, but you must understand that that family history stands behind my husband, all of his ancestors, and all of his descendants like a rock. It brings with it a value system that simply precludes something as selfish and unthinking as suicide. There has never been a suicide in the history of the Sewall family, and I can tell you without a doubt that my husband was not the first. We are also not just churchgoing Episcopalians but devout Episcopalians, despite that Church's unfortunate political agenda. Martin was a member of the Vestry at Saint Paul's. As you can imagine, the Church teaches that suicide is a sin and forbids it. The whole matter is just unthinkable. But I also imagine," she said, a trace of humor lighting her eyes, "that, despite all that, you have perhaps more mundane questions that require answers."

"I did have a few questions, ma'am, if you don't mind, and I hope that you won't find them intrusive."

"I would only find them intrusive if I thought that either I or my husband had anything to hide, which we do not. I am also desperately anxious to get to the bottom of this."

"Thank you, ma'am," said Mayhew. He hesitated momentarily. "Ma'am, would you consider your marriage a happy one?"

"Sergeant, I know that to many, our marriage must have looked like an arranged union between two elite Boston families meant more to consolidate fortunes and pass the wealth on to yet another generation of privileged children than it was to unite two young lovers; but I can assure you that was the furthest thing from the truth. I met Martin thirty years ago at a dance at Harvard when he was a first-year law student, and I was a sophomore at Radcliffe. I know this sounds like a scene borrowed from *Romeo and Juliet,* but it was literally love at first sight. We were inseparable from that moment on, and we married two years later. Ours was a truly happy marriage."

"I'm sorry to ask this, ma'am, but was there ever any infidelity?"

"Certainly not on my part, and I can also tell you for a fact that if my husband had ever been unfaithful here in Boston or even the surrounding area, I most definitely would have known about it. It would have affected my husband's reputation and our family's, not to mention my own. That simply would not have been allowed, and I would not have let it escape my notice."

"But you also sound like you wouldn't be surprised if it happened elsewhere."

"Surprised, Sergeant? I'm fifty years old, and there is very little in this world that surprises me anymore, especially when it comes to the behavior of men. You are an impulsive bunch, and your touching refusal to grow up makes it laughably easy for women to manipulate you. So is it possible that my husband had at one time or another been physically unfaithful to me? Of course it is, although I doubt it. But I will tell you that he was emotionally devoted to me, as I was to him; and that we were as much in love with each other the last time I saw him as we were the first time I saw him." Her voice faltered.

"I'm sorry, ma'am."

"Please go on," said Abby, rapidly regaining her composure.

"Did he have any health problems that you know of?"

"None. He didn't take a single prescription medication. The only pills I ever saw him take were Zantac for heartburn after a heavy meal, and aspirin. He drank very little and took no illegal drugs of any kind."

"Just so you know, ma'am, there were no drugs found in his body, illegal or otherwise, at the time of his death other than the poison that killed him."

"I am unsurprised."

"Was your husband having any financial or legal difficulties?"

"In order to maintain our position in Boston Society, and especially to maintain the credibility of our philanthropic activities, it is absolutely essential that we remain above reproach legally and ethically. Boston elite society is small but unforgiving, unlike in New York or on the West Coast." The way she said "West Coast" made Mayhew think that Abby Peabody Sewall didn't approve at all of California, perhaps unsure if it should have been admitted to the Union in the first place.

"And how about the family's finances. No problems?"

Much to Mayhew's surprise, Abby hesitated. Sitting in this beautiful room, inside this exquisite home, knowing the Sewall family's reputation for philanthropy, he couldn't imagine that there was any question of the family's financial stability, but her expression now made him suspect otherwise.

"Let me be honest with you, Sergeant. I make the reputation of this family my business; I guard it zealously, and I make sure I know everything I need to know in order to do that. But money is another matter. My mother and father taught me that in our society a family's finances were taken for granted. Our fortunes were made centuries ago, and it was the sacred duty of the men in the family to exercise proper stewardship over them. It was Martin's full-time job to perform that duty, and I did not interfere with it. I can, however, tell you that at present, it seems that our family's fortune has never been in better condition, so I can't imagine that it could have had anything to do with his death."

"But you hesitated when I asked."

"I . . . I can't tell you anything concrete, Sergeant, which is why I hesitate. But I also have an obligation to be completely open with you, especially since I desire even more than you to understand what happened to my husband. I need you to understand, however, that what I am going to tell you is simply based on impressions and a few fragmented incidents, not facts."

"I understand."

"This goes back seven or eight years now. Around 2007 or 2008."

"About the time the Great Recession began?"

"I would say so, even though I don't follow politics or the economy much. I remember because about that time we were about to embark on a major renovation of this house. The plumbing, electricity, and heating systems were badly out of date and there were structural repairs that were urgently needed. We had identified contractors, established a schedule, and had made plans to stay at our home in Kennebunkport for the better part of the six months that would be required to complete the project. Then, one night after dinner, about a week before we were scheduled to leave for Maine, Martin shocked me by saying that the project had been delayed, and that we wouldn't be leaving for Kennebunkport after all."

"Did he give you any explanation?"

"Yes and no. He made some vague remarks about the contractors having scheduling difficulties, but that made no sense to me because the schedule had been meticulously negotiated months prior."

"Did you question him about it?"

"No, I didn't. I didn't feel that it was my place. But I also couldn't help noticing that about that same time he was taking an inordinate number of private calls in his office, and that he was also going out of town frequently on what he called 'business trips.'"

"Was that unusual?"

"It wasn't just unusual, Sergeant; it simply made no sense."

"Why?"

"Because he had no business out of town. His job was to manage the family's finances, under the guidance, of course, of a professional investment advisory firm. He did all of this in Boston; there was absolutely no reason to go out of town."

"How did he explain the trips?"

"He didn't. I didn't ask."

"I don't understand. I thought you and he had an open and honest relationship."

"I just didn't think it was my place. And perhaps, Sergeant, because I didn't want to know."

"But why not?"

"Because I was afraid, that's why. I'm not stupid, Sergeant, and I could only conclude that he was involved in some kind of personal or financial crisis, and I couldn't bear the thought of the implications of either."

"So what happened?"

"Nothing."

"Nothing?"

"One day, whatever had been going on was suddenly over. The trips stopped, the home renovations moved forward, and we suddenly had more money than ever for our philanthropies. And more importantly, he seemed happier and more relaxed than he'd been in ages. Our marriage was wonderful. I convinced myself that whatever had been going on hadn't been so serious after all. I put it behind me and moved on."

"Until last week."

"Yes, Sergeant, until last week. And now I have this awful feeling that whatever happened all these years ago somehow had something to do with his death."

Sergeant David Mayhew could not disagree. After asking her for the name of the family's investment firm, he left Abby Peabody Sewall and her beautiful home not knowing much more than when he'd arrived.

But good cops learn how to listen to their stomachs. David Mayhew may have been young and inexperienced, but he had all the instincts of a good cop. And his stomach was now telling him that Charles Martin Sewall had been murdered, and he'd been murdered over money.

15

THEY'D HAD ANOTHER FINE BREAKFAST TOGETHER AT THE FARM ON TUESDAY MORNING, but the meeting with Maas & Maas had not gone well.

Jill Maas had repeated her offer from Rensselaer Partners to buy the farm for $1.1 million, and had handed Sarah the business card of an agent at Sotheby's in Manhattan. Sarah once again rejected the offer for the farm, now more firmly inclined to keep it, not out of antagonism toward Jill but out of a genuine personal desire to hold on to the property, at least a little longer. She loved it now more than ever, and after further conversation with Julie and Levi she was becoming convinced that she could easily afford to hang on to it for as long as she desired. At Julie's prompting she had taken the Sotheby agent's business card.

At the end of the conversation, Walter had tried to catch the Maases off guard by casually asking what they knew of a man named Charles Martin Sewall, but their blank expressions, even to his practiced detective's eye, had seemed genuine.

They had all gone over to Avery's after the meeting, and after another sampling of his fine food they all felt better. In addition to pleasing adults, Adam also had a gift for cooking for kids. Beth, now eight, and Robin, a precocious five-year-old kindergartner, had both wolfed down tuna melts while one-year-old Daniel guzzled chocolate milk and seemed to eat his weight in scrambled eggs laced with a little local cheddar cheese. Once again, they were the only patrons, but the four adults and three kids at least seemed to give the illusion of a thriving eatery.

"I'm going to miss your business, I'll tell you that," said Adam as they prepared to leave, "and I'm going to miss your friendship as well. You know, for a bunch of city slickers, you sure do seem to fit in well up here."

"Oh, you'll be seeing more of us," said Sarah, "you don't have to worry about that."

"So the Maases haven't talked you into selling the place already?"

"So far we have been impervious to their charms," said Sarah.

"Good for you."

"So, what is it with those guys?" said Walter. "Why are they so anxious to get rid of us?"

"Oh, I wouldn't take it personally if I were you," said Adam. "Remember, if they act as the attorneys on both sides of the sale of the farm, get a fee from Sotheby's for sending you in their direction, plus collect a fee for executing and probating your great-uncle's will, that'll add up to about $50,000 in revenue for a week's work. I doubt they collect that in six months normally. I really don't think it's anything more than that."

Sarah had decided that she wanted to have one last chance to drive Julie's Mercedes, which Julie thought was a brilliant idea, so Walter and Levi loaded the three kids into the back of the Saturn.

"Jesus," said Walter and Levi simultaneously as they watched the Mercedes roar out of town.

"Something tells me," said Walter, "that those two women are going to develop a wonderful friendship with at least one New York State policeman before they get back to the city."

⸺⬥⬥⸺

The kids fell asleep almost immediately, having had more fresh air and sunshine in the past few days than they'd had in their entire lives. Sarah and Walter couldn't imagine living in Dutch River year-round, but looking in the rearview mirror at his children's brown faces, even Walter had to admit that the idea of selling the farm was becoming less and less appealing.

How easy it is, he thought, to get used to the idea of having money, and how difficult it becomes to contemplate no longer having it, even though until two weeks ago they had rejoiced if there had still been twenty-five dollars in the checking account when the next payday arrived. He recalled all of the stories that he'd read in the newspaper during the Great Recession about the desperate, illegal acts committed by formerly law-abiding people in order to save the houses, the cars, and the lifestyles that just a few months before they had taken for granted. People had taken those things, Walter now realized, as affirmation of who they were, as reflections not just of their financial worth but of their human worth; without them, they had been forced to accept hard truths about themselves. People, he now understood, would do a lot to avoid those truths.

"Life is funny, isn't it?" said Levi, reading Walter's mind.

"I guess it's all a little much to absorb," said Walter.

"Walter, remember, two years ago when we first met, I was penniless and recently divorced. I'd been unemployed for almost three years, and I was clinging to a new job I hated with a company I didn't trust simply because I had no alternatives. Then my whole life was turned around because I found poor Peter Lee dying in an alleyway in Midtown. And because of that I met you, and everything changed."

"And you met Julie."

"Yes, I did. I still can't get over all that."

"Not to mention the fact that you're the only guy I've ever known who fell in love with a woman who was pointing a pistol at him."

"In retrospect that seems like the least surprising part of the whole thing. Look, Walter, what I'm trying to say is that I know what you're going through. You're asking yourself, 'Why me?' You're convinced that you did nothing to deserve all this, and you're going to wake up one morning and find out that the whole thing was some pipe dream."

"Just about."

"My advice to you is . . . don't think about it. Take it for what it is and enjoy yourselves. No one can predict the future, and you shouldn't waste any time trying."

"So how would you feel if it all disappeared?"

"I guess I'll never know unless it happens. What I do know is that the best thing that ever happened to me was meeting Julie, long before the Sheikh left her a fortune. I'd at least like to think that I could stand losing everything as long as I had Julie. But Walter?"

"Yeah?"

"Do yourself a favor and don't think about it, okay?"

"Okay, Levi."

"Think about trading in this heap for something a little nicer, maybe," said Levi as they both listened to the suspicious gurgling noises coming from under the hood.

About a half hour later, they saw a state police car with its lights flashing parked behind a black Mercedes SL550 in the breakdown lane up ahead. They waved as they drove by.

16

"**L**OOK AT ME, MR. GRAY," said Walter Hudson. "Do I look like someone who could give a rat's ass about the privacy of your guests?"

Herbert Gray, the assistant manager of the Hotel Grenadier, looked like his name: Gray thinning hair; a gray jacket with "Hotel Grenadier" stitched into the breast pocket with a maroon thread; a shirt that was supposed to be white that wasn't and a collar at least an inch too big for his thin neck; a gray necktie with a maroon "G" embossed on the front, and a grayish complexion that led Walter to conclude that he spent far too much time behind the front desk of this dim lobby for far too little pay. He'd feel bad for the guy later, he thought.

"Please, Officer, try to understand," said Gray, a thin film of perspiration breaking out on his forehead, "our clients depend on our discretion, especially our cash-paying clients."

"I understand perfectly, Mr. Gray. But you have to understand that if you don't cooperate with me to the fullest extent possible right now, I will come back like a bad rash, and I will do so in full uniform. So I strongly suggest that you turn the desk over to your capable assistant over there and take me to your office where we can have this conversation in private." He pointed at a chubby, feckless-looking young man whose nameplate announced his name to be "Nestor," never taking his eyes off Herbert Gray.

"Nestor, you're in charge," said Gray. Nestor stared at him dumbly with his mouth open, looking scared. Gray came out from behind the counter and led Walter toward a door off to the side of the lobby.

The office was about what Walter had expected: cramped, dim, and stuffy. There was a gunmetal-gray desk that looked like government surplus pushed as far back from the door as possible with one beat-up-looking chair behind it and one off to the side. There was a lone poster of Manhattan at night on the wall, the Twin Towers still dominating the skyline in the distance, at least here at the Hotel Grenadier. Walter's tiny cubicle at Midtown South Precinct headquarters compared favorably; a first, he thought. Thankfully, Herbert Gray offered no coffee.

"We believe," said Walter, pulling out a photograph sent to him by Sergeant Mayhew, "that this man stayed in this hotel on the night of Monday, September 9th, and that he departed the next day."

"Can you at least tell me why you're asking?" said Gray, trying not to look at the photo.

"He died the following day on his way back to his home in Boston, and we are investigating."

"Do you think he was, like, murdered?"

"I've told you all you need to know. Now please, look at the photo and tell me if you recognize him."

Gray stared hard at the photo with an expression of agonized concentration. He looked up at Walter, then back at the photo.

"Yes. I recognize the man. I remember that he had a funny accent, like he wasn't from around here. He sounded like the Kennedys."

"And I assume he paid with cash?"

"I don't really remember."

"Try."

"Okay, yes, I believe he paid with cash."

"Was he accompanied by anyone?"

"Not when he checked in, I remember that."

"How about during his stay? A woman, perhaps?"

"Lieutenant, you have to understand. A lot of women come and go here, and, frankly, men, too. Our customers depend absolutely on our discretion, and I make it my business not to interfere with their business."

"Answer my question, Mr. Gray."

"Please believe me, Lieutenant. I do not know. I would tell you if I did."

"I guess it's pointless to ask if he filled out a guest form."

Gray stared back at him, mute. Walter thought he saw a flicker of amusement on the man's face, but he could have been wrong.

"One last question, Mr. Gray, and then I'll leave you alone. If this man had driven here, where would he have parked his car?"

"Well, of course, most of our clientele arrive here by cab or on foot, and we do not provide valet service. But the most convenient parking garage is adjacent to the hotel just around the corner on Thirty-fifth Street. The hotel used to own it, but we sold it off a few years back. You'd have to walk four or five blocks farther to find another one."

"Thank you, Mr. Gray, you've been very helpful," said Walter, rising to leave.

"Should I expect to see you again?" said Gray as they walked across the lobby.

"I don't think you need to worry about that," said Walter. It was the first time he'd seen Herbert Gray smile since he had met him.

⚬⚬⚬

"If this was Butt Crack, Minnesota, maybe I'd be able to help you, Lieutenant," said the young garage attendant with the kind of wiseass attitude that reminded Walter of himself during his youth in Greenpoint, Queens, "but this is Manhattan. Do you know how many Mercedes-Benz E-Classes we park here every day?"

"But you've got to have a surveillance system here, right?"

"Of course, we do," said the attendant, whose nametag identified him as "Stevie." "It's state of the art."

"So can you pull up the tapes from Monday and Tuesday, the 9th and 10th of September?"

"No, I cannot."

"Why?"

"Because we only keep the tapes for a week, and then we record over them."

"State of the art?"

"State of the art."

"OK. Let's move on. Were you working here on those days?"

"Yes, I was. Me and James were here both days," said Stevie, pointing to a young black man who was looking on curiously from a few feet away.

Walter pulled out the photo of Martin Sewall and showed it to Stevie as James sidled over. "Do you recognize this man?"

"Sorry, no, I don't," said Stevie. "He wouldn't exactly stand out in a crowd around here. Kind of like his car, you know?"

"I recognize him."

Walter wheeled around and looked at James. "You do?"

"'Course I do. I don't get many $50 tips, and that guy gave me one. Made him hard to forget, you know?"

"How often do you get a tip like that?"

"Most days, never. That Monday, I got two $50 tips. One from this guy, and one from some lady who, as I recall, didn't look bad for her age."

"Jeez, James, thanks for sharing the wealth," said Stevie, looking peeved.

"Hey, you're on your own, man. You ain't got my charm and good looks, that's your problem."

"What about the next day?" said Walter before they got into a full-blown tiff.

"Same thing," said James, "same two folks, two more Grants."

"Damn," said Stevie.

"Do you remember what she looked like?"

"Not really," said James, "like I said, just a pretty decent-looking white woman, that's all."

"Is there anything else you remember about the two of them?" said Walter, his excitement growing.

"Now that you mention it," said James, "they were both driving the same model car, 2013 black Mercedes E-Classes."

17

"SO, YOU'RE TELLING ME," said Sergeant Mayhew, sitting in his cubicle in the Sturbridge, Massachusetts, State Police Barracks with a phone cradled to his right ear, "that you think there were two identical versions of the same car, and that Mr. Boston Brahmin Charles Martin Sewall and some mysterious female accomplice from upstate New York met in this no-tell hotel in Midtown Manhattan and switched them in a parking garage around the corner. That's what you're telling me."

"That's what I'm telling you," said Lieutenant Hudson, sitting in his cubicle at Midtown South Precinct Headquarters.

"The hell of it is, I can't come up with any better theory."

"Neither can I, and I especially can't figure out what the hell Dutch River, New York, could possibly have to do with any of this." Walter had explained to Mayhew the odd connection that he had with the small town and had told him of his weekend visit.

"I've never visited the place like you have," said Mayhew, "but judging from the way you described it, it doesn't exactly seem like a hotbed of high finance or criminal activity."

"Not at all. But the facts keep staring us in the face, and I'm not willing to write them off to chance, at least not yet."

"Me either. Hey, do you want me to send you the coordinates up in Dutch River that we pulled off the GPS system in Sewall's car? They don't relate to a specific address. It's just a dot on a map, but it may help."

"Trust me, everything in Dutch River is just a dot on a map, but yeah, send them to me; it may be just the middle of a cornfield, but maybe I'll stumble on something. You never know."

"No problem. Anyway, the conversation I had today with the Sewall family's investment advisor might help us."

"Tell me about it," said Walter, although money was the last thing he wanted to talk about. He and Sarah had just come from a meeting with a financial advisor recommended to them by Levi and Julie, and Walter's head was still spinning. Fortunately, Sarah seemed to be absorbing at lightning speed all of the information that was so bewildering to him, so while she happily carried on a conversation with the advisors about the inverse relationship between interest rates and bond prices and something called yield to maturity, which sounded to Walter like a topic best reserved for a sex education class for the elderly, he had zoned out. But this was business; he had to pay attention.

"This advisor, a guy named Barclay Hollis, works for a firm called Safe Harbor Securities, but it sounds like they didn't exactly live up to their name."

"Never trust anyone with two last names, I always say."

"You could be right. Anyway, it seems that this investment firm talked Martin Sewall into some very dicey investment strategies that at the time they thought were foolproof, and I'm willing to bet that's how they represented them to Mr. Sewall."

"Mr. Sewall should have known better," said Walter. "Even my old man, who never had two nickels to rub together in his entire life, always taught me never to bet on a sure thing."

"Well, this guy Hollis tried to turn it all back on Sewall, said that Sewall had wanted to 'adopt a more aggressive investment strategy,' because he kept on hearing all this chatter at his club about how rich some of his friends were getting from investing in the real estate market, which at the time was red hot. He talked about stuff like mortgage-backed securities, collateral debt obligations, and swaps, at which point I put down my pencil and asked him to speak English. So he said the bottom line was that all these strategies would have worked beautifully as long as real estate prices kept going up, which everybody was positive they would. All the fancy models these geniuses were using back then were based on that one big assumption."

"So I'm assuming Mr. Sewall bit."

"Big time, and you know what?"

"Real estate prices went down."

"You should be a financial guru, Lieutenant. They didn't just go down, they collapsed."

"And Mr. Sewall lost a lot of money."

"No, Lieutenant, he lost all the money. By the time the dust settled, he was down to a cash reserve that would last about six months, at which time he would have to sell the Beacon Hill town house and their summer home in Kennebunkport at fire sale prices and move the family into a double-wide in Kentucky. The family fortune that had lasted for over three hundred years was gone, and it was his fault."

"But they seem to be doing fine now. What did this guy Hollis do to help him dig out?"

"Nothing. He said that the firm had issued all the usual disclaimers about the inherent risk of investing and that there was nothing they could do."

"Despite the fact that he'd sold these investments as foolproof."

"You know what they say about a fool and his money, Lieutenant."

"I'm beginning to learn," said Walter, thinking that he was going to have to start paying better attention at his and Sarah's meetings with their financial advisor. He was beginning to realize that investing was like police work: you always wanted someone to have your back. He didn't want to put that type of burden on Sarah.

"But, like I said, the family seems to be richer than ever now, so I asked Hollis what Sewall did to make that happen."

"And?"

"He said he didn't know. He said one day Sewall showed up with a cashier's check for $25 million and asked him to deposit it in his brokerage account."

"Did he ask him where the money came from?"

"Nope. He said it was none of his business. I also think that he didn't want to know. He wanted to be able to claim ignorance in case anything ever went south, although I talked to a guy in the Financial Crimes Division over at the local FBI office, a nice guy named McIntire, and he said that would never hold up in court."

"So Hollis must be getting nervous now that Sewall's turned up dead."

"Sweating bullets, although he was trying not to show it."

"But back then he just took the money."

"Oh yeah. Safe Harbor Securities was just barely hanging on back then. He wasn't about to turn down the management fees on $25 million."

"So was that it?"

"Oh no. The next year, he showed up with a check for $50 million, and the year after that, another one for $65 million. He said he's been averaging about $50 million a year since, and with the rising stock market, the Sewall family is now in billionaire territory. Not exactly hedge fund manager kind of money, but it'll keep the family in clam chowder and baked beans for a long time."

"And you think Mrs. Sewall was being honest with you when she told you that she didn't know anything about all this?"

"I think she was, Lieutenant, but in all honesty I've got to admit that Abby Sewall could probably talk me into believing in the Easter Bunny if she were so inclined."

"She's really something, huh?"

"She most certainly is, Lieutenant."

"Wasn't she at least curious about his trips to New York?"

"She said no. She knew he made the occasional trip there, like once a year, but he said that it was just an annual meeting sponsored by some big brokerage house for large investors that he found helpful. She said she had absolutely no reason not to believe him."

"I guess it's hard to argue with her about that. So where do we go from here?"

"I asked the FBI guy, McIntire, if there was anything that we could do to trace the checks, and he said that since they were cashier's checks, probably not. He could go back and check through Federal Reserve records for bank transfers for that amount around the dates of the checks, but he said that transfers of that size are routine, and it would be like finding a needle in a haystack."

"Besides," said Walter, "if Sewall was just getting a cut of a larger deal, the amounts wouldn't match anyway."

"Hey, you're getting good at this," said Sergeant Mayhew. "That's exactly what McIntire said."

"So I guess that leads us right back to the beginning of this conversation. What the hell could all this possibly have to do with Dutch River? I've got to tell you, Sergeant, there's no one up there who's getting rich."

"Apparently somebody is."

"Well, at least I'll have a place to stay when I go back up there."

"And all those new friends that you can get to know better."

"Yeah, except I'm thinking that one of them isn't a friend."

18

"WHERE DID YOU LEARN TO DRIVE LIKE THIS, LEVI?" said Walter, hoping that his voice didn't betray the fear that was tying his stomach in a knot. They were in Julie's Mercedes, driving north on the Taconic Parkway on yet another spectacular autumn day. Levi wasn't driving with Sarah's abandon, but he was certainly putting the little monster through its paces.

"Remember," said Levi, unable to suppress a smile at Walter's discomfiture, "I spent twenty-five years of my life living on Long Island. If you can survive Route 110 on a Saturday morning, you can manage just about anything. And I never thought that I'd ever in my life have a chance to drive a car like this one. It's fun; you ought to try it."

"I think I'll take a pass for now."

"OK, but remember, Sarah's probably going to have one of these things of her own pretty soon."

"Don't remind me," said Walter as Levi hit a sharp, downward sloping curve at 85.

"So tell me again how you convinced Captain Amato to let you follow up on this?" said Levi. "I mean, the guy died in Massachusetts and he was probably poisoned in Connecticut."

"I reminded him that it's extremely likely that whatever happened in the Hotel Grenadier between Charles Martin Sewall and our mystery woman was most likely a factor in his murder, and that it probably involved a great deal of money. I also told him that at this point the New York State Police are showing no interest because they have no evidence that any crime was committed in their jurisdiction, so it's not like I'm going to cause a turf war with our brother law enforcement professionals."

"And then you told him that I'd be coming along with you since the Intelligence Division was taking an active interest because of the possibility of a financial crime being committed, since financial crimes are so often linked to terrorist activity."

"Well, yeah, I guess I did that."

"Which came as news to Deputy Commissioner Strickland. You know . . . my boss."

"I guess I got a little bit out in front of myself there. Sorry."

"No you're not. But that's okay, I smoothed it over, and once Strickland heard what was going on, he got really interested anyway."

They pulled off the road to refill their coffee cups. Before they pulled away, Levi said, "Hey, didn't you say that Sergeant Mayhew gave you the GPS coordinates for where in Dutch River that car started its trip?"

"Yeah, he did, but he said it was just a dot in the middle of nowhere. But I've got it, hang on." Walter pulled out his smartphone and logged into his e-mail. "Here they are," he said.

Levi pulled out his own phone and pulled up his "Maps" app. "Why don't you give them to me," he said. Walter gave him the coordinates and waited while Levi punched them into the app.

"Well," said Levi after just a few seconds, "I guess we know where we're going to start our investigation."

"What do you mean?"

"Sergeant Mayhew was right; the coordinates just land you in the middle of an empty space on the map, but look." He handed the phone over to Walter.

"Holy crap," said Walter.

"I'm not wrong, am I?"

"No, you're not. That's Armin Jaeger's farm."

"No," said Levi. "That's your farm."

———

"It's good to see you guys again," said Adam Avery as he handed menus to Levi and Walter, "though I didn't expect to see you so soon. Where are Sarah and Julie?" As usual, Avery's Restaurant was empty except for them, but the shining sun pouring in through the front window casting a golden glow over the tables, along with the aromas coming from the kitchen, made Avery's Restaurant seem warm and friendly anyway. The air outside was decidedly more autumnal than before, but still pleasant.

"Sarah and Julie had to stay back this time," said Walter, "but don't worry, they'll be back soon."

"I hope that means that you haven't come here to sell off the farm."

"Oh no," said Walter. "That's Sarah's decision, not mine, and she is nowhere near ready to sell the place. As a matter of fact, she's more determined than ever to keep it."

"Well, that'll make a lot of people around here happy. You were a big hit at the dinner last week. I know my wife, Sally, will be really pleased. I don't know if you noticed, but our kids really hit it off."

"I did notice that, and I also know that Sarah and Julie really hit it off with Sally."

"Sally and I have lived our entire lives up here, and we can't think of anyplace we'd rather live and raise our kids, but it's always nice to meet some different folks, I've got to say. Anyway, I hate to be nosy, but if you're not here to sell the farm and your families couldn't come with you, what are you guys here for? I'm pretty sure it's not so that Fred Benecke can get more free labor out of you."

"We're still sore from that last visit," said Walter. "I don't know how that guy does it at his age."

"Well, I'll tell you, he misses all the help that Armin used to give him, so watch out. He'll be putting you back in harness the minute he sees you if you're not careful."

"Actually, I'm looking forward to that," said Levi, "but unfortunately, we're here on police business this time."

"You're kidding me, right? New York City cops here in Dutch River on police business?"

"Nope, we're not kidding, Adam."

"Look, I'm being a pretty poor host here. Why don't I bring you your lunches and you can tell me more about it, if you're so inclined."

"That sounds great," said Walter. "I think a lot better on a full stomach."

They both ordered roast beef sandwiches and a bowl of Adam's homemade vegetable soup, and they dug in hungrily when the food arrived. Adam had put thick slices of excellent local cheddar cheese on the sandwiches along with generous dollops of freshly made horseradish. The soup was thick with local vegetables, and Adam had seasoned it perfectly with herbs raised in his own garden.

"Adam," said Levi, "if you served this soup in Manhattan, you'd be the talk of the town."

"Thanks, Levi. That means a lot to hear you say that. But if I were serving this soup in Manhattan, I wouldn't have just had the vegetables delivered an hour ago from a farm a mile down the road by a farmer I've known all my life, and I wouldn't have picked the herbs from my own garden while I was heating the broth. That is the basic experience of cooking that means so much to me, that direct connection with the food and where it comes from. And besides, it wouldn't taste the same, at least to me."

"And the cheese in these sandwiches is amazing," said Walter, his mouth full.

"Our friends across the border in Vermont like to brag about their cheese, but to my taste, a good, sharp, New York State cheddar is one of the finest cheeses in the world."

"No argument here," said Walter, reaching for the second half of his sandwich.

"So now that you guys have some food in your stomachs, do you mind telling me what this police business is that you're here for?"

Before Walter and Levi could start to talk, the door of the restaurant opened and Officer Bert Steffus squeezed himself through the opening.

"Aw, Bert," said Adam, "you're not here to make more trouble, are you?"

Bert stared at the men with a surprised expression on his face, clearly having expected to find Julie and Sarah sitting in the restaurant.

"Officer Steffus," said Walter, before Bert had a chance to say anything, "we haven't had the pleasure of meeting you. I'm Detective Lieutenant Walter Hudson, and this is Captain Leviticus Welles, both NYPD. I'm just your average flatfoot, and Captain Welles is a big shot in the Intelligence Division. Come sit down." It wasn't an order, but coming from Walter, it sounded like one. Bert almost snapped to attention, making his stomach jiggle, and his face turned bright pink. He opened his mouth as if to say something, but then closed it and came over and took a chair next to Adam and across from Levi and Walter.

"I'm not here looking for any trouble," said Bert, looking more at Adam than at the two cops.

"I didn't assume you were," said Walter, eliciting a suspicious stare from Bert. "Actually, I'm glad to meet you. We've heard a lot about you."

"Now, look, like I said—"

"We've heard that you are a conscientious police officer, and we would like your assistance," said Levi, now eliciting an incredulous glance from Adam. "Adam, why don't you bring this man a slice of that apple pie of yours."

"What?" said Bert.

"As we were just beginning to explain to Mr. Avery," said Walter, "we are here on official police business."

"And you want *my* help?" said Bert, his chest puffing out. Walter couldn't help but notice that it looked like the buttons on the blouse of his uniform were about to surrender to the enormous strain being placed on them.

"No," said Levi, "we *need* your help. And we need Adam's help."

"I don't get it," said Adam and Bert in unison.

"We are investigating the suspicious death of a very prominent man from Boston," said Walter.

"Did he die around here?" said Bert, digging hungrily into the slice of pie that Adam placed in front of him. "I haven't heard anything about it, but nobody tells me anything anyway . . ."

"No, Bert," said Walter, "he didn't die around here. He died in Massachusetts. But the day before he died, we have strong reason to believe that he met with someone in a New York City hotel, a woman who, it seems, drove down to New York from Dutch River in a black Mercedes-Benz."

"Well, we don't have people driving around in Mercedes-Benzes around here," said Bert. "It must have been somebody from out of town who stopped here on her way back from Saratoga or something."

"That's a really good point, Officer Steffus, but we don't think so," said Levi. "First of all, the GPS record in the car doesn't indicate any other recent trips were made, and the other thing is that the trip the car took didn't start from here in town, like it would have if this woman was just stopping off for a meal."

"Then where did it start from?" said Adam.

"It started from Armin Jaeger's farm."

"What?" said Bert.

"That makes no sense," said Adam.

"You're right," said Walter, "especially since the trip took place after Mr. Jaeger died and the house was most likely empty."

"I know it was empty," said Bert.

"How would you know that?" said Levi.

"Because after he died, I made sure to drive by the farm at least once a day. I also popped in once or twice. It was a valuable place, and it had a lot of expensive stuff in it. I thought it was my duty to make sure that it was protected."

"How did you get in? I thought nobody had the access code to the security system but Armin and Fred," said Walter.

"I had it, too," said Bert, a look of pride brightening his face as he saw the surprised expressions coming from the other three men. "Mr. Jaeger trusted me, believe it or not. He said that someone besides him and Fred needed to have the code in case of an emergency, and because they were both old. He chose me. He said I was a good man." His voice almost cracked on the last words.

"I'm sure he was right," said Levi.

"Which is all the more reason why we need you," said Walter, "and you, too, Adam. Do you guys have a little more time?"

"Sure looks like I do," said Adam, casting a glance around the still empty restaurant.

"I've got all the time you need," said Officer Steffus, looking like he'd have to be dragged out of the restaurant in cuffs if forced to leave.

"Good," said Walter.

"Do you think I could have another slice of pie?" said Bert, holding up his plate.

"On the house," said Adam, making Bert smile.

19

"DO YOU THINK IT COULD HAVE ANYTHING TO DO WITH THE ART?" said Walter as he, Levi, and Fred Benecke sat out on the back porch of the farmhouse sipping beer. The air was cool and the light was fading, but the south-facing porch was still warm. They had spent the afternoon helping out a grateful Fred with chores around the farm, and they'd invited him to stay for a beer and a bite to eat. The beer was Armin's home brew, and it was delicious: malty and rich without being heavy, crisp without sacrificing substance. Fred had brought over some steaks for grilling and some produce to make a salad.

"I don't see how it could have been," said Levi. "The money doesn't add up."

"What do you mean?" said Walter.

"Martin Sewall's financial advisor told Sergeant Mayhew that Sewall was depositing $25 million, sometimes $50 million a year into his brokerage account. Sotheby's estimated that the total value of Armin's entire art collection was maybe $35 million."

"And it's still here," said Fred.

"So you're saying that you haven't noticed any changes in his collection over the past seven or eight years?" said Walter.

"Those paintings have been on the wall for sixty years or more now. If anything, he's added a couple of the more modern-looking pieces over the years. But I can't recall a single painting that I've seen on the walls that isn't there anymore."

"Could he have been storing some in the attic?" said Walter.

"Perhaps, but I doubt it. I've been up to the attic plenty of times to help him move furniture, and I've never seen a single painting up there. And the attic isn't climate controlled, so he wouldn't have stored any artwork of any real value up there. But I guess that's not the real point."

"What do you mean?" said Levi.

"Armin wasn't a trader. He didn't collect that art for the money. He collected it because he loved it, because it gave him pleasure to look at it.

He wasn't interested in buying or selling, and I'm pretty sure he never even got an estimate on the value of his collection."

"So we must be looking at this all wrong," said Walter as Levi put the steaks on the grill. "Maybe I've been trying too hard to make a connection between Martin Sewall's murder, the money he's made, and his visit with this woman in New York. Maybe the guy was just having an affair."

"I don't think you really believe that," said Levi.

"No, I guess I don't. From everything Sergeant Mayhew had been able to learn from Mrs. Sewall, he made these trips to New York just once a year, and those annual deposits were usually made within a week or two of the trip."

"I'm no detective," said Fred, "but for all you know, this was the only time this Sewall guy ever met up with a woman who drove down from Dutch River."

"I hadn't thought about that," said Walter, "but you're right. Maybe this woman was just some Internet hookup, and he'd arranged to meet her in New York on his annual trip. The pattern fits. I bet ninety percent of the clientele at the Hotel Grenadier on any given day are there for just that reason. If you're a prominent man, you don't carry on an adulterous affair at the Waldorf-Astoria."

"But still," said Levi, "let's not forget that our theory is that there was a rather elaborate scheme set up involving two identical cars being switched out as part of this rendezvous. You wouldn't do that if you were just having an affair. At most, you'd just stay in separate parking garages. To me, the only logical reason for that type of a switch is because something was being handed off, and those two didn't want to be seen making an exchange."

"I can't disagree," said Walter.

"But what were they exchanging, then? There was nothing found in Sewall's car, and it was torn down to nuts and bolts."

"The obvious answer is that Sewall brought something to New York and the woman drove off with it. And whatever he dropped off is what he got a huge sum of money for. That makes a lot more sense to me than this woman from a poor town in upstate New York bringing something to Sewall that would be worth that much. And besides, if she were the one bringing something, he'd be paying her, not the other way around."

"And I hate to complicate things for you young men," said Fred, "but all this makes me more suspicious than ever about Armin's death."

"What do you mean?" said Walter.

"I don't care what that doctor said about Armin being ninety and dying a natural death from 'massive systemic' whatever. Armin Jaeger was a healthy man right up to the day he died. Please don't take offense, but that day he put in a day's work that would've landed the two of you in the hospital."

"How did he seem afterward?" said Walter.

"He seemed fine. He seemed more than fine. He looked like he could head back out to the fields and do it all over again. And then he said to me, 'Good day's work, Fred. Come on in and have a refresher with me.'"

"Refresher?"

"That's what he always called his afternoon cocktail, his 'refresher,'" said Fred, smiling at the reminiscence. "I said, 'Fine, but I'll stick with a beer if you don't mind.' Armin said, 'Fine, Fred, but you're too young a man to be going soft.' We both got a laugh out of that."

"But you said he wasn't feeling well by the time you left."

"That's true, but that wasn't until just before I left. We sat out on the porch for an hour or more, just chatting about anything and everything. Armin would just as likely strike up a conversation about the latest symphony he'd just listened to as he would about the price of corn. Like I keep saying, he was a funny guy."

"Let me ask you," said Levi, "did Armin ever start sounding short of breath?"

"No."

"Did he ever start sounding congested, like he had a bad chest cold?"

"No."

"Did he ever complain about having heartburn, or pains in his arms or neck?"

"No."

"What are you getting at, Levi?" said Walter.

"What he's getting at," said Fred, "is that those are all signs of congestive heart failure or an impending heart attack. I know that, and Armin knew that. If he felt like he was going to have a heart attack or if he was going into heart failure, he would've told me, and he didn't. And he didn't because he wasn't."

"Did he say anything other than he just wasn't feeling good?" said Walter.

"No. He just felt that he was starting to feel a bit poorly and all he wanted to do was get his boots off. He said he thought he might have laced them a bit tight in the morning."

"And what did you make of that?"

"Nothing. I took it that he'd laced his boots too tight that morning. It happens."

"And now you're starting to think that he didn't die of natural causes, and that his death had something to do with Martin Sewall's death and all this other stuff."

"Yes," said Fred Benecke, his jaw set. "And I'll tell you one other thing."

"What's that?" said Walter.

"We better eat those steaks before your friend there turns them into shoe leather."

———————

After dinner, they decided to go upstairs and look once more at Armin's bedroom, which Walter and Levi had only peeked into on their first visit. They were struck, as Sarah and Julie had been before them, by the simplicity of the room and by the sophistication of the books in the bookcase.

"I don't think you're going to find much here," said Fred.

"I'm beginning to agree with you," said Walter.

"Fred," said Levi, "is there anything about this room that you find unusual? Anything out of the ordinary?"

"Look, I spent very little time in here. The only times I was in here was when I was fiddling with either the climate or the security systems. And I was usually in here by myself when I was doing that stuff."

Levi walked over to the nightstand and picked up the book on it, Will Durant's *Life of Greece*. "I guess Armin was quite a reader, huh?"

"Oh yes he was. Those books weren't in the bookcase for show, let me tell you. I'll bet he read every book in that bookcase at least once." Then he did a double take on the book Levi was holding. "Hey, wait a minute."

"What?"

"That's not one of his Bibles."

"No, it's a book about Greek history. Why?"

"It's just that Armin always said that the last thing he did every night before he went to sleep was read a passage from one of his Bibles. Every time I've been in this room, the only thing I've seen on that nightstand is a Bible, usually his German one."

"But you've said you weren't in here very often," said Walter. "And he may not have meant every night."

"When Armin said 'every night,' he meant 'every night.'"

"Hmmm, that's interesting," said Levi, opening the book to the bookmarked page.

"What?" said Walter.

"Walter, what poison did Sergeant Mayhew tell you Martin Sewall died of?"

"Aw, I don't remember. But wait," said Walter, pulling a small notepad from his shirt pocket. "I wrote it down." He flipped through the pages until he came to the one he was looking for. He looked at the writing in concentration. "It says, 'conium maculatum.' Do you want me to spell that for you?"

"Please," said Levi, pulling his smartphone out of his pocket. He punched in the words, and then stared at the screen.

"So?" said Walter.

"That's what I thought. The common term for 'conium maculatum' is 'poison hemlock.'"

"Uh-oh," said Fred.

"What am I missing here?" said Walter, looking back and forth between the two.

"Poison hemlock," said Levi, reading from his phone, "is a slow-acting poison that tends to progress from the feet up, which might explain why Armin was complaining about his boots the night he died. His feet were probably starting to go numb."

"But what does that have to do with the book?" said Walter.

"The book was marked at a page describing the trial and death of Socrates. Legend has it that when the Greek court wrongfully sentenced him to death for treason, he chose to die by drinking poison hemlock, talking with his friends while the poison progressed."

"So Armin put that book there for a reason," said Fred.

"Yes, he did," said Levi, closing the book and placing it back on the nightstand. "He was trying to tell someone that he had been poisoned, and that the poison was poison hemlock."

"The same poison that killed Martin Sewall," said Walter.

"The very same."

"Fred, I'm beginning to think that you may have a point."

20

"**Y**OU HAVE TO UNDERSTAND, SERGEANT, that I am not a well-traveled woman," said Abby Peabody Sewall to Sergeant David Mayhew. They were once again sitting in Abby's office on the third floor of the Beacon Hill townhouse, once again with a coffee tray between them, though this time, since it was afternoon, a tray of delectable-smelling pastries had also been served.

Abby must have been profoundly shaken by Mayhew's revelations that her husband most likely had a rendezvous with a woman on his last trip to New York, but she had barely shown it. Her face had almost imperceptibly paled, and her erect posture had sagged just for an instant, but long enough for Mayhew to notice. Once again, he had been almost overcome with the impulse to take the fragile-looking woman in his arms, and once again, he had resisted, but it had been more difficult this time. He silently chastised himself, though he really didn't know exactly what for.

"So you haven't visited New York City recently with your husband?" said Mayhew.

"I have never visited New York City with my husband, Sergeant."

"I'm not saying that I don't believe you, ma'am, but I find that surprising."

"Why should that be surprising to you, Sergeant? My entire life: family, friends, all my charitable activities, are right here in Boston. Boston has fine museums and libraries and one of the greatest orchestras in the country. The number and quality of the restaurants in this city is astonishing. Why should I leave? Many New Yorkers are the same way, you know. City dwellers are very provincial in their own way."

"If you say so, ma'am. So I'm guessing then that you've also never been to a town in upstate New York called Dutch River?"

"I have never heard of such a place. Should I have?"

"It just seems that the woman your husband met with in New York City drove down from there."

"Sergeant, I am vaguely aware that there is a region called 'Upstate

New York,' but that is the limit of my knowledge. Do I seem to you, Sergeant," she said, a glint of humor lighting her hypnotic eyes, "to be the type of woman that you would expect to meet in a place called 'Dutch River'?"

"No, ma'am, I guess not." He knew that she was toying with him, but he didn't know if it was because she realized how utterly under her spell he had fallen, or if it was just out of habit, something she had learned to do to elicit the maximum donations from wealthy donors at cocktail parties. Or both. All he knew was that the moment could not have been more intimate if she had leaned over and kissed him, and it left him utterly flustered. She smiled for just an instant, and was once again all business. He collected himself as best he could.

"Would you know how many automobiles your family owns?"

"I certainly would not. I do know, of course, that we own a car that I use for my travels around the city, and my husband must have had one as well. I'll ask Jeffrey, my driver, if you'd like."

"Perhaps we can do that later. Would you know the make of the car that you use? Would it be a Mercedes-Benz?"

"I'm not sure, but I don't think it's a Mercedes. One sees so many of them, and mine doesn't look like that. But we'll ask Jeffrey."

"Sure. Did your husband ever serve in the military, ma'am?"

"No, he did not," she said, looking a little surprised at the question. "He was not what one would call the martial type, and, besides, his father tragically passed away while Martin was still in law school, and he was completely absorbed in the business affairs of the family from a very young age. But please don't think that the Sewall family has ever been unwilling to serve. His father served in Vietnam, and his grandfather served in World War II. Duty to Country has always been an important element of the family's value system. But why do you ask?"

"Sometimes people make connections in the armed services that they wouldn't have made otherwise. You know, kids from Kansas becoming lifelong friends with kids from Wisconsin, that type of thing. I'm just trying to figure out how your husband ever would have come to know anyone from Dutch River, New York."

"I don't see how that would have made sense in any event, Sergeant. This woman that my husband seems to have met with was apparently quite a bit younger than he was."

"I know I'm stretching, but there has to be some kind of connection between the two, somewhere. And to be perfectly honest, ma'am, I do not think that he was meeting with this woman merely to carry on an affair."

"I don't know if you are saying that simply to defend my sensibilities, Sergeant," said Abby, reaching over and lightly touching the back of his hand, sending an electric thrill through his body. "If you are, thank you, but it is unnecessary."

"It's just, you know, the whole car switching thing doesn't sound like something people do just to carry on an affair, that's all."

"It doesn't seem that way to me, either, but at this point, I'm not certain we're ever going to know for sure."

"We're doing the best we can, ma'am."

"I'm sorry," said Abby, once again reaching over to touch his hand, "that wasn't meant to be a criticism of you or anyone else. It's just that I've been told that if these matters are not solved quickly, they are often never solved at all."

"It is true that the probability of solving a murder case goes down over time, but we are not even close to giving up on this, ma'am."

"Especially, I suppose, since you suspect that my husband's murder has something to do, perhaps a great deal to do, with the restoration of our family's wealth. Money always seems to keep people interested, doesn't it?"

"No one is saying that your husband did anything illegal or improper to restore your family's fortune, ma'am. What we are saying is that there is a strong suspicion that his death was due, perhaps, to someone else's envy or greed."

"Perhaps, Sergeant. Now, I do not want to rush you, but I have an appointment across town in a half hour. Should I postpone it, or do you think we are finished here, at least for the moment?"

"I think we're just about finished for the time being," said Mayhew, rising to leave and thinking that he would have stayed the rest of the afternoon if she hadn't said anything. He looked down at the tray of pastries and realized that they were untouched. He'd been hungry when he'd arrived, but had lost any awareness of his appetite while he'd been talking to Abby.

"Sergeant, you never touched any of these lovely pastries," she said, noticing his glance. "What a shame. They're fresh from an Italian bakery in the North End, and they are always delicious. Please take some with you. I would hate for you to leave my home with an unsatisfied appetite."

The smile she gave him wasn't seductive, but it didn't have to be.

"Well, ma'am, sometimes these things can't be avoided," said Mayhew, feeling his face flush. He grabbed a couple of the pastries and wrapped them in a napkin. He saw himself out.

———

It hadn't been difficult to find the garage in the lower level of the town house in the back. It had two bays; one occupied by a late-model Bentley and the other by a Range Rover Evoque. Off in one corner a small office had been constructed, and sitting in it was a man whom Mayhew presumed was Jeffrey.

Jeffrey looked to be about sixty, and to Mayhew's eye had probably been a cabdriver or an employee of a limousine company after a previous career, perhaps in insurance, had ended badly. How he had landed this job with the Sewall family was probably an interesting story told often over drinks at his favorite pub; he looked like a man who had gotten lucky and knew it. He also looked like a man who appreciated a good pub.

"Hi," said Mayhew, poking his head into the office, "are you Jeffrey?"

"The one and only, and judging from the uniform and the phone call I just got from upstairs, I assume you are Sergeant David Mayhew of the Massachusetts State Police, an organization of which I think very highly."

"Yes, I am. Mrs. Sewall probably already told you why I wanted to see you."

"She wasn't too clear, but it sounds like you want to know if Mr. or Mrs. Sewall owned a Mercedes E-Class?"

"That's right. Apparently, Mr. Sewall was sitting in one when he was found dead on the Massachusetts Turnpike."

"All I can tell you, Sergeant, is, if he owned a Mercedes, it's news to me." He pointed at the cars sitting in the bays. "These are the only cars the Sewalls own to the best of my knowledge. On top of that, does this family look like it would be caught dead driving around in an E-Class?"

"I hear you, Jeffrey. But all I can tell you is that Martin Sewall was found dead in one."

"I'm sure you guys must've run the tags on it."

"Yeah, we did, but it was registered to some funny-sounding corporation. I didn't think about it much because I know a lot of these guys set up leasing corporations to own their cars for tax purposes."

"I wouldn't know anything about that, Sergeant, not being in that kind of a tax bracket myself. All I know is they don't own an E-Class, and I've never seen either Mr. or Mrs. Sewall in one."

"Did you see Mr. Sewall the morning he left for New York two weeks ago?"

"Yes, I did. I was down here having my morning coffee when he came down. They usually call ahead so I can warm up the car, but that morning he just showed up. It was about seven o'clock, which is early for himself, you know, and he asked me to take him down to the Ritz Carlton. He said he was meeting someone there. So I fired up the Rover and drove him down. I was back before my coffee got cold."

"Oh, I would have thought that the Rover was Mrs. Sewall's car."

"Nah, Mrs. Sewall rides around in the Bentley. It keeps that skinny little fanny of hers nice and warm and comfortable, you know?" said Jeffrey giving Mayhew a sly wink.

"No, I don't know," said Mayhew, surprised at the anger he heard in his own voice.

"Hey, sorry," said Jeffrey, looking alarmed. "I didn't mean any offence, you know? Hey, please don't tell her I said that, okay? I need this job."

"Don't worry. Did you see him meet anybody when you got to the hotel?"

"No, he just got out of the car and walked straight into the lobby, and I drove away."

"Okay, Jeffrey," said Mayhew, turning to leave. "Thanks for your help."

"No problem, Sergeant. Anything I can do to help, you just tell me, okay?"

"Okay, thanks."

"And you're not going to tell Mrs. Sewall about what I said, right?"

"Don't worry about it."

"Thanks, Sergeant. I'm a big supporter of the state police, you know?"

"I'm sure you are."

21

"YOU REMEMBER ME, GRANDDAD? I'm Adam, your grandson."

"You are?" said Oscar Avery, looking slightly dubiously at Adam.

"Yes, you know, Clayton's son."

"Clayton, you say? I have a son named Clayton."

"Yes, you do."

"Do you know my son?"

"Yes, Granddad, he's my father."

"He is?" said Oscar Avery, a look of sly skepticism animating his blank face.

This was not what Walter had been hoping for. Adam had been honest with him about his grandfather's condition and had recommended against the visit, saying that it would be a waste of time. But Walter had insisted, thinking that perhaps the stimulation of a visit might prompt at least a few brief moments of mental clarity. Levi had stayed behind, arguing that more than two people would probably overwhelm the old man. He had clearly been right, and Walter's only regret was that he hadn't been the one to stay behind.

If Armin Jaeger had been a remarkably robust ninety-year-old, as all the evidence indicated he had been, then Oscar Avery was the polar opposite. He was completely wheelchair bound, his stick-thin legs sticking out pathetically from the bottom of his pajamas, marble white against the black of the wheelchair, his slippered feet strapped to the foot supports. His hands rested, unmoving, on the armrests. His head tilted slightly to one side, his thin neck no longer up to the task of keeping it straight.

And his mind was even worse. The attending nurse had told Adam and Walter when they had arrived that Oscar was "having a good day." It made Walter wonder what a bad day was like for the old man.

The nursing home itself was not bad, as nursing homes go, and Oscar's room was clean and bright with the autumn sunshine that streamed through the window. But the window was closed and the air was stuffy and overly warm, smelling of that combination of disinfectant, food odors, and bodily effluents that no amount of cleaning could ever quite eradicate.

"Do you think we could ask him about Armin?" said Walter.

"I don't see what harm it could do," said Adam.

"Maybe you should do the talking. At least your voice isn't completely strange to him."

"Okay," said Adam, turning to his grandfather, a resigned look on his face. "Granddad, do you remember Armin Jaeger?"

Suddenly Oscar's head straightened and his eyes lit up. "Corporal Jaeger? Of course, I know Corporal Jaeger."

"How do you know him, Granddad?"

"What do you mean, 'how do I know him'? For heaven's sake, we grew up together, we enlisted together, went through basic training together, and now we're fighting side by side for the greatest general this army has ever known."

"When is the last time you saw him, Granddad?"

"Saw him? I saw him this morning at the mess tent, of course. You can ask him yourself. He's right down there." Oscar flung his left arm straight out in a loose-jointed manner that reminded Walter of the Scarecrow in *The Wizard of Oz*. "He pitched his tent right down that path last night. Not twenty yards from here."

Adam and Walter's heads reflexively swiveled in the direction of Oscar's pointed hand, and as they did they noticed that the nurse had entered the room.

"That's where he lives now," she said. Her nametag identified her as "Becki."

"Lives where?" said Walter.

"Back in World War II. You see it a lot. For guys like Oscar here, you know, 'The Greatest Generation' guys, that was the defining time of their lives. Then, after the war, they spent their adulthoods not talking about it, just moving on; but when they get near to the end, they start to talk, and when they get to the point where your grandfather is, they go back there, and they stay there."

"Does he talk to you much?" said Adam.

"Oh yes. Your grandfather is a wonderful man. I spend as much time as I can with him. It's my job, but it's more than that. He's a fascinating person, and I never get tired of his stories."

"Jeez," said Adam, flinching with guilt.

"Do you think any of what he says to you is true, or do you think it's all just a fantasy in his mind?" said Walter.

"Of course, it's impossible to know for sure, but if you ask me, it's all real. The rest of his mind may be shot; I mean, I can't remember the last time he actually knew where he was, but that part of his memory is crystal clear. He's happy there, and that's where he stays."

"What does he talk about?"

"Mostly he talks about himself and this guy Armin. He tells me how the two of them were best buddies growing up and that they'd sworn an oath that they'd stick together during the war and take care of each other as best they could. One of the reasons I'm glad you guys came today is because it finally confirmed to me that Armin was real. I was positive he was, but I never knew absolutely for sure until today. It just makes me more positive than ever that all the stories he tells me are true."

"Does he talk about anybody besides Armin?"

"Not really, except every once in a while he'll talk about somebody he calls 'The Major.' But I've got to tell you, 'The Major' is the one part of his stories that I'm not sure is really a genuine memory."

"Why not?" said Walter.

"Because he only comes up from time to time, and he doesn't have a name, just 'The Major,'" said Becki, making air quotes with her fingers. "He remembers the names and nicknames of all the other men in his company, but 'The Major' is never anything but 'The Major.' He could just represent some authority figure who had intimidated him somewhere along the way."

"What does he say about him?"

"Just things like, 'The Major stopped by today, but I didn't talk to him.' The other reason I don't think he's real is that he never recounts any conversations he had with him. He always says that Armin talked to him. If the guy was real, he would have had his own conversations with him, but he always let Armin do all the talking to him. But we'll never really know."

"The Major?" said Oscar suddenly, a look of alarm on his face. "Did you say the Major was coming?"

"It's all right, Oscar," said Becki in a soothing voice, but it didn't work.

"I've got to find Armin," he said, helplessly trying to grasp the wheels of his wheelchair. "The Major doesn't like to be kept waiting. Where's Armin? I've got to find Armin!"

"I'm sorry, gentlemen," said Becki, "but I'm going to have to ask you to leave. When he gets overwrought like this, it takes a while to calm him down, and it's really not good for him."

"We understand, ma'am. We're sorry if we caused you trouble," said Adam as he and Walter rose to leave.

"It's okay, I'll manage. And it's so good for him to have some company. Thank you so much for stopping by."

"Jeez," said Adam once more.

It was a quiet ride back to town.

⚯

"I don't know how much longer we can go without reporting our findings to the state police, Walter," said Levi, as he, Walter, and Bert Steffus sat at the kitchen table at the farmhouse. In a triumph of hope over experience, Adam had asked to be dropped off at his restaurant so that he could prepare for the lunch hour, in case anyone showed up.

"I'm starting to agree with Mr. Welles," said Bert. "My old high school buddy over at the crime lab was willing to do me a favor and test the whiskey, but he was really nervous, and he doesn't want to get in trouble." Bert, as Walter had suspected, had turned out to be a resourceful and capable ally once he realized that, for once, someone was taking him seriously. There was a good mind lurking behind that clownish exterior, and his temperamental behavior had moderated considerably. Walter had seen it over and over again: Respect to a human being is like water to a flower, and Bert Steffus was blossoming.

"I know that," said Walter, "but I also know that the minute the state police find out Armin was poisoned, they're going to take it out of my hands, and I'm not willing to let it go yet."

"Walter," said Levi, "it'll take them a couple of weeks to exhume the body, do the tests, and get the results back. If we can't solve this whole thing by then, we probably deserve to have it taken away from us."

"You're both right. I don't want to get anyone in trouble, and I also don't want to do anything that would get in the way of Sergeant Mayhew's investigation. But my biggest concern, and you know this as well as anyone, Bert, is this is a small town, and I'm not sure how fast I want news of this to spread."

"Because?" said Levi.

"Because," said Bert, "Lieutenant Hudson thinks that someone around here is up to their neck in something that caused the death of Armin Jaeger and also Martin Sewall. And so do I."

"That's right," said Walter, "and we should give them as little chance as possible to cover their tracks."

"I guess I'm not sure I agree with you," said Levi. "My guess is that whatever is going on here is being done by outsiders, and Dutch River is just some kind of accidental intersection where these outsiders met. My guess is that poor Armin probably got in the way of something he knew nothing about."

"I can't argue with you, Levi," said Walter, "but my stomach is telling me otherwise."

"So what do we do now?" said Bert.

"We're going to do what we can, and see where that leads us," said Walter.

"What does that mean?" said Bert.

"It means we're going to follow the poison."

22

FRED BENECKE HAD TOLD THEM that, like everything else in his life, Armin Jaeger's purchases of bourbon had been done according to a strict routine: On the first business day of every other month, he had driven up to a place called Colonie Fine Wines and Spirits on Shaker Road in an area northwest of Albany called Loudonville, where he would buy a case of his favorite bourbon and, if necessary, refresh his supply of Angostura bitters.

The drive took about a half hour, but the morning was sunny and pleasant, and Bert Steffus felt excited about doing important police work for an important policeman. He knew that Sergeant Stanley Barry of the Columbia County Sheriff's Department looked at him as a nuisance and gave him nothing more than make-work assignments designed to make him look foolish in the eyes of the other cops. They knew he could hear their snickers, but they didn't care.

What would they say if they saw me now? he thought. Those other guys had never participated in a real murder investigation. That would wipe the snide grins off their faces! The only disappointment was that he couldn't tell them. But someday they'd know, and that would be a fine day in the life of Officer Bert Steffus.

But now he had work to do.

He pulled into the parking lot and got out of his cruiser, twisting his weak ankle in the process, but managed to walk into the store without limping. He stepped up to the counter and said to the sales clerk, "I'd like to speak to the manager, please."

"Yes, sir," said the young clerk, a skinny young man with a bad complexion who didn't look old enough to be working there, "he's in the storeroom doing an inventory right now. I'll show you the way."

"No need, I can find my own way."

"Yes, sir."

"Who should I ask for?"

"What?"

"What is the manager's name?"

"Oh! I'm sorry, sir," said the clerk, reddening. "His name is Harry Roach."

"Thank you, young man," said Bert, relishing the respect the young man accorded him. He walked to the back of the store and through a swinging door with a sign that said "Management and Staff Only." The air was stuffy but cool; the lighting was dim. Cases of wines and liquors appeared to be stacked haphazardly on the floor and against the walls. Three men, none of whom looked old enough to be managing the store, were huddled together off in a corner, smoking and whispering conspiratorially to each other.

"Any one of you guys Harry Roach?" said Bert, causing all three men to jump. They all wore the expressions of young men who, on any given day, had been guilty of something since they were in grade school.

"Hey! What the . . ." said one of the young men, but a glimpse of Bert's uniform stopped him cold. "Uh, may I help you, Officer?"

"Are you Harry Roach?"

"Yes, sir, that's me."

"And you're the manager here?"

"I'm the assistant manager, sir. My father is the manager, and my grandfather owns the place." One of the other young men snickered; the other sniffled.

"Are either of them here?"

"No, sir. They usually get here after lunch."

"Yeah, when the customers actually come in," said one of the other young men, the sniffler.

"Shut up, Boonesy!"

"Boonesy?" said Bert, enjoying the discomfiture he was causing the young men. It was a rare pleasure.

"My name is George Boone," said the young man, sniffling again, "but everybody calls me 'Boonesy.'" The other young man snickered once more. His jaw hung open, and he breathed through his mouth, like he had a permanently stuffed nose.

"And what's your name, kid?"

The young man's mouth closed so hard Bert could hear his teeth click.

"Alan, sir, Alan Griffin."

"And what's your nickname?"

"Grifter, sir."

"That fits," said Bert.

"It does?" said Grifter, his face lighting up like this might be good news for him. The other two cackled, and Grifter turned beet red.

"Okay, guys, settle down. I need to ask you a couple of questions," said Bert, causing the young men to assume a defensive posture that indicated to him that this was not the first time that they had been questioned by the police.

"I need you to tell me," said Bert, pulling a photograph of Armin Jaeger out of his pocket, "if any of you recognize this man." Harry and Boonesy kept their mouths shut, but Grifter, like a second-grader looking for a pat on the head from the teacher, couldn't help himself.

"Hey, that's the old guy who comes in here and buys that special bourbon by the case!" he said, looking at Bert for approval. "Right, guys?"

"For chrissake, Grifter, shut up!" said Boonesy.

"What are you afraid he's going to say?" said Bert, staring hard at Boonesy.

"Nothing, I guess," said Boonesy, as Bert heard Harry whisper, "Shit," under his breath.

"You sure about that?" said Bert, "Because I'm not."

"Pretty sure," said Boonesy, looking desperately at Harry for some help. Harry looked away. Bert knew it was time to move in while Boonesy felt isolated and before he had any time to recover what may have existed of his wits.

"Let me tell you what I think you're afraid he's going to say," said Bert, pointing at the photo of Armin but still staring at Boonesy. He was guessing now, but he knew he was right. "I think one of you got a visit from someone just before this guy came in to buy his case of bourbon last month. I think this person asked one of you to help him play a joke on the old man for his birthday or something. He showed you how to spike one of the bottles of this guy's whiskey, probably with some big old syringe that would go right through the cork. Probably said it was going to do something funny like make the guy pee his pants. Said it would be no real harm."

Boonesy was now sweating profusely and wiping constantly at his nose. The other two were so still that Bert wondered if they were still breathing.

"Need to blow your nose, Boonesy?" said Bert.

"I'm okay."

"No, Boonesy, you're not okay. You know why?"

"No."

"Because this man is dead, that's why. And we think he died because that shit you put in the bottle of whiskey was poison." Boonesy's body began to shiver, and his knees began to buckle. He sat down on a case of wine.

"Hey, watch it, Boonesy," said Harry, exercising managerial stewardship, "that shit's expensive!"

"Shut up, Harry," said Bert. He turned back to Boonesy. "It was pretty easy, wasn't it? And I bet this guy paid you more money than this place pays you in a month, right? Enough to keep that nose of yours happy for a long time."

"Look, Officer—"

"No, you look, Boonesy. If you're honest with me right now, right here, I'll be able to testify that you were just an ignorant accessory, that you really believed that it was all just an innocent joke, and I'm sure a judge will buy that. But if you won't talk to me, right here, right now, then I'm going to have to take you to the county jail, a place I'm sure you're familiar with, and I might be inclined to think that what you are is an accessory to murder, and a judge will probably agree. So, which is it, Boonesy?"

"I didn't know nothing, Officer, I swear!" said Boonesy, his nose now running freely, his whole body shuddering violently, his voice breaking. "She told me it was all just a fucking joke! A fucking harmless joke, okay?"

"It was a woman?"

"Yeah," said Boonesy, "it was a woman who put me up to it, not a man."

When Officer Bert Steffus walked back to his car twenty minutes later, his weak ankle was aching, and when he sat down behind the wheel, he realized that he was sweating and his legs were trembling. He felt slightly nauseous.

It was the happiest moment of his life.

"Were they able to give you any description of the woman?" said Walter, sitting at the kitchen table in the farmhouse with Bert and Levi. It was late morning, and they could hear Fred's tractor off in the distance. It was a good day to be outside, thought Walter, making him wonder if he was turning into a farmer. He shook his head to clear it.

"No," said Bert, "sorry, but I'm not sure I would have trusted any description they would have given me anyway. They just said she wasn't young, but she wasn't old, she wasn't a knockout but she wasn't 'a hag,' as they put it, and she had 'awesome knockers.'"

"That describes an awful lot of women around here," said Levi.

"It describes a lot of women just about anywhere," said Walter. "When I was that age, I don't think I ever knew a girl who didn't have 'awesome knockers.'"

"I'd like to see you say that with Sarah around," said Levi.

"Not if you wanted to see me alive again, you wouldn't," said Walter, grinning.

"So where do we go from here?" said Bert.

"I got a call from my boss, Captain Amato, this morning, and he's getting impatient with this whole thing. I made the mistake of telling him about our poisoning theory, and he jumped on that and said that it was now a state police matter, or even a federal one, since this whole thing seems to have crossed state lines. But he made it clear that it's no longer an NYPD case, and that he wants me back at the precinct forthwith."

"I got the same message from Deputy Commissioner Strickland," said Levi.

"So, what are you guys going to do?" said Bert.

"I'm going to obey my orders, of course, and go back to the city," said Walter, "but I just may get a little lost on the way back. I'm really not too familiar with the area, you know? And those GPS systems can be awfully unreliable sometimes."

"I'm going to head straight back, too," said Levi, "but I think I'll stop off and have lunch at Avery's first. Walter, you take the car. I can take the train and have Julie pick me up at Penn Station when I get in."

"Thanks. I'll try to get it back in one piece."

"Just remember, you'll have to answer to Julie about that, not me."

"I'll obey the speed limit, I promise."

"What do you guys want me to do?" said Bert.

"Bert, I want you to keep an eye on the farmhouse, and I need you to keep searching for the mysterious second black Mercedes. I'm not sure when either one of us is going to be able to get back here, so we need you to be our eyes and ears. But you need to do it without attracting attention."

"Don't worry, Lieutenant, I can do that."

"I know you can, Bert. I know you can."

23

"**D**O YOU KNOW WHAT A 'POTEMKIN VILLAGE' IS?" said Levi between bites of locally raised chicken breast that Adam had braised in a white wine sauce and served with a saffron risotto and roasted Brussels sprouts. He was washing it down with a glass of the same surprisingly tasty New York State Riesling that Adam had used to make the sauce. Adam was sitting across from him drinking a cup of coffee since, as usual, he had no other customers to serve.

"Isn't that some place up near Lake George?"

"Not exactly, Adam. They were fake villages created to make Catherine the Great think the Ukrainian countryside she'd just conquered was prosperous. Potemkin villages were like movie sets. Facades of houses and barns were built, and soldiers would put on peasant clothing. Then, as soon as she passed through, everything was torn down and transported to another spot she'd be visiting the next day. The whole region was actually devastated, but Catherine didn't want to know that, so her underlings made sure she didn't have to."

"That's interesting," said Adam, taking a sip of coffee, "but I know you well enough by now to know that you never come up with these interesting tidbits for the fun of it. So why are you telling me all this?"

"Adam, please don't take this wrong, but there's a lot that just doesn't make sense around here, especially from an economic perspective, that makes Dutch River feel like a Potemkin village to me."

"I'm sorry, Levi, I don't know much about economics. What do you mean?"

"Well, just look at your restaurant here," said Levi, putting down his fork and knife. "You serve these delicious meals and you are a fabulous chef, but face it, you have no customers. I've never seen anyone in this restaurant besides Julie and me and Walter and his family. Oh, I know you have the Tuesday night gatherings, but that's not really paying business. But despite that, the restaurant stays well supplied and you somehow seem to be doing okay financially, despite the fact that your wife doesn't have a paying job."

"I do get customers in the summer."

"I'm sure you do, but it's hard to believe that you get enough to make this place a going concern, no matter how good the food is. And it's not just you. Margie's is always empty, but the store is always well stocked, and Margie and Mike seem to be doing okay, even though Mike has been unemployed for years. You told me that the only way Mel Williams keeps his medical practice going is with subsidies from the town. Bert Steffus, for heaven's sake, draws a nice salary and drives around in late-model police cruiser that must have cost $50,000. I could go on, but you get my point."

"I get your point, Levi."

"So what am I missing?"

Adam hesitated momentarily, then leaned forward slightly over the table and began to speak with a lowered voice. "Look, Levi, I don't know much about economics, and I can't speak for anyone else. All I know is that when I came back to town a few years ago and was considering taking over the restaurant, Peter Maas came over and paid me a visit."

"Would that have been Mayor Peter Maas or Attorney Peter Maas?"

"You never really know which hat he's wearing, but it doesn't really matter, I guess. Anyway, he told me that the town was really anxious to keep the restaurant going. He called it 'one of the real anchor businesses of our downtown,' whatever that meant. He said that the state had an economic development program specifically designed to aid towns like Dutch River, and that my restaurant would receive any subsidies necessary to keep it in business."

"I never heard of that before, but it sounds like a great program. I take it your subsidy is pretty generous."

"Let's just say that your assessment of my business activity is pretty accurate."

"And I guess the other businesses in town have the same type of arrangement?"

"I don't really know, Levi, but I've got eyes just the same as you, so I assume they do. And I know that Sally, because she's on the board of education, sees a lot of the same kind of subsidies coming to them. There's no way we can still afford our local elementary school. I mean, for heaven's sake, there's only seven or eight kids in each class. But the state money keeps rolling in, and from what Sally tells me, they're not just operating on a shoestring. There's all kinds of enrichment programs and nutrition programs that they're able to offer as well."

"I'm glad things have worked out so well for you all here. I guess sometimes the state government actually uses all that tax revenue for a useful purpose. I guess the only downside is the paperwork."

"What do you mean?"

"Well, I know the amount of paperwork I had to file just to get a new desk chair at work. I can't imagine how much time you all must have to spend to get all these subsidies reviewed and renewed every year."

"I guess Mayor Maas must do all the paperwork stuff, because I don't."

"You mean, none?" said Levi, astonished.

"I never had to file a single piece of paper, Levi. Never."

"You mean all you had to do was submit your financial results to the mayor?"

"I've never had to do that either."

"So how do they calculate your subsidies?"

"I don't know. I never thought about it. Like I said, I'm not much of a businessman. Now I guess I'm a worse one than I thought. You don't think I've done anything wrong, do you?"

"No, I don't, Adam. I just think you're on the receiving end of one hell of a deal, and there's nothing wrong with that."

"I'm glad to hear that," said Adam, looking greatly relieved. "Are you going to talk to Peter Maas about all this?"

"No, I'm not. You've told me all I need to know, and, besides, it's really none of my business. You know me; if I were a cat my curiosity would have killed me by now. I'm just glad the state saw fit to help all of you out the way it has. This is a wonderful town, and you're all wonderful people. You deserve every penny you get, as far as I'm concerned." He rose to leave.

"So when do you think we'll be seeing you again?" said Adam. "Soon, I hope."

"I don't know when, Adam, but we'll be back. I think Sarah and Walter have really fallen in love with this place, and I don't think they're going to be selling that farm anytime soon."

"That's great news, Levi. Hey, do you need a ride to the train station?"

"I don't think so. It's only two blocks down the street, right?"

"That's the one. We thought it was going to close down, but just last year we got a grant from the state to renovate it. It's really beautiful now."

"I'm sure it is," said Levi.

24

THE DRIVE FROM DUTCH RIVER to Vernon, Connecticut, had been an easy one, a simple matter of taking the Massachusetts Turnpike over to Springfield and then picking up I-91 South to Hartford, Connecticut. The Berkshire Mountains were breathtakingly clad in their autumn foliage, and the little Mercedes had been a joy to drive, although Walter had to set the cruise control to 70 after he'd unknowingly let his speed drift up to 90 a couple of times. He pulled into the modest shopping plaza where Rein's Deli was located a little after noon, and was surprised to see that the parking lot was almost full. When he walked in the front door of the restaurant he discovered why: every table was occupied and there was a waiting line extending almost out the front door. A good omen, he thought; people don't stand in line for bad food.

Mayhew and Hudson had never met before and both were in mufti, but cops know how to spot other cops, and the two big men recognized each other immediately.

"Sergeant Mayhew," said Walter, shaking the man's hand, "it's a pleasure to meet you. Thanks so much for coming down here on such short notice."

"No problem," said Mayhew, "my barracks are only about a half hour from here, and I never pass up a chance to get a free lunch at Rein's. And please call me Dave."

"And you can call me Walter. Do you think we're ever going to get a table?" he said, staring at the long line.

"Oh yeah. They move people in and out of here real quick, but you never feel like you're being rushed, you know? We'll be sitting down and ordering in about fifteen minutes. And trust me, the food's worth it."

Walter thought that it would be hard to impress him after his meals at Avery's, but a glance at the offerings in the deli case made him feel like he was somewhere on the Lower East Side instead of the Connecticut suburbs, and his skepticism faded. The line moved along and, just as Mayhew had predicted, they were sitting down in less than fifteen minutes.

"So what's good in here?" said Walter.

"Well, it's probably nothing special to you, being from the big city and all, but I always get the pastrami on rye with Swiss cheese and a side of slaw."

"Sounds fine to me," said Walter. A waitress soon appeared who announced her name to be "Penny," and took their orders.

Mayhew ate like a man who loved his food, but he put his sandwich down when Walter told him that the GPS coordinates that he'd extracted from Martin Sewall's Mercedes had come from Armin Jaeger's farm, and what they'd discovered about how Armin had died.

"You know what this means, don't you?" said Mayhew.

"Yeah, it means the feds are going to take this over in about the same time that it takes for the Red Sox to lose a ballgame. No insult intended."

"None taken, Walter, especially since not even the feds could move in less time than it takes the Mets to lose."

"Who knows? Maybe it's all for the best. Besides, my boss is all over me to dump this case anyway."

"I'm starting to get the same kind of flak, believe me, but I hate to let a case go, you know? Especially one like this."

"They get under your skin, don't they?"

"Yeah, they do."

"Speaking of getting under your skin, Dave, it sounds like Abby Sewall is doing a good job of getting under yours."

Mayhew sat back. "Look, she's just been my best source of information, that's all. She's been very forthcoming and helpful. What am I supposed to do, ignore her?"

"But?"

"But what?"

"It just sounded like there was a 'but' at the end of that sentence, that's all. But look, it's none of my business. Sorry, it's just the detective in me being nosy."

Mayhew sagged. "Maybe it isn't any of your business, but I've got to tell you, you're not the first person to bring Abby up."

"Don't tell me. Your wife brought her up, right?"

"How did you know that?"

"Been there, Sergeant. You want to tell me about it?"

"I don't know what there is to tell. I know it must all be pretty routine to you, but this is the first time I've ever had the chance to be part of a murder investigation, and it's been really interesting. So I've been talking a lot to Joanie, you know, my wife, about it. And last night, all of a sudden, she sits up and out of nowhere says, 'So, are you interrogating this woman or just angling for a date?'"

"Ouch."

"Damn right, ouch. I told her Abby was close to twenty years older than me and I didn't know what she was talking about, and she said that's because I was a fool. But I was her fool, and she intended to keep it that way, so if I wasn't careful I would, you know . . ."

"Find yourself in an altered state of manhood?"

"That's right," said Mayhew, his eyes widening.

"We all live and learn," said Walter, thinking back to his own painful memory. "I won't bother you with the details of my particular learning experience. All I'll tell you is that you can't ever forget that you and I are men, and that means we know nothing about women, and that puts us at their mercy."

"Funny, Abby said kind of the same thing."

"I bet she did. She knew that she could tell you right to your face that she knew how to manipulate you, and you'd never even hear what she was saying."

"But, Walter, she's been my most cooperative witness."

"Sure, she has. So cooperative that you'd never suspect that she was holding anything back."

"I just don't know what she could be holding back. She's been so open with me."

"You're the same guy who told me that she could make you believe in the Easter Bunny, right?"

"I guess I am."

"All I can tell you is that I've learned from hard experience that the witnesses that seem to be the most cooperative are sometimes the ones with the most to hide. So my professional, and personal, advice is to be careful, okay?"

"Thanks, Walter."

"No problem. But now that we're here, we might as well try to get as much accomplished as we can before we have to hand it off to the damn feds."

"Yeah, I hate those guys."

"You and the rest of the universe."

Their waitress came over and refilled their coffee cups. "You guys interested in dessert?"

"You got any ruggalach?" said Walter.

"Of course we've got ruggalach."

"You got the kind with apricot jam in them? And the ones with honey and nuts?"

"Of course."

"Why don't you give us three of each of them."

"We've also got the ones with chocolate in them."

"I was wondering when you were going to stop holding out on us."

"What's a ruggalach?" said Mayhew, prompting an incredulous stare from both Walter and Penny.

"Ignore him," said Walter. "We'll have two of them, too."

"You mean you want eight, just for the two of you?"

"I think we can manage, don't you?"

She looked at the two big men and smiled. It was a nice smile. "Yeah, I guess you can. I'll be right back."

When she returned with the pastries, Mayhew said, "Penny, do you think you could do us a favor?"

"Depends," said Penny, looking a little suspicious. "What kind of favor?"

"Could you tell us if you recognize the man in this photo? It's official business. We're police, ma'am."

"Tell me something I don't know," said Penny, reaching for the photograph. "Look, I serve a lot of customers, I probably won't recognize . . . Oh."

"You recognize the guy?" said Walter, sounding surprised.

"He's hard to forget. He left me a $50 tip on a $15 order. I like to think I'm a good waitress, but that doesn't happen very often, you know?"

"Do you remember when this was?"

"Not exactly, but it was a couple, maybe three weeks ago."

"Did you ever see him again?"

"Yeah, I actually saw him the next day."

"Did you wait on him again?"

"No, I didn't."

"Do you remember who did?"

"Yeah, I do. It was Iris. I remember thinking that poor Iris finally got lucky."

"Why did you think that?"

"Because Iris has a gambling problem, and she doesn't seem to get lucky very often."

"Is Iris here today?"

"No, she's not here at all anymore."

"What, she quit?"

"No, she got fired. She kept on missing shifts because she was always down at Mohegan Sun Casino spending her last paycheck. This is a nice restaurant, you know? The owners are really great to the staff, but they couldn't put up with it anymore, I guess. So you guys liked the ruggalach, huh?" said Penny as she picked up the empty plate.

"They were great," said Mayhew.

"You want anything else? More coffee?"

"No, I think we're all set, thanks. Thanks for all your help."

"No problem," said Penny. "You guys have a good day." She put the check on the table and moved on to the next customer.

Walter picked up the check and left a twenty on the table. He hoped Penny wouldn't be too disappointed.

The NYPD frowned on excessive tipping.

25

"**N**O, I DON'T RECOGNIZE THE GUY," said Iris Stanton, looking at Walter with large brown eyes that had probably been pretty before the desperation had settled into them. She was probably forty but looked a decade older.

If this is Iris's poker face, thought Walter, no wonder she's a lousy gambler. They were sitting on folding chairs in the middle of the living room of her apartment in a small but well maintained complex a couple of miles down the road from Rein's, which a sign at the entrance had informed them was "*Doe Haven—A Residential Community.*" The chairs, along with a mattress on the floor, seemed to be the only furniture. The sun coming through the front windows failed to brighten the room, succeeding only in highlighting the dust in the air and the cigarette burns on the carpet. Iris had been on the way out when they arrived, but a quick flash of their badges had convinced her to give them a few minutes of her time.

"Ms. Stanton," said Walter.

"It's 'Mrs. Stanton,' at least for the next few weeks."

"Excuse me, ma'am. Mrs. Stanton, we have reason to believe otherwise. We believe that you waited on this man at Rein's Deli approximately three weeks ago. From what the manager tells us, it was the day before your employment there was terminated."

"Then maybe I did. I don't know. Anyway, I don't remember."

"Mrs. Stanton, please take another look at the photo and try to remember. It's very important. He may have left you a large tip. Maybe you remember that," said Walter, but Iris resolutely looked away from the photo.

"Ma'am," said Mayhew, "the manager we spoke to, and another waitress confirmed this, said that you left before your shift was over that day without punching out or informing anyone."

"It was probably that busybody Penny."

"It doesn't matter who it was, ma'am. The manager says that you were scheduled to work until 5 p.m., but that you left just after 12:30 p.m., which we have reason to believe is approximately the same time this man would have left the restaurant. He says the receipt indicated that you waited on him."

"Well, the manager's never wrong, is he? So maybe I did wait on the guy. So what?"

"The manager further told us that you were scheduled to start work the next morning at 8 a.m., but that you didn't arrive until 11 a.m., and that you were, according to him, in no condition to work. He said that you were wearing the same clothes from the day before and that you appeared disheveled and exhausted. He said that your breath smelled of alcohol."

"Look, what do you want me to say? Yeah, I showed up a little late. Maybe I'd had a couple of drinks the night before. So what? And then the bastard fired me."

"Had you been gambling the night before, ma'am?" said Walter.

"I may have played with the Indians a little that night. So what? It's legal in this state, you know."

"Indians, ma'am?" said Walter, who'd never wagered a nickel in his life.

"You know," said Iris, staring at him in disbelief, "down at Mohegan Sun Casino. It's on an Indian reservation, right?"

"If you say so, ma'am. How long were you there?"

"I don't remember. I was there a while, I guess."

"What did you play?" said Mayhew. He and his wife had been down to Mohegan Sun for a concert once so at least he was vaguely familiar with the facility. It had been designed so that it was impossible to go to a restaurant or to the arena without walking through the casino, so on their way out they'd taken a couple of turns at the roulette wheel. They'd lost.

"Blackjack."

"Blackjack, huh? No slots?"

"Slots are for losers. Real players hit the blackjack tables. You keep your head and play smart, you can beat the house."

"So how did you do?"

"I should've won, but I got screwed."

"Ma'am?"

"Look, I was all in. I had 19 on the table and I knew, I mean I knew that the deuce was the next card. It had to be."

"What happened? Did the deuce come up?" said Mayhew.

"The seven came up, and I was busted. But I'm telling you, Officer, that dealer was crooked. I'll swear that he dealt that seven out of his sleeve. I went to the floor manager, and I said, 'Look, I won't make a formal complaint as long as you give me credit so I can win my money back.' All I wanted was a couple thousand dollars. I was being very reasonable, right?"

"And what did he say?"

"He said 'no,' of course. They knew I was a player, and they didn't want to give me a chance. I'd been five thousand up just an hour before that, you know? I was one card away from the jackpot. So they screwed me."

"How much did you lose that night?"

"I don't know."

"It'll take us twenty minutes to call the casino and find out, Mrs. Stanton, so why don't you just tell us?"

"Ten thousand."

"Ten thousand?" said Mayhew, looking around the room.

"Oh, I know what you're thinking," said Iris, seeing both Walter and Mayhew scanning the apartment. "You're just like my husband; you're just like my boss at Rein's; you're just like the bastards who repossessed the furniture and my car; you're just like my prick of a landlord who's telling me I've got to be out of here in a week. You're going to give me the same lecture they did, about how I have a problem and I've got to get help."

"But you don't have a problem," said Mayhew.

"Of course I don't," said Iris. "Haven't you been listening to me? If they'd given me that couple thousand of credit I asked for, I would have been driving a Caddie and living on a beach house down on the shore by now. I'm a player. I'm a winner, dammit."

"Mrs. Stanton," said Walter, "where did that money come from?"

"None of your damn business."

"I'm afraid it is, ma'am. This man," said Walter, holding up the photograph of Martin Sewall, "this man was murdered. He was poisoned, and we have reason to believe he was given that poison in something he ate or drank at Rein's that day—the day you were waiting on him. The day you left as soon as you'd finished serving him his lunch."

"I don't know anything about anybody being murdered!"

"We're willing to believe that, Mrs. Stanton. We're willing to believe that someone told you that it was all going to be a joke. Or maybe it was a woman; a woman who said her husband had just left her for another woman, just like what happened to you. She probably said it would be harmless, that it would just embarrass him. Just something to help her get back at him, maybe like you'd like to get back at your husband. And then maybe she said that she'd pay you ten thousand dollars if you would just help her."

"What do you want me to say?"

"We want you to tell us the truth, Mrs. Stanton."

"And what's in it for me if I do?"

"Let me put it this way," said Walter. "If you come clean with us right now, it will be easy for us to conclude that you were just an innocent victim, a dupe. We'll be able to smooth things over with the prosecutors, and we'll have no need to discuss your situation with the casino. But if you don't, if you continue to stonewall us, we'll have to conclude that you were an accessory to murder, and we don't think you'd be able to find anyone who disagrees with us. You will then be all alone dealing with the judicial system on criminal charges. And then we'd have to alert the casino that you were playing with dirty money, after which you will never get inside any casino in this country ever again. That's what we have to offer. What we're offering you is a choice. So what will it be, Mrs. Stanton?"

"I thought maybe my information might be worth some money, that's all. I only need a couple thousand, you know?"

"I can't promise anything, but I'll see what I can do."

This is what police work comes down to, thought Walter. It comes down to finding the weak spot, that spot that is already so bruised, so raw from so many beatings over the course of a lifetime that all you have to do is touch it just one more time. Walter knew what he was doing to Iris Stanton, a woman who was a slave to an addiction that she could not overcome, an addiction for which she had been receiving beatings since the day she lost her first dollar. It was his job, he told himself, a job that was necessary and a job he was good at. But how much longer could he bear the sight of the Iris Stantons of the world cracking and crumbling at just the lightest touch of his finger? How much longer would he be able to commit the unspeakable cruelty of walking up to a person on the precipice and extending his hand, not to save her, but to give her that last, gentle nudge to oblivion, before it destroyed his own soul?

He watched her crumble. He watched her fall.

"So you'll help me?" said Iris, her lifeless eyes fixed on his.

"Sure, ma'am, of course we will."

26

"SO IT SOUNDS LIKE we've pretty much got the same story on both ends," said Walter. He and Sergeant Mayhew were in the Mercedes talking to Levi Welles, who was back in his office in New York, and Bert Steffus, who was calling from his patrol car. They were using the Bluetooth connection built into the car, and it sounded like they were all in the same room.

"Yeah, it does," said Levi. "Whoever this woman was, she was pretty good at sniffing out people with weaknesses she could exploit. I mean, the tale she told about being a wronged wife who was just looking for a little innocent revenge was pretty lame, but when your body's screaming at you for a hit of cocaine, or the blackjack tables are whispering in your ear, you'll believe just about anything."

"But how did she know that Sewall would sit at one of Iris's tables at Rein's?" said Bert. "The whole thing could have fallen apart right there."

"Actually, that was pretty easy," said Mayhew. "Iris just went up to the hostess and pointed Martin out. She said she knew the guy, so could she steer him to one of her tables. Our unidentified lady was waiting at a Chinese restaurant in the same shopping plaza. As soon as Martin finished his meal, Iris ran over to the restaurant, picked up the $10,000, and drove off to the casino without ever punching out at Rein's."

"She must have been pretty desperate," said Bert, "just like 'Boonesy' at the liquor store."

"Yes, she was," said Walter, trying not to think about it.

"Were you able to get any better description of the woman than the guys at the liquor store were able to give me?" said Bert.

"No," said Mayhew, "same thing as you got: thirties, kind of attractive, nothing remarkable to go on. I think the problem is that the people we're dealing with had too much else on what was left of their minds to pay much attention to what anybody looked like. All she looked like to them was an answer to their problems."

"Well, like the old saying goes," said Bert, "appearances can be deceiving."

"So, Levi," said Walter, "how did your conversation with Adam go?"

"Actually, it was an extremely productive conversation, although I didn't realize just how productive until I got back here to New York where I could do some snooping."

"It's good to be an NYPD Intelligence Officer, I guess," said Mayhew.

"You've got no idea," said Levi.

"This sounds like it's going to be interesting," said Walter. "Why don't you tell us what you've got."

"Well, I laid it all out to Adam what our concerns were, that we couldn't understand how the town was surviving, how the economic equation just didn't balance."

"Please tell me you didn't torment him with your Potemkin village story."

"Of course, I did. He's fresh meat for all of my trivia, and I wasn't about to pass up an opportunity like that."

"So what did he say?"

"He told me that the state of New York had some special program to aid small towns like Dutch River, and that the town and its businesses, including his, were being subsidized. But it just didn't add up."

"Why not?"

"First of all, he told me that he never had to fill out any paperwork or submit any financial statements for his restaurant to qualify for his subsidy."

"That sure doesn't sound like the state of New York I know," said Walter, "especially since that must be one heck of a subsidy, judging from what we've seen of his restaurant's business."

"I always wondered how they were able to afford me and my police car and everything," said Bert. "I guess I feel pretty stupid."

"There was no way you could have known," said Levi, "so don't feel bad."

"And you've been doing some terrific police work for us, Bert," said Walter, "so don't get down on yourself, okay? As far as I'm concerned, you're earning every penny of your pay, no matter who's paying it to you."

"Thanks, Lieutenant."

"The other thing that bothered me," said Levi, "was that, as everybody who lives in New York knows, the state's budget is a mess, and they've been cutting programs left and right. I can't imagine that they'd have a program like that, or if they did have one once, that it hadn't been chopped by now."

"And every time I pick up a paper or watch the local news on TV, I see another story about all the dying towns upstate," said Walter.

"Right," said Levi, "so I did a little research when I got back here, and you know what?"

"I can't wait," said Walter.

"There is no program like that. So I took a look at the town's banking transactions to see what I could find out."

"You can do that?" said Bert.

"It's not that tough," said Levi.

"And what did you find out?" said Mayhew.

"For the past eight years, there has been a large annual deposit to the town's bank account, about $10 million every year. That's not a huge amount, but it's enough to keep the town and its business community afloat."

"And from what I learned from Martin Sewall's investment advisors, that means that Sewall was taking an extra slice of whatever pie they were divvying up," said Mayhew.

"So were you able to find out where the money was coming from?" said Walter.

"You'll find this interesting, Walter. The money was coming from an organization called Rensselaer Partners."

"Why do I recognize that name?"

"Because that's the same outfit that keeps trying to buy the farm out from under you and Sarah, that's why."

"That's right! So were you able to find out who's behind Rensselaer Partners?"

"Not yet. It was established as a 501(c)(3) organization."

"A what?"

"I won't bore you with the details. The important point is that because of the way it was organized the people behind it don't have to disclose their names."

"So does that mean we just hit another dead end?" said Bert.

"Nah," said Levi, "it just means that it'll take me a little time and effort to find the names, that's all."

"How long?" said Walter.

"Not long, probably a day or two."

"Hey, hold it just a minute," said Sergeant Mayhew, furiously flipping through his pocket notebook. "Yeah . . . That's what I thought."

"What?" said the other three simultaneously.

"You said 'Rensselaer Partners,' right?"

"Yes," said Levi.

"That's the name of the company that Martin Sewall's Mercedes was registered to."

27

OFFICER BERT STEFFUS usually just drove by Armin Jaeger's farmhouse to make sure that he didn't notice anything unusual: a light inside that shouldn't be on; a car he didn't recognize parked in the driveway; or any suspicious movements. He knew that just the sound of his car and the glare of his headlights would be enough to scare away kids looking for trouble or even a petty thief. He also knew that the security system in the house was first rate, and that even a professional intruder would probably be deterred by it.

But a lot had been going on in Dutch River lately, all of it troubling, and too much of it involving this farmhouse to be a coincidence. So tonight, he had decided to take the time to disarm the security system and inspect the house.

The disarming process was tedious and time-consuming, involving punching in multiple sequences of code, each containing nine digits. Each one had to be accurately entered and accepted before moving on to the next, making it virtually impossible to disarm the system by guesswork or simple luck. Bert had an outstanding memory, especially for sequences of numbers. He could still recite the first 75 digits of "pi" from memory, and he had long ago memorized the codes. Still, it took him a full five minutes before he was able to open the door and step into the dark kitchen.

At first, he thought he would use only his flashlight for illumination, but he'd never been comfortable in the dark, and he couldn't afford to trip over anything, what with his weak ankle and large girth: Either he, something of value, or both, would undoubtedly be a casualty if he fell, so he decided to turn on the kitchen light. Besides, the flashlight was large and heavy and his arms tired easily. He really didn't want to have to hold it out in front of him as he inspected the house. He promised himself that he'd start doing pushups again.

As his eyes wandered around the kitchen, he was once again puzzled, as he had been on his previous visits, by Armin Jaeger's determination to furnish such a beautiful house with old furniture and decorations. It looked like he'd picked it all up at a tag sale, for heaven's sake! If he were ever lucky enough to own a house like this, he'd furnish it with some good stuff, brand new, off the showroom floor from some classy furniture store in Albany. And he'd replace the dingy, old paintings on the walls with bright, colorful posters of the national parks he'd always dreamed of visiting, and perhaps some depicting wild horses. He'd always loved horses. But there was no explaining taste, as his mother used to say.

He knew that Lieutenant Hudson, Captain Welles, and their wives had stayed at the house a couple of times recently, but everything was neat and in place. No dirty dishes or leftover food left thoughtlessly on the counter the way some people would have done. He liked the two men, and he was thrilled at the professional respect they had shown him and the responsibilities with which they had entrusted him. He didn't want to let them down. He moved through the kitchen and living area, and after determining that all appeared to be in order, he headed upstairs, turning on lights as he went.

He saw nothing out of place or suspicious as he went through the rooms. He was impressed, as Walter, Levi, and their spouses had been, with the immaculate condition in which the old man had been able to maintain such a large place. Someday, when he owned a beautiful home like this, he'd take good care of it, too. Thanks to Walter and Levi, his ego had undergone such a profound transformation over the past couple of weeks that he had once again begun to imagine a life for himself less lonely and more successful than the one he now led. Perhaps there would be a wife after all, and children. He picked up the heavy book that lay on Armin's night table, making sure not to lose the page it was opened to. He should start reading more, he thought. But all that was something to ponder at another time. Besides, despite the lightness of his heart, his legs were beginning to feel heavy, and there was really nothing to be seen here in any event. It was time to leave. He left the bedroom and headed down the hallway, turning off the lights behind him as he went.

He stopped still as he turned out the last hallway light at the top of the stairs.

The house was suddenly pitch dark.

But how could that be? He was positive that he hadn't turned off the lights behind him when he'd climbed the stairs. But he must have, he thought. It was late, he was tired, and he just hadn't been thinking. Still, he stood silently at the top of the stairs and listened for a minute.

He suddenly realized that he hadn't rearmed the security system behind him after he had entered the house. He had to learn to be more careful, he thought. It was the kind of sloppy mistake that Lieutenant Hudson would surely never make, and he was glad the big cop wasn't there to witness his gaffe. But he heard nothing. He had excellent hearing, and he was sure that if there was anything to hear, he would hear it. He reached for his flashlight.

It wasn't there.

Damn! He must have left it sitting on the kitchen table after he'd turned on the kitchen light. He felt sweat begin to trickle down his neck. His hearing might have been excellent, but his eyesight was not. He remembered the eye doctor telling him that he had particularly poor night vision and that he should drive extra carefully in the dark.

He reached for the stair rail and luckily found it on the first try. Good. He took a tentative step and found the first step down. Good again. He was starting to feel better. He could do this. He made his way slowly down the stairs. By the time he was halfway down, he realized that he could have left the hall light on upstairs and he would have been able to see where he was going. But now it was too late. Damn! He hadn't counted the number of steps on the way up, but there seemed to be a lot more of them on the way down. Finally, his foot reached out for another step and instead, found level flooring. He'd made it. He breathed a heavy sigh of relief. The night was moonless, but there was just enough starlight coming in through the kitchen window to allow him just barely to make out the shape of the old Shaker kitchen table. He couldn't make out the shape of his flashlight, but he knew that was where he'd left it, so he made his way over to it and started to feel around the surface.

But it wasn't there. He felt the panic start to well up within him and the sweat once again start to trickle down his back. He hated the dark. Maybe he'd left it on the counter. He started to edge his way over to it, trying to keep at least one hand on the table as a guide.

It wasn't there either.

He could feel the perspiration start to trickle down his cheeks and under the collar of his shirt. Where the hell was the kitchen light switch? He'd forgotten. *Stop it!* he thought. *Lieutenant Hudson wouldn't panic, and you shouldn't either!* He stood by the kitchen sink and tried to collect his wits.

"Lose something, Bert?" came the voice from behind him. It was female, and he thought he should recognize it. "Don't worry, I found it for you."

He tried to turn around, but his legs were frozen. He tried to say something, but his throat had gone bone dry. He felt a sharp pain in the back of his head.

And then there was nothing.

28

"WHOEVER HIT HIM, HIT HIM HARD," said Adam Avery. "He was barely conscious when Fred Benecke found him this morning about five."

"How is he now?" said Walter. He was sitting in his cubicle at Midtown South, but he was on his personal cell phone since that was the number he'd given to Adam before they'd left Dutch River.

"I'm not going to lie to you, Lieutenant," said Dr. Mel Williams. "He took quite a shot to the head, and he's in pretty rough shape."

"Has he regained full consciousness?"

"Yes and no. He's drifted in and out, but we've had to keep him pretty heavily sedated."

"So he hasn't been able to tell you anything about what happened, I suppose."

"Not a thing," said Doctor Williams, "and I wouldn't get my hopes up. Even when he does regain full consciousness, I doubt he's going to remember much. He sustained a severe concussion, and that usually wipes out any short-term memory."

"Do you know how long it might be until he's recovered enough to talk to us?"

"It's hard to say. I talked to the docs up at Albany County Medical Center just about twenty minutes ago, and the brain scans they did indicate that he has a large subdural hematoma on the right parietal lobe of his brain."

"In English, please, Doc."

"There was bleeding in his brain, beneath his skull on the right side of his head. It was a pretty significant bleed, and it's putting pressure on his brain. They're starting the process of draining the blood, but they have to be careful, and they have to do it slowly. In the meantime, they have to keep him sedated. It might be a few days before he'll be fit to talk to, and like I said, I doubt he's going to be able to tell you much anyway. Frankly, Lieutenant, he's just lucky to be alive. I've seen less severe blows than this kill people."

"Are the docs at the hospital going to stay in touch with you?"

"Yes, they are. And you may remember that my wife, Evelyn, is a registered nurse. She's been up there with him since he got to the hospital. She's not employed by the hospital, but as a professional courtesy the hospital medical staff are sharing all their information with her."

"Keep me up to date, okay?"

"No problem, Lieutenant."

"Adam, did Fred tell you anything about what he found when he got to the farmhouse?"

"Not a lot. He said he'd gone over there to feed the cows, and he noticed that the front door to the house was ajar."

"What did he say about the alarm system?"

"He said it was disarmed. There was no sign of forced entry, at least as far as he could tell."

"And he's positive that he and Bert are the only ones who know the entry codes?"

"That's right."

"Which means that Bert got there first and whoever knocked him out just followed him in."

"I guess he should have reset it once he was in the house, huh?" said Adam.

"Yes, he should have," said Walter, "but don't forget, Bert may wear a police uniform, but he has no real experience, and from what I can tell no one ever bothered to give him any formal training."

"But I guess the important fact is," said Mel Williams, "that he wasn't investigating a break-in, which says to me that whoever it was who attacked him didn't just follow him *into* the house, they followed him *to* the house when he did his routine check."

"Which says to me," said Walter, "that someone knew Bert's patterns and had been following him for a while, just waiting for this kind of opportunity. Which probably means that whoever it was knew enough about the alarm system to know that they wouldn't be able to get past it without using brute force."

"Which would have set off every alarm in the place."

"What did Fred say about the condition of the place when he got there?"

"He said it had been ransacked," said Adam, "but the funny thing was that it didn't look like anything had been stolen. And even stranger, all the paintings had been taken off the walls and placed on the floor and all the antique furniture was still there, but it looked like it had been moved. He also said that every book had been removed from Armin's bookcase, and it looked like someone had leafed through all of them. But as far as he could tell, they were all still there. They'd also taken all the clothes out of his closet."

"Well, if they were thieves, they were probably just looking for cash, right?" said Dr. Williams. "A lot of people don't trust banks these days, and they keep it stashed somewhere in their house they think is safe. That's what it sounds like to me."

"If they were just a couple of random crooks, you might be right," said Walter. "I could believe that people like that wouldn't have any idea that the furniture was valuable, and they wouldn't have a clue what to do with the art, but whoever this was doesn't impress me as that kind of crook."

"So what do you think, Lieutenant?" said Adam.

"I think whoever followed Bert into that house was looking for something specific."

"And what makes this really interesting," said Adam, "is that if they ignored the paintings and the furniture, whatever they were looking for must be pretty valuable."

If he only knew, thought Walter. To his knowledge, only he, Sarah, Levi, and Julie had any idea what those paintings were worth, or the furniture. Assuming, of course, that the Maases didn't have big mouths.

"Do you think they found what they were looking for?" said Mel.

"I don't know, but I'd bet not," said Walter.

"Why?" said Adam.

"Because from what I've learned about Armin Jaeger, he was an extraordinarily intelligent man, and he installed about the most sophisticated security system I've ever seen in a private home in his farm in the middle of nowhere. He was the type of man who would have taken extraordinary care to make sure that whatever he was hiding was very well hidden."

"And the fact that our thief was looking behind pictures and emptying closets indicates that they didn't have even a clue where to start," said Mel.

"And they didn't bring any sophisticated search equipment with them," said Adam.

"You're both right," said Walter.

"So where does that leave us?" said Adam.

"It leaves us frustrated right now," said Walter. "Do either of you guys know if there is going to be any kind of thorough investigation into this by the local police?"

"I really don't know," said Adam. "I think you'd have to talk to the County Sheriff's Department to find out."

"Okay," said Walter, pulling a pencil and notebook out of his pocket, "do you have a name for me?"

"I'd start with Sergeant Stan Barry," said Adam. "He's the officer in the sheriff's department who oversees Bert, and I think Fred told me that he was one of the officers who arrived on the scene after he called 911."

"Okay, I'll give him a call."

"Do you think you'll be back up here anytime soon?" said Adam.

"Adam, the only official connection I currently have to this case is the fact that Martin Sewall stayed in a hotel in my precinct the night before he was murdered. The fact that my wife just inherited her great-uncle's house is just a personal coincidence. My precinct is understaffed and buried under cases that my boss considers far more important than this one, and he's told me in no uncertain terms that he wants me off it."

"So I guess that means we're not going to be seeing you."

"Did you hear me say that, Adam?"

"No, I guess I didn't."

"That's right, Adam, you didn't."

29

"**S**O TELL ME AGAIN," said Captain Eugene Amato, Lieutenant Hudson's boss and chief of the Midtown South Precinct, "why you think the Midtown South Precinct should be leading the investigation into the murder of a man from Boston that took place in Connecticut, and an old farmer from upstate New York who probably never set foot on Manhattan Island, never mind this precinct?"

Walter paused, regarding his boss. He knew he had to be careful here. Captain Amato was only forty, but he looked younger than his years, his blond hair carefully combed, his white shirt impeccably pressed, and his imported suit hanging perfectly on his broad shoulders. Captain Amato was a hard charger, a man who had been gunning for the commissioner's office since the day he had joined the NYPD; and every step he took, every decision he made, was made through the prism of that goal. Walter knew that if he was going to get his boss to go along with him on this, it would only be if Walter could convince him that it would further his career.

The discussion was complicated even more by the fact that Amato viewed Walter not as a junior officer who reported to him, but as competition. For it was well known that Lieutenant Walter Hudson was one of Police Commissioner Sean Donahue's favorites. He had been invited to Donahue's private "office," in fact a perfect recreation of an Irish pub tucked down the hall from his office at One Police Plaza, more often than any other officer on the force; and he had helped Donahue, not to mention Mayor Deborah Kaplan, gain renown and popularity by solving some high-profile cases. Amato had been invited there precisely once, and it had not gone well. Donahue had been heard to mumble to his secretary after the meeting that he'd never had his Irish ass kissed so thoroughly in his life.

"Captain, the New York State Police, especially upstate, are underfunded and undermanned. At this point, all they see is a dead ninety-year-old man, and they say, 'So what?' Even when we showed them the poisoned bottle of bourbon, they said that they were going to have to wait for Mr. Jaeger's body to be exhumed and autopsied before they made the case a priority, and that's going to take weeks. And by then, this case will be as cold as ice. The Massachusetts State Police are staying involved, but so far, the most senior officer they have assigned to it is a sergeant from a small barracks in Sturbridge with absolutely no training or experience in the investigation of a murder. He's a good guy, but he may be in a little over his head, and I think the fact that the state police haven't assigned anyone else to the case tells you just how eager they are to get involved."

"I've heard of Sturbridge," said Amato, his glance drifting toward the window. "I think my kids went up there on a school trip once."

"Yessir. Anyway, I think both the New York and the Massachusetts State Police are stalling. This is a potentially very-high profile case in Massachusetts because of Mr. Sewall's wealth and social standing, but they're short of staff and funding, and I think they're genuinely convinced that this is a federal issue because it involves multiple states. I don't think they're going to budge."

"Maybe we should be doing the same thing. I've never seen any upside to messing with the FBI."

Walter sensed that the discussion was starting to slip away from him. It was time to roll out the heavy artillery. "Sir, you know how Commissioner Donahue hates it when the FBI sticks its nose into an NYPD case."

"Well, you have a point there," said Amato, his attention suddenly refocused.

"And sir, when this thing finally blows up, it's going to be big. I mean, the murder of one of the most prominent men in Boston and hundreds of millions of dollars in the mix. If we were able to solve this case, it would bring a tremendous amount of excellent publicity and credit to, ah, the Midtown South Precinct, and, of course, the NYPD. And remember, the nexus of this whole case is right here. Whatever happened at the Hotel Grenadier was the trigger for all of this."

The words "publicity" and "credit" seemed to sharpen Amato's attention even further.

"You may have a good point, Lieutenant. The NYPD has a hard-earned reputation for stepping in and taking on the tough ones when no one else will."

"That's right, sir."

"And you make a good point about the commissioner. He'd love to step in and solve this case before the feds have a chance to grab it and take all the credit."

"I think he would, sir."

"And after all, we have a public duty here. There are two dead men and evidence of large-scale financial crimes. For all we know, citizens of this city, this precinct, even, could be the victims of a massive swindle. We can't just stand back, can we, Lieutenant?"

"Of course not, sir."

"Okay, I'll give you a little more time on this one. Don't worry, I'll manage the commissioner for you."

"Thank you, sir," said Walter, inwardly cringing.

"And Lieutenant?"

"Yes, Captain?"

"Make sure you keep me in the loop. I wouldn't want to see any major breakthroughs announced on the front page of the *Times* without my prior knowledge and consultation. These things have to be managed very delicately, you know."

"I understand perfectly, sir."

⚊⚊⚏⚊⚊

As soon as Walter got back to his desk he picked up his phone and punched in a familiar number.

"Leviticus Welles," said the mild voice that Walter had come to know so well.

"Hi, Levi, it's Walter."

"Hi, Walter. Why am I already smelling trouble?"

"Not at all, Levi. Have you and Julie got any plans for your weekend yet?"

"It sounds to me like even if we do, we ought to change them."

"I was just wondering if you guys were up for another road trip to Dutch River, that's all."

"To help Fred Benecke with the harvest, I suppose."

"I don't know about harvesting, but I'm pretty sure we'll be doing some digging."

30

"YOU GOT A STICK SHIFT?" said Walter, sitting in the passenger seat of their new car. "I don't know how to drive a stick shift!"

"Sure, you do," said Sarah as she carefully guided the car onto Union Turnpike. "You're a man. It's hardwired into your gonads. Don't worry, you'll love it. Now, sit back and watch and learn." In just a few minutes, they were crossing over the Whitestone Bridge and cruising up to the Taconic Parkway.

The first thing Sarah Hudson had purchased with her newfound wealth was this car. With Julie Remy's help, she had worked with her financial consultant and the experts at Sotheby's and had selected the surprisingly few paintings she needed to sell in order to pay the taxes on her great-uncle's estate and establish an investment fund that would easily cover the costs of maintaining the farm and also supplement Walter's modest NYPD income.

And buy the car of her dreams.

She had quite virtuously, she thought, decided that a Mercedes sports coupe would not be practical for her family, so she had instead purchased a BMW 535i. She had selected the all-wheel drive "X" model, explaining to Walter that it would be safer for the children. He had pointed out to her that it would also help her avoid leaving the car languishing in the garage during the winter months. She had replied that she hadn't thought about that, but that it was a good point.

But there was no rationalizing the 6-speed manual transmission. It wasn't for the kids, and it wasn't for Walter. It was for her. She had learned to drive in her father's treasured '67 Pontiac GTO with the "four on the floor" transmission and Hurst shifter, and she knew from the beginning that for her, as with her father, nothing else would ever be true driving.

Walter had long ago stopped being surprised by his extraordinary wife, a woman who still fascinated him and whom he still craved as much as he had almost twenty years ago when he had first laid eyes on her in high school. He tried to observe her hand and foot movements closely, so that when it was finally his turn to get behind the wheel of this amazing machine, he wouldn't make a complete fool of himself. But mostly he found himself watching Sarah, the alert eyes looking out of her serene face as she negotiated the twists and turns of the Taconic Parkway; the practiced movements of her hands and feet as she seemingly unconsciously kept the car in the ideal gear. He became mesmerized watching her hands as she almost caressed the stick shift through the gears. He realized too late that he was becoming aroused, and that Sarah was looking over at him, an amused smile on her face.

"I know," she said, giving him a wink.

"What do you know, Mommy?" said Robin from the backseat.

"I know that buying this car was a really good decision, and so does your daddy. Right, Daddy?"

"Right," said Walter, staring straight-ahead, hoping the kids would go to sleep early tonight.

<hr />

Levi and Julie arrived at the farmhouse about the same time as Walter and Sarah. It was early afternoon and, although the calendar indicated that it was mid-October, Indian summer had arrived and the weather in upstate New York was gloriously sunny and mild. Beth and Robin immediately disappeared, racing around the corner of the barn toward the orchard.

"Bring back some apples!" called Sarah after them, but she doubted they heard.

Levi and Walter brought the luggage into the house while Julie hauled some groceries they'd bought before they left town into the kitchen and Sarah took charge of Daniel, who badly needed a diaper change, though he was the only one who didn't seem to mind the smell. Once everything was unloaded, Walter and Levi headed out the door to visit Officer Steffus at the Albany County Medical Center.

"Didn't you forget something, Walter?" said Sarah just as they reached the door.

"What?" said Walter, turning around to face her.

"You forgot these, didn't you?" said Sarah, dangling the keys to the Beemer from her index finger.

"I was thinking we'd take Julie and Levi's Mercedes," said Walter, the mildest hint of panic in his voice.

"I'll tell you what," said Levi, "I've been looking forward to taking that new car of yours for a spin. Why don't I drive it up to the hospital, and on the way back we can find a nice stretch of empty road, and you can get some practice in."

"Sounds good to me," said Walter, looking at Sarah hopefully.

"That's fine, but I want to see you pulling that car into the driveway when you get back, Walter. Deal?"

"Deal," said Walter, knowing that buying time was his only option.

"And remember, Walter," said Sarah, her voice turning sultry, "there's a lot riding on this. I mean, a lot." She tossed him the keys.

31

OFFICER BERT STEFFUS FELT MISERABLE, but at least he was conscious and alert. The huge bandage on his head made him look like an extra in an ER rerun, but otherwise he seemed good.

"I'm so sorry, guys, I really messed everything up, I guess."

"Actually, Bert, you and your rock-hard head wound up telling us a lot we either didn't know or couldn't be sure of up to now," said Walter.

"It did?"

"Sure," said Levi. "It tells us that whoever attacked you had tried to get into the house before and had failed, and had learned enough about the security system to know that the only alternative was to follow someone else in once the system had been disarmed."

"And it also told us," said Walter, "that whoever this was had been following you around long enough to know that you had the code."

"They must have been following me around for a pretty long time then, because the last time I actually disarmed the system before the other night was a few weeks ago, just after Armin died. I decided that since the house was empty, I'd better make sure that I still had the code right so that I could protect the property."

"Which all suggests to me that whoever did this to you was a local," said Levi, "because a stranger spending a lot of time in Dutch Village would have been noticed."

"Did you mention to anyone that you were going to be checking on the house that night?" said Walter.

"I don't know, but I'm having a hard time remembering," said Bert. "If I told anyone it would have been Sergeant Barry. I just feel stupid that I let someone follow me around for all that time without noticing I was being followed."

"One of the first rules of spotting a tail," said Walter, "is that you have to be reasonably suspicious that someone might be following you. You had no reason to suspect that, so don't feel bad about it, okay?"

"I guess so, but I still feel like an idiot."

"There's no time for that right now," said Walter, "because I think the other thing we can conclude from all this is that the key to two murders and potentially a large-scale financial crime is somewhere in that house."

"And someone in this town is up to their neck in all this," said Levi, "and they're desperate not to get found out. Desperate enough to try to make you the third murder victim, Bert."

"Is there anything that you remember that may help us?" said Walter.

"I wish like heck there was," said Bert, "but so far there's nothing. The last thing I remember is walking into the kitchen after disarming the alarm system and turning on the light."

"Well, maybe things will start coming back to you," said Levi.

"I think they might," said Bert. "When I first woke up, my last memory was eating supper that night. Now I remember getting in my car, driving out to the farm and walking into the kitchen, so I'm making progress, at least."

"That's good," said Walter, "because we're going to need you."

"So what's the plan from here?"

"Well, your plan is to stay here a couple more days and make sure you're over the concussion you got," said Levi.

"And what are you guys going to do?"

"We're going to go back to the farm and find whatever we've been missing up to now."

"Any idea how you're going to do that?"

"Not really."

"Apparently, that's not all we're going to be doing," said Levi, staring at his cell phone.

"What do you mean?" said Walter.

"I just found out who's behind Rensselaer Partners."

⸺◈⸺

"Levi, we don't have time for this right now," said Walter, having just stalled the BMW for the third time in the parking lot of a Walmart they'd found just outside Albany.

"Judging from the look on Sarah's face when she handed you the keys, you don't have time for anything else, Walter."

"I just don't understand why this is so important to her, that's all."

"You mean, as opposed to all those things you *do* understand?"

"I guess you have a point there."

"Look, I barely scratched the surface of a very long e-mail. We're going to have a long night deciphering it all, so for now, put it out of your mind and concentrate on learning to feel the clutch engage."

"Yeah, you're right, especially if I want to engage in anything else tonight."

"That's the spirit."

⚬

Julie and Sarah were waiting out by the driveway as expected when Walter, sitting triumphantly behind the wheel, pulled the BMW into the driveway. He even remembered to disengage the clutch before bringing the car to a halt and emerged with the keys dangling from his fingers and a smile on his face.

"Well?" he said as he handed the keys back to Sarah.

"We have something we need to show you guys," she said, unsmiling, as she pocketed the keys.

"What," said Walter, "no congratulations?"

"Yes, yes, honey, I'm very proud of you, but we're serious. We really need to show you something. Come on." She and Julie started to walk toward the back of the house.

"Where are we going?" said Levi.

"Just follow us, please," said Julie. "It'll take a lot less time to show you than to try to explain it."

"This evening could be even longer than I thought it was going to be," said Levi to Walter as they followed their wives.

They arrived at the back of the house, and the girls brought them over to the electric meter attached to the exterior wall at about eye level.

"Look," said Sarah.

"Okay," said Walter, "I'm looking. It's an electric meter."

"Look closer."

"Sarah, I'm getting a little frustrated here. What is it that you want me to see?"

"See that little disk on the inside?" said Julie.

"Yeah."

"What's it doing?"

"It's, you know, spinning."

"Right."

"Isn't that what it's supposed to do?"

"Yes, it is," said Julie, "at least when the house is using electricity."

"Julie," said Levi, "could you guys tell us what you're getting at? I'm as confused as Walter."

"Look, today has been a wonderful, mild day. It's not warm enough for air conditioning, and it's not cold, so there's no reason to run the furnace. It's broad daylight, so there's no need to have any lights on. We're not cooking anything, and it's a gas stove anyway. And just before you got here, we went in and unplugged the refrigerator. There is nothing, and I mean nothing, drawing any electricity in that house. And look at that thing." Julie pointed her finger at the meter.

"It's not just spinning," said Sarah, "it's spinning like there's a lot of electricity being used."

"I don't spend a lot of time staring at my electric meter," said Levi, "but you're right. That thing should be barely moving, if at all. So what's going on?"

"We don't know, but there's something that's using an awful lot of electricity around here, and we'll be damned if we can figure out what it is."

32

"**I**'VE GOT A HEADACHE," said Walter, staring at the piece of paper that Levi had spent the last two hours scribbling on.

"Hey, that's my line," said Sarah.

"Not tonight, it isn't," said Walter, miming the motion of dangling keys from his finger.

"Okay, guys, let's concentrate," said Levi.

As Levi had predicted, it had been a long evening. They had spent over an hour scouring the house for the source of the mysterious electrical consumption, but they'd come up empty. By that time, Beth and Robin were rightfully complaining that they were starving after an afternoon spent climbing through every fruit tree in the orchard and hauling back at least a bushel of apples to the house; and Daniel desperately needed another diaper change.

Fred Benecke had shown up just in time with two freshly plucked and cleaned chickens and a basket of potatoes and green beans from his garden. He was invited to stay for dinner, and he made drinks for the adults while Walter and Levi fired up the grill and Julie and Sarah prepped the vegetables. In no time, everyone was sated and happy, especially Daniel, who managed to consume what looked to be his weight in mashed potatoes and barbecued chicken. All the kids ate like farmers when they were up here, and the sight of them wolfing down their dinners after a day in the fresh air and sunshine made Sarah more determined than ever to keep the farm.

They'd quizzed Fred about the strange consumption of electricity, but he had been as mystified as they were. He'd gone so far as to shut down the security system temporarily to make sure that nothing in the house was drawing any current, but upon inspection, the electric meter was still whirring away.

"I don't know what to tell you," he'd said. "Armin completely updated the electrical service to the house before I ever installed the climate and security systems, so I'm sorry to tell you I don't know much about it. And, of course, he paid all the bills himself and kept all the records, so I'd have no way of knowing how much electricity this house normally uses."

Fred left after dinner, and after cleaning up and getting the kids to bed, the four of them had sat down at the kitchen table and started to unravel the e-mail that Levi had received.

"Here's what we've got," said Julie, turning the paper so that they all could look at it. Julie, it turned out, had a brilliant mind for tracing elaborate money trails, and she'd done most of the heavy lifting deciphering the e-mail.

"You're going to have to talk us through this, hon," said Levi.

"The best way to do it is to walk it back," said Julie. She put her finger at the bottom of the page. "Okay, here's the final step: The money is transferred from Rensselaer Partners to the town of Dutch River."

"But less than half of what we saw come into the Rensselaer Partners account went to the town," said Sarah.

"That's right," said Julie, moving her finger further up the page, "the rest of it went back into an account that Levi and his geniuses at NYPD Intelligence identified as belonging to the Sewall Family Trust, without going through any intermediate steps."

"What does that tell you?" said Walter.

"It tells me that Martin Sewall had no desire to get into a tussle with the IRS, and that he reported all the income that went to him and paid taxes on it."

"That's swell of him," said Sarah.

"Don't forget, Sarah," said Julie, "that you guys are wealthy yourselves now. You'll soon discover the fine art of keeping your tax bills to the minimum."

"Don't worry," said Sarah, "our financial adviser keeps telling us the same thing."

"But the funny thing is," said Levi, refocusing their concentration, "I thought Adam Avery said that the town was getting about $10 million a year, but the transfer to the town account is about twice that."

"That could just mean that Adam was wrong, but what I'm hoping it means is that the town is establishing some type of investment account that will allow it to keep the its finances healthy on a long-term basis," said Sarah, whose financial acumen continued to astonish Walter.

"But here's where it gets interesting," said Julie. "The money is deposited into the Rensselaer Partners account by a real estate investment trust domiciled in Luxembourg."

"And that real estate investment trust, which in financial speak, is called a REIT," said Levi, "is an enormous investment fund that appears to be entirely legitimate. It's so big and gets inflows from so many different sources that it is impossible, even with the resources of the NYPD, to figure out exactly where or who the money that goes to Rensselaer Partners is coming from."

"The perfect money-laundering operation," said Julie, a look close to admiration on her face.

"So at the end of the day," said Walter, scratching his head, "all we know is that the town of Dutch River is getting enormous sums of money from someone, we don't know who, from a REIT that we'll never be able to unravel, for some reason that we don't understand."

"And I'm more convinced than ever, especially since Bert was attacked, that it has something to do with this house," said Levi.

"My house," said Sarah.

"Your house," said Julie.

"I'm with you, Walter," said Sarah, "I'm starting to get a headache."

Walter glared at her.

"Well, at least we know who we're going to talk to next," said Levi.

"Who's that?" said Sarah.

"The president and vice president and treasurer of Rensselaer Partners."

"And they would be?" said Walter.

"That's right, I forgot to write that down here," said Levi. "They would be Peter Maas, Jill Maas, and Evelyn Williams, in that order."

"Evelyn who?" said Julie.

"You remember," said Sarah, "Dr. Mel Williams's wife, the one with the MBA from Columbia, remember?"

"Oh yeah."

33

"**I**'M SORRY, DO YOU HAVE AN APPOINTMENT?" said Dot Ferguson, looking up as Julie, Levi, and Walter walked into the offices of Maas & Maas. She was once again wearing a blouse that was at least two sizes too small over an overworked brassiere.

"No, we don't," said Walter looking around at the empty waiting area, "but it doesn't look like that's going to be much of a problem."

"We'll see what we can do to squeeze you in," said Dot, popping her wad of gum and leafing through the empty appointment calendar in front of her. She got up and headed toward Jill Maas's office. The only things being squeezed in at this office, observed Walter, were Dot's breasts into her brassiere and her ample hips into her too-tight, too-short skirt. But he had to admit her legs looked good. He wanted to tell her that he had high confidence in her ability to squeeze things in, but he bit his tongue. "I'll be right back. Can I get you folks any coffee?" said Dot, turning back toward them.

"Thanks," said Walter, averting his eyes, but probably too late, "that would be great. And please tell Ms. Maas that Evelyn Williams will be joining us in just a few minutes. I called her just before we got here."

"Can I ask what the subject of the meeting will be?"

"Just tell them Rensselaer Partners."

"Oh, have you decided to sell the farm, then?" said Dot, suddenly puzzled at Sarah's absence. Sarah had, in fact, volunteered to remain at the farm to look after the children. Walter had offered to stay behind instead, arguing that Sarah would probably be better equipped to follow the conversation, but Sarah had said, "Walter, you're the cop. You have to be there." He couldn't argue.

"No, we're not selling the farm."

"Then what should I tell them?"

"Please, Ms. Ferguson," said Walter, "just tell them that we're here to see them about Rensselaer Partners."

"All right, then," she said as she disappeared into Jill's office. She came out just a few minutes later.

"Ms. Maas said that this is highly unusual and she would have preferred an appointment, but she and Mr. Maas will be able to see you in
just a few minutes. Please take a seat in the conference room and I'll bring
some coffee in."

Dot was just getting the coffee served when Peter Maas arrived followed by his daughter. He looked dapper in a light gray tartan plaid suit
and a subdued tie. Jill was wearing what appeared to Julie to be the same
dark, pinstriped pantsuit that she had worn to their first meeting. They
had no sooner sat down than they heard the door to the law offices open
and close, and momentarily Dot entered the conference room accompanied by another woman.

"Ms. Williams is here," said Dot.

"Please, come in and sit down," said Jill. "Help yourselves to some
coffee. Dot, please stay here and take notes."

"Sure," said Dot, pouring herself some coffee, ostentatiously adding
some Splenda. She tugged at her skirt as she adjusted herself in the chair.

"What a surprise! What a surprise!" said Peter, giving them his bright-
est politician's grin, "although a pleasant one I can assure you."

"I'm not too sure why I'm here," said Evelyn, looking to Jill for help,
"but these folks said it was important, so I thought I'd better come over."
She was a small woman with a slight build. Short, honey-colored hair
framed a pretty face with delicate features that needed little makeup. She
wore a casual blouse and jeans and a pair of Nikes on her feet.

"I'm as confused as you are, Evelyn, so don't feel bad," said Jill, looking nervous but trying to sound all business.

"We're here to talk to you about Rensselaer Partners," said Levi.

"Rensselaer Partners? Rensselaer Partners?" said Peter. "What could
you possibly want to know about Rensselaer Partners?"

"Dad, why don't you let me handle this, okay?" said Jill.

"Fine with me. Fine with me," said Peter, his politician's smile turning
into one of bemusement.

"But I'll ask the same question my father just asked," said Jill. "What
could you possibly want to know about Rensselaer Partners?"

"Like I said! Like I said!"

"Ms. Maas," said Levi, "I've been doing some research into Dutch
River's finances—"

"And what business would that be of yours?" said Jill.

"Ms. Maas, Lieutenant Hudson and I are assisting the Massachusetts

State Police in an investigation into the apparent murder of a man from Boston named Charles Martin Sewall."

"Good for you. What can that possibly have to do with Dutch River?"

"We are also looking into the apparent murder of Armin Jaeger, and we believe the two deaths are related," said Walter.

"What are you people talking about?" said Jill, her milky complexion turning bright red, her blue eyes widening in disbelief. "Armin Jaeger was a ninety-year-old man who died in his sleep of natural causes. I saw the coroner's report. Have you people all gone nuts?"

"He was poisoned, Ms. Maas."

"He was what?" said Jill, suddenly looking unsteady.

"Please, let me explain," said Levi.

"It better be a damn good explanation, or this meeting is over." Jill put her hands palm down on the table, like a sailor trying to regain her equilibrium on a rocking boat.

"As you may or may not know, Ms. Maas, I work for the Intelligence Division of the New York City Police Department, and using the resources available to me, I have been investigating Rensselaer Partners."

"But why?"

"But why? But why?" murmured Peter Maas, his eyes drifting to the window.

"Because the finances of this town just didn't add up to us. We were initially told by Adam Avery, apparently because he believed it, that there was a state program to assist struggling towns like Dutch River, but that turned out to be false. So I looked further, and that is when I discovered Rensselaer Partners and the role it has been playing in supporting this town."

"I don't understand what this could possibly have to do with your murder investigation," said Jill.

"Because Rensselaer Partners not only deposited significant sums of money into the accounts of the Village of Dutch River," said Levi, "it also deposited even larger sums of money into investment accounts that we have traced to Charles Martin Sewall."

"Who knew? Who knew?" mused Peter Maas.

"What?" said Evelyn Williams, suddenly sitting up. "Jill, you told me—"

"Please, Evelyn, please," said Jill, holding her hand up, then slowly lowered it as her eyes rested on the tabletop. She slowly looked up.

"Okay, enough," she said. "I'm assuming you are asking us these questions because my father, Ms. Williams, and I appear as the operating officers of Rensselaer Partners in its organizing documents."

"That is correct," said Levi.

"That's fine. But you're crazy if you think Ms. Williams, my father, or I had anything to do with the murder of this Mr. Sewall. I never heard of the man; none of us did. And as for Armin Jaeger, well, excuse me, but I still don't believe he was murdered. I don't know where you got that."

Walter opened up a folder that he had placed on the table and took out a recent photo of Charles Martin Sewall. He turned it toward Jill. "Do you recognize this man?"

"I've never seen him in my life."

Walter turned it toward Evelyn, and then Peter Maas. "Do either of you recognize this man?"

"Absolutely not," said Evelyn.

"Of course not, of course not."

"I'm assuming you're going to tell us that he's Charles Martin Sewall," said Jill.

"That is correct."

"Well, then, I'm sorry. We can't help you."

"You have to do better than that," said Walter. "You are a licensed, practicing attorney in this state. You signed the formation documents for Rensselaer Partners. Your father is the mayor of this town, and I'm willing to bet that you give him quite a bit of help in carrying out his duties."

"Dad is sharper than you might think."

"That is neither here nor there," said Walter. "I need you to tell us what you know about Rensselaer Partners."

Jill Maas paused, slowly picked up her cup of coffee, took a long sip, and put it carefully back down. She looked up with a resigned look on her face.

"Look. Eight years ago my father got a phone call. The person who called, a man, said that Dutch River had acquired an anonymous benefactor, a benefactor who wished to help the town survive and maybe even thrive. He instructed us to create a 501(c)(3) charitable organization to receive funds from this benefactor. He also told us that this same benefactor wished to help other unnamed towns, and that we would be asked to wire transfer money to certain other accounts for the benefit of these other entities. That's all I know. Other than those basic functions, we all play what would charitably be called a passive role in the entity."

"Weren't you curious at all about this mysterious benefactor? Weren't you at all concerned, as an attorney, about the integrity of a setup like this?" said Julie.

"Ms. Remy. Mr. Welles. Lieutenant Hudson. Let me explain something to you," said Jill, looking at them all with a steady gaze. "Like most of the people around here, Dutch River is where I was born and raised. It's where my parents, my grandparents, and my ancestors going back generations were born and lived their lives. Just about every relative I ever had is buried in the cemetery a half-mile down the road from here. I was accepted at Princeton for college and Harvard Law School after that, but I went to SUNY Albany and Albany College of Law, two fine schools, by the way, so that I wouldn't have to go away to school. I graduated summa cum laude from college, and I was first in my law school class. I could have gotten a job with any top law firm in this country. But I didn't. I didn't because this is my home. It's the only place I could ever imagine living my life, and the only reason I became a lawyer was so that I could practice with my father, as he did with his father."

"So you didn't want to look too hard into this mysterious new setup," said Julie.

"You're damn right I didn't! Would you? This town, my home, was dying, dying right in front of me, me with all my education, and there was nothing I could do about it. And then that first deposit came, and it took my breath away. And then a year later, another one came. And all of a sudden, Dutch River wasn't going to die anymore. Adam could keep his restaurant going. Margie could keep her boutique up and running. We could bring in Mel and Evelyn to provide health care, and we could keep the local elementary school open. And Dad and I could keep our firm open. What would you have done?"

"I don't know," said Levi. Next to him, Julie just shook her head.

"But we still have two murders to solve, Ms. Maas," said Walter.

"Pardon me if I don't give a warm crap about your murder investigations, Lieutenant."

"I'm not sure you really mean that," said Walter, "especially since one of those men was someone just like you."

"I knew Armin Jaeger my entire life, Lieutenant," said Jill, her eyes suddenly welling with tears. "I picked apples on his farm. He taught me in Sunday school, for God's sake. He taught us all, every year, how to sing 'A Mighty Fortress Is Our God' in the original German. I loved that man, and I'd do anything to bring him back for just one more day. But I can't, and I don't think Armin would want anyone nosing around into his death if it meant destroying this town."

"I sympathize, Ms. Maas, but my job is to seek justice, justice for two murdered men. It's not just my job; it's my duty, and Mr. Welles's duty. And, might I add, it is also your duty."

Peter Maas suddenly sat up in his chair so abruptly it made everyone jump.

"Now you listen here, Lieutenant," he said in a strong, clear voice. "My daughter and I know our duty, and we don't need you to tell us what it is. We will assist you in any way possible with your murder investigations. Armin Jaeger taught my Sunday school class, too, you know. But we will also do everything in our power to protect our town. That's our duty, too, though I understand it's not yours."

"I understand, sir," said Walter, as Jill rested a hand on her father's shoulder. She stared at Walter with defiant pride.

"Good," said Peter Maas, "so let's get on with it. And no more of this nonsense about who has the higher calling here. Do you understand, Lieutenant?"

"Yes sir," said Walter.

"Good. Good."

They all rose to leave. As Walter walked around the table to leave the room, he looked down at the steno pad lying on the table that Dot Ferguson had brought into the room with her.

She hadn't taken a single note.

34

"**W**ELL, THAT SHOOTS MY THEORY ALL TO HELL," said Walter, digging into the rich lamb casserole that Adam had served him. Adam was sitting with them at the booth, but with only a cup of coffee in front of him. As usual, he had insisted that he had to be ready in case anybody else showed up.

"And what theory would that have been?" said Levi, after swallowing a mouthful of his subtly seasoned, fork-tender veal piccata.

"I would have bet money that Jill Maas was up to her neck in this. She was one of my prime candidates for the mystery woman who poisoned Charles Martin Sewall and Armin Jaeger."

"I never suspected her of the murders," said Bert, who had already finished off his bacon cheeseburger and fries with the happy abandon of a man for whom eating food—any food—was a joy. He still had a bandage on his head and his color was still off, but he had insisted on checking out of the hospital as soon as the doctor would clear him.

"Why not?" said Levi.

"Because neither 'Boonesy' nor Iris gave a clear description of the woman who gave them the poison. Jill has that headful of red hair, and they at least would have noticed that."

"That's a good point," said Walter, making Bert beam.

"And I don't think she was lying about her involvement with Rensselaer Partners," said Levi.

"I don't either," said Walter. "Everything she said sounded like it came straight from the heart. I think the only thing we can accuse her of is remaining willfully ignorant."

"That probably goes for her father, too," said Levi, "although with that vague old man routine he puts on it's hard to tell."

"Peter Maas has been using that vague old man routine for as long as I can remember," said Bert. "On the rare occasions that he has a court case, he uses it very effectively. And Jill and I were only a grade apart in school. I know she can rub people the wrong way, but so do I. Deep down, she's good people."

"Just like you," said Levi.

"I hope so."

"So did you go to Armin Jaeger's Sunday school class too?" said Walter. A bright smile lit up Bert's face. He looked at Adam who smiled back.

"Are you ready?" said Bert.

"You bet," said Adam, as they broke into the first verse of "A Mighty Fortress Is Our God" in the original German. Adam had an adequate baritone, but he had a good ear, and he sang accurate harmony as Bert sang the melody in a surprisingly clear, sweet tenor voice. They stopped after one verse, but continued to grin like children on Christmas morning.

"He not only taught you how to sing," said Levi, "he taught you excellent German."

"Aw, that's the only German we ever learned," said Adam, "and I don't remember what the words mean anymore, but nobody in this town ever forgets how to sing that hymn."

"I don't think I ever heard it before," said Walter.

"It's not exactly a favorite in the Catholic Church," said Levi, "but that's a long story. Someday I'll tell you all about the Reformation."

"No, you won't."

Levi laughed. "You're right, I won't."

"So where do we go from here?" said Bert.

"I don't know," said Levi. "We've apparently hit a dead end on the Rensselaer Partners angle. There is simply no way that we will ever be able to identify who, out of the thousands of investors in the Luxembourg REIT, was funneling money to Dutch River and the Sewall family. Most of the investors in the REIT turned out to be blind trusts that are absolutely impenetrable, and Luxembourg still has pretty strict privacy laws."

"Someone out there has to know," said Adam.

"Of course. But they've gone to great lengths to keep themselves well hidden, and I don't think they're just suddenly going to pop up and raise their hands."

"Do you think Mr. Sewall knew?" said Bert.

"I think he may have," said Walter, "but that doesn't do us any good now."

"What about Mrs. Sewall?"

"Sergeant Mayhew doesn't think so, but I'm not sure."

"Why not?"

"First of all, the Massachusetts State Police have basically told him to stop working the case. They've got budget and manpower issues, and I think they've decided they're going to stand back and wait for the feds to take over, since there's pretty convincing evidence that this was an interstate crime. So Mayhew never really had a chance to dig in."

"Has the FBI assigned anyone to the case?" said Bert.

"Not that I know of," said Walter, "but it's not like they'd tell me if they had. The FBI and the NYPD are not exactly on warm and fuzzy terms. And right now, they're using all their resources to soak the big banks and Wall Street firms for billions for their roles in the Great Recession. The money that's going through Rensselaer Partners may sound like a lot of money to us, but to them, it's small beer."

"But what about the murders?" said Adam. "They have to care about the murders, right?"

"I hate to sound like a cynic, but the murders are not their priority, especially if the state police in New York and Massachusetts can't give them any solid leads."

"And the state guys are standing back waiting for the feds," said Bert.

"Right, so we have a great big stalemate that's not going to end soon, and I doubt it will end well," said Walter. "But all that's not the biggest reason why I'm not convinced Sergeant Mayhew is right about Mrs. Sewall."

"So what's the other reason?" said Adam.

"I think he may have a little bit of a crush on her," said Walter, immediately regretting it. "I'm sorry, I shouldn't have said that. Sergeant Mayhew is a fine police officer, and I have no right to say something insulting like that. Please forget I said it." The others all nodded.

"So, once again, where does that leave us?" said Bert.

"It leaves us back at the farmhouse. Armin Jaeger was murdered, and you were attacked there for a reason, and we're just going to have to figure out what that reason was and hope that it leads us somewhere."

"What do you want me to do?" said Bert.

"I can't think of anything you can do other than to go about your normal duties. Just observe everybody and everything as carefully as you can. You never know when someone will make a mistake, even a small one. I know you might find that a little frustrating, but we're all a little frustrated right now."

"Do you think we might never be able to solve this case?"

"No, Bert, I don't think that. One of the toughest parts of any case like this is not letting yourself give up. This has happened to me plenty of times before. Something will come up, I'm sure of it. But right now, all we can do is keep our eyes and ears open and plow ahead. So please be patient."

"Sure," said Bert as they all rose from the table. Bert headed back to his patrol car while Walter and Levi stayed behind to settle the check for lunch. Just as Adam finished giving them their change, a sixtyish-looking couple pulled up in a car with Connecticut plates on it. They opened the door to the restaurant and poked their heads in, scanning the empty booths.

"Is this place open?" said the woman.

"Of course it is," said Adam, "may I show you to a booth?"

"Do you serve anything other than burgers here?" said the man.

"We most certainly do," said Adam.

Walter winked at him as he left.

———————

"I know you backed off in there," said Levi as he and Walter settled into the BMW. Walter had grabbed the keys and volunteered to drive, starting to love the machine. "But you're not sure how much Abby Sewall really knows, are you."

"No, I'm not. I just felt like a shit insulting a fellow officer like that. It was totally unprofessional."

"But perhaps not totally uncalled for."

"Perhaps not."

"You really think that she could manipulate David Mayhew? Maybe it was just a passing thing, Walter. The guy has a fine record as a cop. And, besides, he's happily married and Abby Sewall is what, fifteen years older than he is?"

"More like twenty. Look, I'm not saying he's in love with her; I'm just worried that from everything I've heard she's a gifted fundraiser who's able to convince even the high and mighty tightwads in Boston to open up their wallets in a big way for her charities. That means she's a charmer and very manipulative, which can be used in good ways and bad ways. And I think it's expecting a lot from a young guy like Mayhew to be impervious to all that."

"But why do you think she knows anything?"

"Levi, you're married. I'm married. How many men do you know who could keep a secret that big from their wives, especially when it affected the family's welfare the way that this secret did, for this long? And Abby Sewall isn't your average housewife. This money coming in helped to make her who she is. It's just hard for me to believe that she wouldn't have found out all about this deal."

"Especially since, as we've seen here, shit happens. She would have wanted to be sure that the flow of money wouldn't stop in the event that her husband died."

"That's what I think."

"But don't you think she'd do everything she could to help us find her husband's murderer?"

"Levi, do you remember what Jill Maas said about Armin Jaeger's murder?"

"Something about not giving a warm shit, as I recall."

"Exactly, and I think it's at least possible that by now, Abby Sewall could feel the same way about her husband's murder: There's nothing she can do to bring him back, so her first priority is going to be to protect the flow of money, the money that's made her one of the biggest of big shots in Boston."

"So what are you going to do?"

"I think I just might make a trip to Boston and make Mrs. Sewall's personal acquaintance myself. Captain Amato's suddenly giving me a long leash on this, and perhaps I should use it to give our young colleague Sergeant Mayhew a hand."

35

"ABBY, I'M SORRY," said Sergeant David Mayhew as he slowly removed his large right hand from her small left breast. "I never meant for this to happen."

"There's nothing to be sorry about, David," said Abby, rolling her body toward his, a knowing smile of her face. "And it certainly seemed that you were enjoying yourself." Her bed was large and comfortable, and the chilly afternoon sun gave the room a warm glow.

It would be hard for him to argue with that, thought Mayhew as he lay there, reveling in the exquisite sensation of her body against his. She was painfully thin, and her breasts were almost nonexistent, especially compared to his wife's generous bust, which even his enormous paws couldn't contain. But her skin was like silk, and she touched him, talked to him, and aroused him in ways that he had never before experienced or even imagined. In the past hour, he'd had three orgasms, but even at that, he hadn't been able to keep pace with Abby, who'd had at least five. She had seemed insatiable, and her arousal had filled him with more sheer lust than he had ever experienced in his life.

"Abby, I'm a married man," said David.

"Of course you are," said Abby, "and you are going to remain a married man. This is something very private, very special, just between us. You must never tell anyone about it, and you must never allow it to affect your marriage and your family. Do you understand, David?"

"Yes, Abby. Yes, I do."

It wasn't supposed to have been like this, he thought, as his mind wandered back to last evening, when he'd received the phone call from Lieutenant Hudson informing him that he would like to drive out to Boston and meet Abby personally.

His boss, Lieutenant Richards, had made it unambiguously clear to him that he was off the Sewall case and that he was expected to do what his boss referred to as his "day job." Richards had reminded him that high-profile murder investigations were well beyond his pay grade and his job description, and it would now be handled at the appropriate levels. He knew Richards was right, but he'd rationalized that he couldn't just let Abby get ambushed by the aggressive detective from New York. The lack of professionalism in that thought had not eluded him, but it hadn't stopped him, either.

The next day was a scheduled day off, but he told his wife that he'd been called in at the last minute to cover for another cop who'd called in sick. Then he'd taken off for Boston, calling Abby on the way. He'd been thrilled just at the sound of her voice, which only served to compound the guilt he felt from lying to his wife.

Yes, he reminded himself. He'd lied to his wife. He'd never done that before. Never. He should have known. He should have turned back. But he hadn't, and he'd felt almost outside himself as he completed the drive and walked up the long hill to Abby's town house.

She'd surprised him by answering the door herself, dressed casually in a pair of worn jeans and a tee shirt that accented her fragile frame and slight build. But for Mayhew, it only served to heighten her allure and his already overwhelming sense of her vulnerability; and the simple fact that she had allowed him to see her, the powerful doyenne of elite Boston society, like this created an air of intimacy that he found intoxicating. His heart was pounding by the time he stepped inside the house and, once again, he had to resist the overwhelming impulse to take her in his arms.

She leaned close to him as he entered, almost as if she were going to kiss him, but then merely extended her hand. Her golden hair, not tied back today, cascaded over her shoulders in a way that made her look like a teenager.

"Sergeant Mayhew, what a pleasant surprise! I wasn't sure I'd be seeing you again. Please come with me." She turned and began to walk down the hallway toward the elevator. He couldn't help noticing that she was wearing nothing on her feet.

When they got to the third floor she surprised him as she walked past the door to her office and opened a door a little farther down on the other side of the hallway. He entered what looked like an intimate living area. There was no office furniture and no computer equipment, just a phone. Two richly upholstered love seats and two chairs were arranged in a square, surrounding a mahogany table that gleamed from decades of polishing. On the table, coffee and pastries had already been laid out. Abby closed the door behind them.

She noticed him staring at the coffee and pastries on the tables and said, "I don't normally serve pastries at this time of the day, but I didn't want you leaving my home yet again with an unsatisfied appetite." She poured coffee for both of them, and then settled herself on one of the love seats, tucking her feet under her legs. She motioned for Mayhew to sit in the chair closest to her.

"Sergeant, may I make an awkward request of you?"

"Ma'am?"

"The carpets in this room are ancient and somewhat fragile, and I hope you won't mind if I ask you to take off your shoes."

"Oh, certainly not, ma'am. I'm afraid they make these things pretty heavy duty," he said as he bent to untie them.

"And, Sergeant?"

"Yes, ma'am?"

"The uniform belt? It's enormous and the upholstery on the furniture is original."

"Oh, no problem," said Mayhew after only a brief hesitation.

"And why don't you give me your tie? I feel like you have me at a disadvantage," she said, resting a delicate hand on her flimsy tee shirt.

He removed his boots, belt, and tie, casting his eyes around the room, looking for a place to deposit them but finding none.

"Please give them to me, Sergeant. I'll get them out of your way." She took the tie, the boots, and the belt and walked to a door on the far side of the room. She turned back to him and said, "Do you mind if they are out of your sight for a short while?"

"Oh no, ma'am. I don't think I have to worry about my shoes being stolen in this house."

"Nobody wears your size, I can assure you of that," she said, staring down at them. She opened the door, and Mayhew couldn't help noticing that the adjacent room was a bedroom. She came back into the living area and resettled herself.

"I'm sorry for the inconvenience, Sergeant, but I'm having some new computer equipment installed in my office, and I thought we'd be more comfortable here."

"No problem, ma'am. I'm just glad that you were able to see me on such short notice," said Mayhew. He hadn't noticed any workmen in the building or any noise coming from the office as they'd walked by, but this was an enormous house, and the ancient walls were thick.

"Now, Sergeant, why don't you tell me all about this visit I'm about to receive."

"As I told you over the phone, ma'am, I have been transferred off the case and the Massachusetts State Police have not yet identified a replacement."

"I assume that is because the trail has gone cold, and the state police are placing this case on the back burner, so to speak."

"No, ma'am, not at all."

"That's good to hear, I guess. And, Sergeant, since you are now officially off the case, would you mind if I started calling you David, and would you please call me Abby?"

"That would be fine, uh, Abby." Her name on his lips felt nice. "But, Abby?"

"Yes, David?"

"You said, 'I guess.'"

"I said what?"

"You said, 'That's good to hear, I guess,' when I said that we were still pursuing the case."

"I guess I did, didn't I."

"Can you tell me why?"

"David," said Abby, lingering over his name, "I'm not sure I know how to explain this without sounding insensitive to my husband's memory."

"Please, Abby, I would never doubt the feelings you had for your husband."

"Thank you, David," she said, resting her hand on his. "That means a lot to me. You . . . Your good opinion, means a lot to me."

"And you mean a lot to me, too. I mean, you know, your good opinion means a lot. You know."

"I know, David," she said, giving his hand a squeeze before removing it. "I guess what I meant is that I, I and my entire family, have gone through so much already. And, well, over three weeks have gone by, and I'm beginning to doubt that the case will ever be solved. And even if it is, my husband will never come back to me. I'm beginning to wonder what it's all for. I'm starting to feel like I just want to put it all behind me and be left alone to move on with my life."

"I can understand why you'd feel that way."

"Then can't you tell this Lieutenant Hudson to please leave me alone? Why hasn't he been removed from the case as you were?"

"He's been given a little more time than I have, Abby. And please remember that he has his own murder to solve."

"Yes, a murder that was committed hundreds of miles outside of his jurisdiction. And now I've heard they're digging up that poor old man and poking through his remains. It's ghoulish, and it will accomplish nothing."

"You're probably right, Abby. But Lieutenant Hudson is a stubborn man, and he likes to solve his cases."

"Good for him. But he ought to consider the feelings of the living while he's going about his work. And what does he think he's going to accomplish by coming all the way out here? I'm not asking anyone to drop the investigation, but I don't know why he feels it necessary to drive to Boston and interrogate me personally. Haven't I been completely forthcoming with you?"

"Yes, you have, Abby, and I've told him that. I have no idea what he thinks he's going to learn by talking to you. You've already told me everything you know, and I've passed that all along to him."

"Then why can't you tell him to cancel his visit?"

"Abby, please understand, I'm a junior officer in the state police. Lieutenant Hudson is one of the most experienced and highly regarded detectives in the entire NYPD. I'm afraid that it would just make things worse for you if I tried to convince him not to come. People might start to wonder."

"Wonder what, David?"

"If I'm maintaining my objectivity, I guess."

"But why would they wonder that?"

"Abby, you're a beautiful, wealthy, successful woman. Even hicks like me out in Sturbridge have seen your picture in the newspapers with politicians and celebrities. I can understand why they'd wonder."

"Oh, David, if they only knew."

"Knew what, Abby?"

"How frightened I am, how lonely. I'm not the woman in those pictures in the newspaper, David. My daughter is away at college. My son is in his final year at Harvard Law, but he has his own apartment near the campus, and I never see him. And, honestly, the children were always far closer to their father than to me. I have no other close relatives. I'm all alone in this house, day after day. I don't even answer the phone anymore." She looked up at him with those bottomless blue eyes. They were damp with tears.

There was no more resisting the impulse. He moved over to the love seat and sat next to her. He took her in his arms. He was afraid that she would push him away and throw him out of the house, but she didn't. She melted into him and tucked her head under his chin.

"Oh, David, thank you."

This is okay, he thought. He was just comforting a lonely widow with whom he no longer had any professional relationship. Even his wife would understand.

Abby looked up at him, her eyes inviting him in close, her mouth almost touching his. He never knew who leaned in first, but suddenly he felt his lips brush hers, sending an electric current straight to his groin. Suddenly his mouth was on hers.

Suddenly, it was too late.

His hands began to roam under her tee shirt, and then the tee shirt was gone and Abby was naked from the waist up. His mouth moved down to her small, delicious breasts, and she had her first orgasm while he was kissing them. She reached down and unzipped his fly.

"Jesus, David," she said, looking down. "Come with me." She grabbed his hand and led him into her bedroom. They were both naked before they got to the bed. Her body may have looked frail, but it was agile and strong, and Abby Sewall gave as good as she got with the big cop.

From the day they had met when she was a nineteen-year-old coed at Radcliffe, she had been stubbornly faithful to her husband, a man she had deeply loved. But he had been a conventional, only mildly enthusiastic, lover, and she had always had to suppress a sex drive that was far stronger and more adventurous than his. Her erotic impulses had been awakened by articles she'd read in *Cosmopolitan* from time to time, and by tales told out of school by friends who shouldn't have drunk so much wine at lunch. She had longed to try even the most outlandish suggestions. But she was a Sewall, and wayward impulses had to be repressed. But now it was different. And now it was more than that. All her repressed anger, her bottomless loneliness, and, yes, her unfathomable sense of grief for the husband she had loved and lost in so many ways, had brought her to this moment with this innocent, helpless young man. She was finally doing it her way, and she didn't want it to end.

David loved and desired his wife, but they had been each other's first and only sexual partners, and they had both remained remarkably naïve lovers. In just a few short minutes, Abby Sewall had opened up a world of sensuality that he had never known to exist. He couldn't even think of stopping himself until he was physically depleted. Only then did the regrets start to leak into his conscience, but he found himself pushing them away. This had been too good.

They would have stayed there the rest of the afternoon if it hadn't been for a knock on the bedroom door.

"I thought I left instructions not to be disturbed," said Abby, the sheet falling from her as she sat up.

"Ma'am, I am so sorry to disturb you," came the timid voice of the maid through the door, "but you have a caller downstairs who said he needs to see you."

"That's impossible. I have no appointments this afternoon. Who does this person say he is?"

"He says his name is Hudson, ma'am. Detective Lieutenant Walter Hudson of the New York City Police Department."

36

"LOOKING FOR SOMETHING, LIEUTENANT?" said Abby Sewall, as Walter Hudson cast his eyes around her third-floor office. He'd spent a full twenty minutes cooling his heels in the foyer before being escorted up to the third floor by the maid, but since he'd deliberately arrived at an unexpected hour, he couldn't complain. Abby was modestly dressed in an oatmeal-colored, midcalf-length cotton skirt and a linen blouse under a rose-colored cardigan. Her hair was carefully tied back. She appeared relaxed.

"Oh, no ma'am. I just thought Sergeant Mayhew might be here, that's all."

"Why on earth would you think that, Lieutenant? I've been informed that he is no longer assigned to the investigation into my husband's death." She poured coffee for both of them without asking Walter if he wanted any, and offered him the same untouched tray of pastries she'd laid out for Sergeant Mayhew. At least he hadn't left with an unsatisfied appetite this time, she thought, inwardly smiling.

"It's just that I thought I saw his car parked down the hill, that's all."

"Well, he may be in Boston; I'd have no way of knowing, but he certainly isn't here," said Abby, technically not lying.

"I can see that," said Walter, mentally noting the technical honesty.

"I don't mean to rush you, Lieutenant, but I do have an engagement this evening. What can I do to help you? I've already told Sergeant Mayhew everything I know."

"Mrs. Sewall, I'm going to be blunt," said Walter, knowing that in any battle of subtlety and innuendo with this woman he would be badly outmatched.

"Please do, Lieutenant. I have neither the time nor the patience for game playing, especially when it involves my husband's death. But I repeat: I've already told Sergeant Mayhew everything I know."

"I'm sure you have, ma'am. But here's my problem. From everything Sergeant Mayhew has told me, you are an impressive woman."

"How kind of him to think so."

"He tells me you are smart, articulate, and accomplished."

"Please, Lieutenant, you're making me blush."

"I also know from my own research that you are a, uh, prodigious philanthropist."

"I do what I can."

"And then some."

"Okay."

"And now that's all going to come to an end, isn't it?"

"I don't know, Lieutenant, is it?"

"How can you be sure that it won't? Your husband is gone, and as you've told Sergeant Mayhew, you knew nothing about the source of your family's prosperity."

"Then perhaps you are right."

"I assume that you would care about that money, ma'am. That money makes you what you are in this city. I assume you would have wanted to know where it was coming from, and how it would keep flowing in the unlikely event that something happened to your husband, which it so tragically did. I find it very hard to believe, ma'am, that you remained completely ignorant for all this time about the source of all this wonderful wealth."

"I already explained this to Sergeant Mayhew, Lieutenant. Yes, I was curious about the source of all the newfound prosperity that our family was suddenly so blessed with. And yes, I was concerned that someday it might disappear as suddenly as it appeared, despite my husband's repeated assurances to the contrary."

"So you did talk to your husband about the money, then? I don't think you told Sergeant Mayhew that."

"They weren't discussions about the source of the money, Lieutenant," said Abby after only a brief hesitation. "However, I never committed to a major donation without consulting my husband to ensure that we would never have to renege on any commitment I made. That would have been personally humiliating, and it would have permanently damaged the standing of our family in this city. I would not tolerate either."

"So you're telling me that you know nothing about the source of the wealth that you've enjoyed for almost ten years now."

"That is true, Lieutenant."

"I'm sorry, ma'am, but I just don't believe you."

"I believe that is your problem, Lieutenant Hudson, not mine."

"And what I don't understand," said Walter, ignoring her, "is that you know that learning about the source of that money would help me to solve two murders, one of them your own husband's."

"I know no such thing, Lieutenant, and I will say to you one more time that I have already told both you and Sergeant Mayhew all I know. I have tried to be as helpful as I possibly could be, and I find it painful and insulting that you have chosen, for no good reason whatsoever, not to take me at my word. In my world, that's about as low as a person can sink. As for the money, I have been fortunate to live in wealth since the day I was born. For a few short years, my husband and I have been blessed with enormous, unexpected wealth. We have treated that wealth not as a personal windfall, but as an obligation, an obligation to do the right thing with it. And we have. I will show you all of the records if you haven't already managed to obtain them."

"Mrs. Sewall, I'm not saying—"

"Please be kind enough to let me finish. If, for some reason related to my husband's death, that extraordinary wealth ceases to come to me, so be it. I will still be who I am. I will hold my head high and carry on. Do you understand, Lieutenant?"

"Yes, I do, ma'am."

"Then I believe our discussion has come to an end; unless, of course, you intend to escort me from my home in handcuffs."

"That won't be necessary, ma'am," said Walter, rising. "Thank you for your time. I hope you understand that I'm just trying to do my job."

"Everyone should relish one's job as much as you do, Lieutenant."

"I'm not sure what you mean, ma'am," said Walter, struggling to maintain eye contact as her mesmerizing eyes bore into his, a hint of a smile flitting across her face like a half-remembered dream.

"I'm sure you don't."

"I'll see my way out."

"Good evening, Lieutenant Hudson."

Abby Peabody Sewall reached for the tray sitting on the table and held it out to Walter as he turned toward the door.

"Pastry, Lieutenant?"

Walter stumbled down Mount Vernon Street, suddenly no longer quite so willing to criticize David Mayhew's handling of Abby Sewall. It had been a mismatch for both of them.

He still wasn't sure if she had told him the entire truth, but he also understood that he would probably never know. If he was going to solve the murders of Charles Martin Sewall and Armin August Jaeger, he'd have to find another way to do it.

Fine. He'd solved crimes against longer odds than this.

When he got to the bottom of the hill he noticed that David Mayhew's car, and he knew that it was his, was no longer there.

It no longer mattered.

37

I T WOULD HAVE BEEN A LOVELY DRIVE IN THE DAYTIME, especially this time of year, but Walter had departed as the autumn sun was setting over Boston, leaving the old city in a golden glow that managed to make the Charles River look almost pretty and the drive even more lovely. But he was tired, and day quickly turned to night. After a few miles the long stretches on the turnpike all started to melt into one another.

But at least the trip was short: two and a half hours on the Mass Pike, from downtown Boston to the exit in New York that was a mere ten minutes from both Martin Van Buren's homestead and Dutch River.

He had expected to find only Levi and Julie when he arrived back at the farmhouse at around eight thirty, the plan having been for Sarah to return to New York with the kids, who had already missed so much school he expected board of education officials to show up on their doorstep with warrants any day. Neither he nor Sarah had any regrets, though; the girls could always make up the schoolwork, and they were having an experience that they would never forget. School was overrated anyway, thought Walter, thinking back to his own painful run-ins with the nuns in parochial school.

Instead, everyone was seated around the kitchen table, expectant looks on their faces. Even Daniel was there, seated on his mother's lap, contentedly gnawing on what appeared to be a chicken bone.

"This is a surprise," he said. "What's up?"

"We wanted to show you something that we think you're going to find interesting."

"And you need to show it to me all together, at eight-thirty at night in the dark?"

"Well, the kids actually made the discovery, so I thought they should be here when we showed you," said Sarah.

"It was Daniel, Daddy!" said Beth. "Daniel found it!"

"Found what?"

"Come on, we'll show you. Kids, put on your jackets; it's chilly out-side tonight."

Kids and adults put on jackets and stepped out into the brisk autumn air led by Levi and Julie, who each carried large flashlights, though the harvest moon lit the night sky so brightly their shadows fell on the ground as if it were midday. They walked from the house to the barn, the evening silence being broken only by their shoes crunching against the gravel driveway, and then circled around to the far side of the large structure, the side facing away from the street and toward the orchard and the freshly mown fields. They stopped at a spot near the far corner.

"So what am I supposed to be seeing?"

"The girls had gone out to the orchard to pick apples," said Sarah. "Fred had shown them how to separate out the 'eating apples' from the 'cooking apples,' so when they were done picking, they dragged the apples over here to do the sorting because it was a chilly afternoon, and this spot was sheltered from the breeze, and it was sunny. I came over to see how they were doing, and they told me that they needed a couple of extra baskets."

"Peck-sized, Daddy," said Robin. Walter stared at her blankly as he vaguely recalled getting a question wrong on a test about bushels and pecks.

"So I put Daniel down on the grass, because I was only going to be gone for a minute, and I went off to get the extra baskets for them."

"And then Daniel started humming, Daddy," said Beth.

"What?"

"It's true," said Sarah. "When I got back, the girls started saying, 'Mommy, listen to Daniel.' I crouched down next to him, and he was humming."

"You mean like humming a tune?"

"Of course not. He's only a year old, for heaven's sake."

"He was going 'Hmmmmmmmmm,'" said Beth.

"Hmmmmmmmmm," said Daniel, bouncing in his mother's arms.

"I'm a little confused and a lot cold, guys," said Walter, "can we get to the point here?"

"Just do us a favor," said Julie, "and sit right here." She pointed to a patch of ground near the barn wall.

Walter looked at Julie skeptically, but Levi said, "Go ahead, Walter, this could be really important."

"Right here, Daddy," said Robin, running over and touching the exact spot with her hand.

Walter went over and sat down. The ground was cold and a stone bit into his hip. He was too big for this, he thought.

"Now everybody stand really still and be really quiet," said Sarah.

"I don't know what you guys are . . . oh," said Walter.

He felt it first, almost indiscernible, just a sensation in his butt and legs. Then, as his ears became accustomed to the total silence, he could have sworn that he heard it, too. It was faint, but it was distinct.

It was a hum, the mechanical humming of an electric motor.

"I think we've found the source of our unexplained electrical usage," said Walter.

"Hmmmmmmmm," said Daniel.

38

IT WAS GETTING LATE, and Sarah and Walter got the kids put to bed as soon as they got back to the house while Levi made coffee and Julie found a large piece of paper and a pencil. The excitement of the day and all the fresh air had done its usual job on the kids. They went down without complaining and were sound asleep by the time Walter and Sarah got back downstairs. They all poured large mugs of coffee; it was going to be a long night.

Julie took a seat at the far end of the long kitchen table, and the others took seats on either side. She spread the sheet of paper out in front of her and began to sketch.

"Okay. This," she said, forming a remarkably accurate freehand rectangle on the left of the paper, "is the farmhouse. And this," she said, drawing a larger, square object off to the right, "is the barn."

She quickly sketched in the details of the first floor of the house, showing the kitchen in the upper right-hand corner of the drawing. The lower right corner was identified as the formal dining room, and the left side was taken up by the living room and what Armin had apparently called the sunroom.

"I think," she said, "that there is some kind of vault under the barn, and that it has its own security and climate systems, completely independent of the one for the main house that Fred Benecke maintains."

"A vault that only Armin ever knew about," said Sarah.

"And the vault that contains the key to all the money that we've been chasing," said Levi.

"With so little success," Walter added, thinking back to his conversation with Abby Sewall.

"It's a remarkable misdirection when you think about it," said Levi.

"What do you mean?" said Walter.

"He installed this sophisticated security and climate system in the house for all the world to see, leading anyone snooping around to think that whatever he might be hiding, he'd be hiding in the house."

"And all along it was somewhere else. Not bad for an old farmer, huh?" said Sarah, suddenly proud of the relative she never knew.

"Now," said Julie, "there has to be some kind of physical access to that vault."

"I'd think it would be in the barn," said Sarah.

"I'm not so sure," said Julie. "If I were Armin, I'd want an access way that I would never have to leave the house to use."

"But why?" said Walter. "The house is at least fifty feet from the barn. It would be a whole lot easier to have direct access from the barn."

"Yes, except then you would have to leave the house to get to it."

"And risk detection by some snoop," said Levi.

"That's right. And remember, the winters around here from everything we've heard can be harsh. I'm sure there are times in the dead of winter when it would be a struggle just to get to the barn without a lot of noise and effort. I don't think he would have wanted that."

"Okay," said Walter, "so where, then?"

"Well, the part of the house closest to the barn is right here," said Julie, placing the point of her pencil on the upper right corner of her drawing, in the kitchen.

They all got up from their chairs and walked over to the corner of the room.

"There's nothing here," said Walter.

"Perhaps," said Julie, "because it would be too obvious to put it here."

"Do you think it could be down in the basement?" said Sarah.

"You know, I've never been down there," said Walter, "have any of you guys?"

They all shook their heads.

"Okay, then, let's go." Walter headed toward the door that Fred had told them led to the basement.

"Hold it just a second," said Levi, walking over to the front door. "After what happened to poor Bert, we have to make sure we rearm the security system every time we leave or enter the house."

"Good thought," said Walter.

Thankfully, there was a light switch at the top of the stairs, and the basement lit up when Walter flipped it. They all trod down the surprisingly sturdy stairs, which clearly weren't original to the house. A mouse scuttled by and Walter yelped. He hated mice. Sarah laughed at him, but it was a nervous laugh.

It was the foundation of an old house. The floor was packed dirt, and the walls were built from individual stones, carefully selected to fit into each other closely. Just this foundation must have taken months to build, thought Walter.

"I don't think we're going to find anything down here," said Julie. "It's kind of hard to build a door into a stone wall."

"And this packed earth floor is like cement," said Sarah.

Levi started pacing around the perimeter of the basement, periodically knocking on the wall. Then he walked around it again, this time getting on his knees every few feet and pounding on the floor.

"What are you doing, Levi?" said Julie. "You're going to hurt your arm."

"Hold on," he said, as he started pounding the earth around the far corner. He suddenly paused, cocking his head, then pounded again. Then again.

"Come on over here. Now listen," he said, when they were all standing around him. He turned to one side and pounded on the floor. There was just the dull thud of his fist on the rock-hard floor. Then he rotated back to the area near the wall where he'd been before. "Now listen to this." He pounded again. It was still a dull thud, but slightly different.

"Do that again," said Julie.

"That's easy for you to say," said Levi. He pounded again.

"Am I imagining things, or was there almost a hollow sound to that?"

"That's what I think, too," said Levi. "Walter, come here."

After a few more minutes of pounding, the two men had identified a small square space that sounded different than the rest of the floor when struck. Walter's massive fists made the hollow sound even more noticeable. They then started feeling around the perimeter of the square.

"What's this?" said Levi, poking at something that looked like a root. He began to dig around it and when he had laid more of it bare, he wedged two of his fingers under it and pulled. It lifted straight up, it's shaft still buried in the ground.

"It's a handle," said Sarah.

Walter scooted over to the opposite side of the square and felt around in the packed earth.

"Huh, here's another one." Soon he had uncovered the second handle, about two and a half feet directly across from the one Levi had uncovered. They each stood up and pulled hard on the handles. A square of the packed earth floor pulled away. Beneath the earth was a heavy oak hatch covered by six inches of the hard earth. They all peered down the hole beneath the hatchway. There were five cast iron rungs leading down to another floor six feet below that seemed to lead to a small passageway.

Levi and Walter dropped the hatch door on the ground, where it landed with a hard thud.

"Your great-uncle must have been a strong man," said Walter. "That damn thing is heavy."

"There's no way anyone ever would have guessed that hatch was there," said Levi, "unless you got down on the floor and deliberately pounded the way we did."

"Is everybody game?" said Julie, staring down the hatchway.

"We should go back upstairs and get the flashlights," said Sarah.

"Hold on," said Levi. He edged himself over and placed his foot on the first rung. Lights suddenly illuminated the floor and the tunnel below. "That's what I thought. There's a light switch embedded in the first rung. I'm not surprised; Armin Jaeger was a very clever man."

They all clambered down the hatchway. It was a low, narrow passageway, but at least it was well lit. It seemed to go on forever, though they all knew that they had only traveled fifty or sixty feet when they came to a steel door that looked like the door to a bank vault. There was a large, spoked wheel on the front. Off to the side was a large, rectangular keypad that had more than just numbered keys: It was a replica of a typewriter keyboard.

"From the looks of it, this is where we're supposed to punch in an entry code," said Levi, "but the code is clearly more than a simple sequence of numbers."

"So the possibilities are literally limitless," said Julie.

"That's right," said Levi. "Even if it's just a random sequence of five letters, there are almost 12 million possible combinations."

"So we're screwed," said Walter.

"Not necessarily," said Sarah.

"Why not?"

"I've just gotten the impression that he wasn't a random kind of man," she said.

"What do you mean?" said Walter.

"I just think that he was the kind of man who would have come up with a code that was personally meaningful to him, that's all."

"I agree with Sarah," said Julie.

"Okay, but so what?" said Walter. "Those possibilities are literally endless too."

"Do you think he might have left the code hidden somewhere?"

"I doubt it," said Levi. "I think it would have been something that he committed to his memory."

"So, where do we start?" said Julie.

"We just start," said Levi.

They began to punch in dozens of guesses: *Dutch River. Dutch River Farm. Hudson River. Hudson River Art. Jaeger Family Farm.* But after a half hour they were all discouraged and freezing.

"This is impossible," said Walter.

"Walter's right," said Julie. "Maybe we ought to go back to the house. He must have left the code hidden somewhere; otherwise, whatever is in that vault might have stayed there forever. He must have wanted someone to know it."

Levi suddenly looked up. "You're right," he said, "he did make sure that someone knew the code."

"Who?" said the others in unison.

"Every single Sunday school student he ever had," said Levi.

"Oh my God," said Julie, "you're talking about that hymn, aren't you?"

"That's what I'm thinking. He never actually told them about his vault, and he never told anyone that he was using that as a code; but I think he was pretty sure that someone in this town would have figured out that he would have used it for something like this."

"If they ever found the vault in the first place," said Walter.

"I think he left that up to us," said Sarah.

"What do you mean?"

"I think that's what his letter to me was all about. Think about it. He told us that the farm was mine to do with what I wanted, but he also made it perfectly clear that he wanted us to keep it for a while, that we might fine it 'rewarding.'"

"That's right," said Julie, "and as I recall, he mentioned a couple of times that you were married to a detective."

"A 'fine detective,'" said Sarah.

"And remember," said Levi, "he had that little throwaway line in there about, 'I bet you've never seen the inside of a barn before.'"

"Okay," said Walter, "so what are we waiting for?"

Sarah carefully punched in the words: "A Mighty Fortress Is Our God."

Nothing happened.

"Shit," said Walter.

"Hold it, hold it," said Levi. "Armin Jaeger was a German, and he taught the kids to sing the hymn in the original German."

Sarah turned back to the keyboard. "Don't wait for me, Levi, jump right in anytime you want."

"Oh, sorry. Okay, it's '*Ein feste Burg ist unser Gott.*'" He spelled it out slowly and Sarah punched it in carefully.

Still nothing happened.

"Damn!" said Sarah.

"What did you capitalize?"

"I capitalized the first letter of every word, just the same as the English title."

"Only capitalize the 'E' in '*Ein,*' the 'B' in 'Burg,' and the 'G' in '*Gott.*' That's the way the Germans would do it."

Sarah made the changes.

Nothing.

"Darn it," said Levi, "I was positive that would do it."

"That was a good guess, Levi," said Walter, "but maybe that wasn't it after all."

"Maybe you're right Walter," said Levi, but then his eyes suddenly widened, and he smacked himself on the forehead with the palm of his hand. "What a dummy!"

"What?" the other three all said in unison.

"Sometimes in the old German it wasn't '*Ein feste Burg,*' it was '*Ein' feste Burg.*'"

"What?"

"Let me punch it in, Sarah. It'll be easier." Sarah moved out of the way, and Levi put his fingers up to the keyboard.

He typed in, slowly and carefully, "*Ein' feste Burg ist unser Gott.*"

There was a muffled click.

Levi spun the large wheel to the right.

The door opened. They all peered in.

39

THE ROOM WASN'T LARGE, perhaps twenty feet square, with a low ceiling just high enough so that Walter didn't have to crouch. It was completely unfurnished; but it was well lit, and two large vents delivered air that was fresh and comfortable. The unadorned cement walls were painted white.

But all around the room, propped up against the walls, were paintings. Hundreds of them. Some were in ancient-looking frames, and some were simply pressed between layers of what looked like Plexiglas.

"Are these more of my great-uncle's collection of Hudson River art?" said Sarah.

"Oh no," said Julie. "I'm in way over my head here, but I'd guess that just one of these paintings would be worth more than Armin's entire collection of Hudson River Valley art."

"What are they?" said Sarah.

"Look," said Julie, walking to one. "This is a Renoir."

"How do you know?" said Walter.

"Because I recognize the style and because he signed it, see? And this is a Rembrandt and, oh my God," she said kneeling down in front of what looked like a small pencil sketch drawn on a scrap of discolored paper pressed between two sheets of Plexiglas. She pointed at the signature in the lower right-hand corner. "Look."

"It says, 'M. Buono' something," said Walter. "I never heard of the guy."

"Yes, you have," said Julie. "It says, 'M. Buonarroti.' The 'M' stands for 'Michelangelo.' I bet it's a preliminary sketch for one of his major works."

"What is all this, and what does it all have to do with the murders?" said Sarah.

"I'm not sure yet, but I'm willing to bet your great-uncle left us some clues," said Levi, casting his eyes around the room, searching.

"What are you looking for, Levi?" said Julie.

Levi suddenly walked to the opposite corner of the room. He carefully

moved one of the paintings away from the wall and withdrew from behind it a large, thick manila envelope that, unlike the rest of the contents
of the room, looked new. It was blank on one side and on the other side
was written only one word, in large, bold print: "Sarah."

"I believe this is for you," said Levi, handing it to Sarah, who held it
in both hands, almost at arm's length.

"What am I supposed to do with this?" she said.

"I think you're supposed to open it, hon," said Walter.

"Should we bring it upstairs and look at it?" said Julie.

"No, I think we should keep it right here for now," said Walter. "Let's
all take a seat." They were all past the age when sitting on a hard floor was
easy, but they all got themselves as comfortable as possible and looked at
Sarah expectantly.

"I believe you have the floor, so to speak, honey," said Walter, smiling
at his own small joke.

"Idiot," said Sarah, opening the envelope.

She withdrew a large sheaf of documents held together by two thick
rubber bands. She riffled through them.

"It looks like these are detailed descriptions of each of the paintings in
this room," she said. "Artist, title, dates, all that."

She reached into the envelope again, and this time withdrew a much
slimmer sheaf of paper. The pages were covered in the now familiar handwriting of her great-uncle.

"This should be fascinating," said Levi.

"To say the least," said Sarah, scanning the first page.

"Sarah, please," said Walter, "we're all dying of curiosity."

"Okay, sorry." She began to read.

Dear Sarah,

*Congratulations! I knew I didn't underestimate you and that clever detec-
tive husband of yours. Even up here in little Dutch River I have read of some
of his escapades in the Great Big City.*

I guess I have some explaining to do, don't I?

*Yes, the art is all genuine, and its worth is greater than that of some small
countries. That little scrap of paper signed by Michelangelo is a preliminary
sketch, in his own hand, of one of the panels in the Sistine Chapel. In today's
crazy world, there are people with the money and the inclination to pay a bil-
lion dollars for just that one drawing.*

So how did I come to possess this treasure trove? It's a long story.

I was a typical American young man of my time. I'd grown up on a farm in rural America. I'd gone to school until the age of sixteen, when I was expected to leave school and work full time on the family farm.

The only thing that made me a little different from the other young men I grew up with was that, from the time I was young, I had been fascinated with art. I remember when I was barely five finding a book in the church library called, The Art of Christianity. *I devoured it, and the Italian Renaissance remains one of my favorite artistic periods to this day. But even as a teenager, my interest expanded to the French Impressionists and even to the modernists like Marc Chagall and Pablo Picasso. At a very young age, I realized that I had developed quite an eye for good art versus great art, and for genuine art versus forgeries. I dreamed of leaving the farm one day and becoming the curator of a great museum.*

And then, of course, World War Two changed my life forever.

I was seventeen years old when I enlisted in the Army with my best friend, Oscar Avery, and I was eighteen years old when we washed up on the beaches of Normandy on June 6, 1944, dragging two comrades along with us. They were dead. We were not. In ten short minutes, Oscar and I had grown up.

Before we knew it, we'd been assigned to General George Patton's Third Army, and we were rolling across Germany at a breakneck pace.

It was shortly after we were assigned to Patton's army that I began to notice a strange phenomenon. In almost every town we liberated there was at least one large home that had been occupied by the highest-ranking Nazi in the area. When I explored these homes, they all seemed to have one thing in common: large collections of rare, exquisite, valuable art hanging on the walls. Since I was one of the few men in my battalion who could speak German, I took it upon myself to walk through the towns and strike up conversations with the locals, who, by that time, no matter what their previous questionable allegiances had been, were more than delighted to throw the Nazis to the wolves. I asked them about the houses and their occupants. I heard the same story over and over again.

Before the rise of the Nazis, all of the houses had been owned and occupied by Jews. But during the 1930s, and especially after the start of the war, the Nazis threw the owners out and took the homes, and all their contents, for themselves.

It was while exploring one of these homes in Western Germany that I met the man who would change my life. We had very little in common: He was an officer, a major in the Quartermaster Corps, while I was a lowly infantry corporal; he was in his forties while I was not yet twenty; he had gone to Harvard and Harvard Law School while I was a high school dropout; and he was rich, while I was poor. But we did have one thing in common: a love of art. His name was Wesley Bradford Sewall. He asked me to call him "Brad."

Brad may have been highly educated, but he spoke not a word of German. He was also immediately impressed with my knowledge of European art, which he soon declared to be far superior to his own. So we began to explore these homes together each time we got to another town.

Brad began to talk to me about his fear of what would happen to all this great art. Rumors were circulating wildly about just how much territory the Allies would cede to the Russians, and Brad was convinced that this art would never be seen again if it fell into Soviet hands. There were also thousands of ex-Nazis fleeing, and they would try to take as much of it with them as they could wherever they went. It was nothing more than a form of hard currency to them, and it would surely once more fall into the wrong hands.

Brad, unlike so many people of his social class today, was driven not by material wealth but by a moral imperative. He was determined not only to save this art for humanity, but to restore it to its rightful owners when the war finally ended. He asked me to join him in this effort, and I enthusiastically agreed.

He said that our main priority had to be to get the art out of Germany until the dust of war settled. I had told him about my family farm, and he decided that a remote, rural area like that would be a perfect place for it. I agreed wholeheartedly, but I also told him that I had no money. He told me not to worry, that if there was something he and his family were not short of, it was money.

So I applied my artistic and linguistic expertise, and Brad used the resources available to him in the Quartermaster Corps, along with his personal wealth, and we began our project in earnest.

By the time the war ended, we had saved over five hundred priceless works of art. It was not enough, but it was better than nothing. Brad had them stored temporarily in a vault at his family's summer home in Maine while I finished the work on the permanent storage facility at the farm.

Then came the heartbreak.

For the next ten years, we worked ceaselessly to find the original owners of the art. We found not a single one. They were all dead, lost in the ovens of Auschwitz, Buchenwald, and Dachau. And then Brad Sewall died, unexpectedly and prematurely. He had traveled throughout postwar Europe, quietly using his family's wealth and personal connections in our attempts to find the owners. I was just a farmer from upstate New York with no wealth and no connections, just an eye for good art. I didn't know what to do, so I'm ashamed to say I did nothing.

At your ages, it's probably hard to comprehend, but the years fly by swiftly, and before I knew it, I was an old man, and all that art was still sitting in the vault.

And then came the Great Recession. My beloved little town of Dutch River had already been struggling, but the Great Recession was the final nail in the coffin, as farms that had been continuously owned by the same families for generations were foreclosed on. Businesses closed left and right as their customers fled the area.

Around that time, I received a strange communication from a man who identified himself as Brad's grandson, Charles Martin Sewall. He told me that before he died, his father had told him the secret of the lost art, which his father had shared with him, wanting someone to know that the Sewalls had done all they could to return it to its rightful owners, so that the family's integrity could never be questioned.

But the grandson told me that, through some unfortunate investments, his family, like Dutch River, was on the verge of financial extinction. He went on to tell me that, because of his social position, he was aware of people, immensely wealthy people, who had an insatiable appetite to own rare art privately and secretly. They would buy stolen art through the underground market at staggering premiums over its appraised value and hide it away in their personal vaults, simply for the sheer pleasure of knowing they possessed it.

He made me a proposal: We would agree to sell only a limited number of the works in my possession, only enough to save his family and my town.

God help me, I agreed.

That was seven years ago, and we have now both agreed that our work is done. My town is saved, and so is his family. Of the original five hundred works, over four hundred remain in the vault.

Now comes the hard part for you, Sarah. I'm sure that you could find some very expensive, very clever lawyers who could make a compelling argument that you now own that art; and if you prevailed, you would be immensely wealthy. But please, don't be tempted. By now, I imagine that you have been made aware of the value of my personal collection of Hudson River Valley School art, which is undoubtedly yours, free and clear. You are already, therefore, a well-to-do young woman. By the way, I bought all those paintings for practically nothing. The world of art is crowded with people of vast wealth but questionable taste, and it wasn't difficult.

Despite my current robust health, I'm an old man, and I will be leaving this earth sooner rather than later, a prospect that does not frighten me except for one thing: I do not want my eternal soul burdened with all that magnificent, stolen art hidden away in my vault.

So please, for the sake of both our souls, do what I should have done many years ago, and make all this brilliant art available for the world to see. Find someone reputable to assist you, and make sure that it is distributed to the great museums of the world.

Make our family proud, Sarah.

Armin August Jaeger

August 28, 2015

"Well, that answers a lot of questions, doesn't it?" said Julie.

"Yeah," said Walter, "except for the only one I want an answer to."

"What's that?" said Julie.

"Who the hell murdered Armin August Jaeger and Charles Martin Sewall?"

40

"LIEUTENANT, YOU'VE GOT TO BELIEVE ME," said Barclay Hollis. "I never knew anything about this, and I have no idea who bought those paintings." Safe Harbor Securities occupied the top five floors of a twenty-story building that overlooked Boston Harbor near the Long Wharf. His large corner office on the top floor looked out east over the harbor and north toward the Bunker Hill Memorial, but he wasn't enjoying the view at the moment.

"You understand that if you're lying to me you could be harboring a murderer," said Walter.

Walter and Levi had driven back out to Boston in Julie's Mercedes after begging and pleading with their supervisors for just a couple more days on the case. They had both reluctantly been won over after Levi reminded them that they now possessed substantial evidence that a large financial crime had been committed at the Hotel Grenadier and that that crime had almost undoubtedly led to the murders of two men. They'd both been given exactly two more days.

They'd also convinced Captain Amato to call Sergeant Mayhew's boss at the Sturbridge Barracks of the Massachusetts State Police to get permission for Walter and Levi to borrow him, just for a day. He'd unenthusiastically agreed. Levi and Mayhew had headed over to visit Abby Sewall while Walter had paid a visit to the Sewall family's financial advisor.

Julie and Sarah were headed home with the kids. But first, they were going to pay another visit to Maas & Maas to see if they could extract any more information from them. They weren't hopeful.

"I'm not lying to you, Lieutenant," said Hollis, "please believe me."

"If you are, it's a federal crime, and I don't think the view through the bars in the federal penitentiary will be as nice as this one," said Walter, nodding toward the window.

"I understand that, Lieutenant, but I'm begging you to believe me. I'm not lying."

"Okay, let's say I believe you."

"Thank you."

"Don't thank me yet. I'm just saying, 'Let's say.'"

"Okay. I'm fine with that. Really."

"Good. So here's what I'm thinking. I'm thinking that you have a lot of really wealthy clients at this firm. Some undoubtedly wealthier than the Sewall family."

"Safe Harbor Securities is proud to protect the financial interests of some of the finest families in Boston, Lieutenant."

"Good for you. And I'm willing to bet that at least a couple of those fine families have what we might politely call a 'private' art collection."

"Lieutenant, I would have no way of—"

"Cut the crap, Barclay."

"I don't know what you want me to say, Lieutenant."

"I don't want you to say anything, Barclay. I want you to give me names."

"Lieutenant, if any of my clients were ever to find out that I had given the police their names, this firm would go out of business overnight."

"Do I look like I care?"

"I'm begging you, Lieutenant," said Hollis, who was now so pale and sweating so profusely that Walter was afraid that the man might have a heart attack or a stroke.

"Stop begging, Barclay, it just pisses me off. Look, I won't divulge your name or the name of your firm. I promise you. But you've got to work with me here. Do you understand?"

"Okay, Lieutenant, okay. But you have to understand something."

"What's that?"

"These are wealthy, intelligent, powerful people."

"Just not very scrupulous."

"Fine. I'll grant you that. But they are very careful people, and they would never do anything that would put their fortunes or their reputations at risk."

"It seems to me that they already have."

"Not really, Lieutenant," said Hollis.

"Why not?"

Hollis leaned forward over his desk and put his hands in front of him, the fingers touching to form a pyramid.

"What I'm going to tell you is all entirely theoretical, of course."

"Of course."

"I have no direct knowledge of anything."

"Surely not."

"So . . . If one of these people were, hypothetically, to want to purchase a piece of stolen art, they would do it indirectly. They would never meet the seller or even know who the seller was; and the seller would never know who the buyer was. They would use cutouts and intermediaries. It would be a totally blind transaction."

"And the money would be thoroughly laundered."

"Pristinely laundered, Lieutenant. So you see, the transaction would be literally untraceable. So if I give you names, what would you do with them? You would have to go barging into their homes and conduct a search to prove anything."

"And there's no way in hell I'd ever get a warrant, because I have no probable cause."

"You're right, Lieutenant. And no judge in this state with any regard for his own career would ever issue a warrant to search the homes of these people unless a warm body was found lying dead on the floor with a knife in its back. And maybe not even then."

"I can't disagree with you."

"So, you see, Lieutenant, I could give you some names if you insist, but I just don't think it would do you any good. And, Lieutenant?"

"Yes?"

"As I said, these are powerful people, powerful enough to be dangerous, if you know what I mean."

"I am not easily intimidated, Barclay."

"I understand that, but maybe you should be. There is a very fine line in this city, and the world, between the world of money and power and the criminal world. A very fine line."

"I've had a chance to learn that lesson on more than one occasion, Barclay, and I'm not disagreeing with you. But I'm still here, and a lot of them aren't."

"As you wish, Lieutenant. I'm just . . . I'm just trying to tell you that there is a brutal element in this city now that wasn't here just a short decade ago. They are immensely wealthy and are working hard to spend as much money as necessary to give themselves at least a veneer of refinement and respect. I'm sure some of them have supported Mrs. Sewall's charities. But make no mistake about it: they are thugs. Brutal thugs."

"Okay, Mr. Hollis, okay. We have the same element in New York, believe me. But I accept your basic point. It's probably useless for me to demand names from you right now."

"I'm so glad to hear you say that, Lieutenant," said Barclay, his body noticeably sagging as he pulled a handkerchief from his jacket pocket.

"But I may be back," said Walter, rising to leave.

"Of course, of course, Lieutenant."

Walter looked out the window at the sailboats scudding across Boston Harbor in the brisk autumn breeze while the sun shone down on them.

It was good to be wealthy in Boston, he decided.

Hell, it was good to be wealthy anywhere.

41

"**I** SEEM TO BE MAKING MORE NEW FRIENDS EVERY DAY," said Abby Peabody Sewall, shaking Levi's hand after the maid had shown him and Sergeant Mayhew into her third-floor office. She was wearing a crimson silk blouse and a pale gray skirt. Her face was impeccably made up and her shining hair cascaded over her shoulders in golden waves making her look half her age. Walter was right, thought Levi: poor Sergeant Mayhew would be no match for this woman. "Please, help yourself to some coffee." She sat down and invited the two men to do the same.

"Thank you, ma'am," said Levi, "and thank you for seeing us once again on such short notice."

"I suppose it would be too much to hope that you are here because you have captured my husband's killer," said Abby, speaking directly to Levi and barely glancing at Mayhew who, in any event, was keeping his eyes resolutely cast to the floor.

"I'm sorry to say we haven't. But we feel that we have made a breakthrough, and we were hoping that with the new information we've obtained, you would be able to give us some further assistance."

"I'll try, Mr. Welles, or, should I say Captain Welles? I'm sorry, you don't look like a policeman to me."

"I'm not much of a cop, ma'am, not like Lieutenant Hudson. I'm in the Intelligence Division, and you should feel free to call me Levi," he said, hoping to put her more at ease.

"I think I'll call you 'Leviticus,' if you don't mind. It's an absolutely delightful name."

"I wouldn't mind that at all," said Levi, feeling like he'd already lost control of the conversation to this extraordinary woman. Sergeant Mayhew continued to stare at the floor.

He proceeded to tell her of the revelations contained in Armin Jaeger's letter. Her expression remained interested but impassive until he got to the part describing her husband's and Armin's sale of some of the art.

"Oh dear."

"I know that Sergeant Mayhew and Lieutenant Hudson have already questioned you, ma'am, and I'm going to take you at your word that you told them everything you knew."

"A courtesy that I'm afraid Lieutenant Hudson was all too unwilling to grant me."

"He's a good officer, ma'am."

"I'm sure he is."

"In any event, I was wondering if, in light of all this new information, there is anything new you can tell us. Sometimes dormant memories of events or things people have said are triggered in situations like this."

"I'm afraid not, Leviticus. I hadn't even been born when Wesley Bradford Sewall died, and Marty only had indirect recollections of the man passed on by his parents. And as far as my husband's activities are concerned, I guess I'm glad finally to have an explanation of his odd behavior all these years ago, but I'm afraid the knowledge doesn't bring back any buried memories."

"Have you had any opportunity to search through his personal and business records to see if there's anything he may have kept regarding these transactions?"

"My husband and I always granted each other complete access to our respective offices and files, in the event that something untoward happened to one of us. So, yes, I have conducted a thorough search, and I have found nothing. Either he has files hidden in places of which even I was never made aware, or he never committed anything to writing, for the obvious reasons. I know every nook and cranny of this house, so I would suspect the latter."

"So would I."

"I'm sorry, but I've done everything I can."

"Then we won't take up any more of your time, ma'am."

"Really, Leviticus, it seems that I have nothing but time these days. I'm only sorry that I can't be of more help to you. Despite what your colleague seems to believe, I would do anything in my power to help you solve my husband's murder."

"I know you would, ma'am, and, believe it or not, so does Lieutenant Hudson."

"I'll take you at your word."

"Thank you, Abby."

"At least I have some certainty about my future now."

"Ma'am?"

"I know now that the extraordinary income that our family has enjoyed in recent years has now come to an end."

"It seems it has. I hope you haven't been left in a precarious financial position."

"Not unless someone tries to recover the income we've received in the past as ill-gotten gains. Much of it has long since been given away."

"That won't happen, Abby. As Brad Sewall and Armin Jaeger sadly discovered, there is no one left to claim the paintings as their property. The legality of the entire situation is murky at best. I'm no lawyer, but I think the only legal activity in the future will revolve around the disposition of the remaining paintings."

"That is a relief to hear. In that event, our family's finances are secure, though I won't be donating any more wings to Massachusetts General Hospital."

"I'm sorry, ma'am."

"Please don't be. There will be plenty of people in this city lined up to take my place, and, frankly, my life is changed now. I'm a widow, and my son will now carry on the family's affairs. I'm looking forward to carving out a new life for myself. I feel that I am shedding an old skin and undergoing a metamorphosis, Leviticus. It's frightening, and it's exhilarating at the same time. My only regret is that I won't have my husband to go on this journey with me."

"You are an admirable woman, Abby."

"And Sergeant Mayhew?"

Mayhew's body seemed to jump as he heard her pronounce his name. "Yes, ma'am?" he said, finally taking his eyes off the floor.

"Cheer up. I'm sure you'll get this case solved, and you have a fine career to go back to."

Mayhew simply nodded, his eyes falling back to the floor.

Levi thought that it was an odd exchange, but he chose not to read anything into it. Instead, he said, "Oh, and, Abby?"

"Yes, Leviticus?"

"In case you need to get in touch with us, here is my card. I also wrote down Lieutenant Hudson's number on it. The cellular service up in Dutch River is sometimes a little spotty, so here's the business card of the law firm we've been working with up there. They'll be able to find us in a pinch. Their paralegal's name is Dot Ferguson. She'll probably answer the phone, and she'll be able to help you."

"What is her name?"

"Dot Ferguson. Would you like me to write it down?"

"No, it's just odd, that's all."

"What do you mean, odd?"

"I take it that her given name is Dorothea?"

"I believe it is," said Levi, thinking back to the diploma he'd seen hanging on the wall behind Dot's desk.

"I once was acquainted with a woman named Dorothea Ferguson, and she was also a paralegal."

"How did you know her?" said Levi, his voice tightening and fear beginning to clench at his stomach. Mayhew looked up.

"She worked for my husband, but that was a long time ago. She left rather suddenly, and I haven't seen her since."

"How long ago?"

"I think it was around 2007 or . . . Oh my God."

Levi pulled out his phone and punched up Walter's number in the speed dial.

"Hey, Levi."

"Walter?"

"Yeah?"

"We've got a problem."

42

"**H**IGHLY IRREGULAR, HIGHLY IRREGULAR," said Peter Maas.

"I'm not sure what you expect us to do," said Jill Maas.

"We don't expect you to do anything right now," said Sarah. "We just wanted to know if any of this made any sense to you."

Julie and Sarah had to admit that they'd put the Maases in an awkward position. They had only told them that they had come across some evidence that the murders of Armin Jaeger and Charles Martin Sewall, as well as the source of Dutch River's recent prosperity, might be connected with the sale of valuable art.

"It makes no sense whatsoever. As I already told you previously, we were never informed of anything except that we had somehow acquired a very wealthy benefactor. We set up the 501(c)(3) as we were instructed, and that was it."

"I know," said Sarah, "and we believe that you've been completely forthcoming with us. We were just hoping that the new information might trigger some ideas or memories, that's all."

"Sorry. This town just doesn't have a lot of people who look like rich benefactors. And the only person I ever knew in this town who had even a remote interest in art was your great-uncle. But all his art is accounted for, and even though it's worth a lot of money by our standards, it's paltry compared to the revenue we've been getting through Rensselaer Partners."

"We're not as concerned about the rich benefactor at this point as we are about finding the person who committed two murders. As my husband always says, murder is an acquired taste, and most people don't simply decide to stop, especially when a lot of money is involved."

"I don't disagree," said Jill, "but we have never had a single murder in the history of this town. At least not until Armin."

"Not a one. Not a one," said Peter.

"I understand," said Sarah. "Look, Julie and I have to get back to the city before the truant officers put my husband and me in jail for child neglect. But please call us if anything else comes to mind. We'll certainly be back up here soon."

"We certainly will," said Jill. She hesitated a moment and then said, "I don't mean to be crass, but does this mean, in your opinion, that the, uh, revenues that Rensselaer Partners has been receiving will no longer be forthcoming?"

"If I were you, I would make that assumption," said Sarah.

"I hope that doesn't mean that Dutch River will be too badly harmed," said Julie.

"Excuse me," said Dot, who had been sitting at the table taking notes, "does anyone want any more coffee?"

"I think we're all set," said Jill.

"Then why don't I clear all this stuff off the table," she said.

"Sure," said Jill, "I think we're wrapping up here."

Dot gathered up the coffee things and left the office.

"Now," said Jill, "where were we? Oh yes. Dutch River's future. Thank you for your concern, but thanks to careful spending and prudent investing over the years, we have managed to establish a trust fund of sufficient size so that we will be able to continue to support the town with the interest from the fund and still preserve, and even grow, the principal."

"That's good to hear," said Sarah.

"May we infer from your ongoing concern that you plan to become a permanent fixture in Dutch River?"

"'Permanent fixture' might be a little strong. My husband's work is in Manhattan, so we won't be coming here to live permanently, but we do intend to keep the farm and visit as often as we can."

"And Levi and I won't be strangers either," said Julie. "We love it here, too."

"I am so glad to hear that," said Jill. "I know my perhaps overeager desire to earn a closing fee from the sale of the property may have left you with the wrong impression, but I think I speak for all the residents of the town when I say that we are looking forward to your family being a part of our little town for a long time to come."

"Oh yes. Oh yes," said Peter Maas.

They were about to say their good-byes when Sarah's phone rang.

"Excuse me, this is my husband calling," she said, putting the phone to her ear. "Hello? No, everything's fine . . . They're over at the restaurant with Adam. We're just about finished here and we're going to take off for

the city . . . No, she's right here. At least, she was until a few minutes ago."
She looked around the office, and then said, "Does anyone know where
Dot went?"

"She isn't at her desk?" said Jill.

"No," said Julie, looking out the office door.

"She probably went to the ladies' room," said Jill. "I'm sure she'll be
right back."

"Can somebody please check?" said Sarah.

"I'll go," said Julie.

"Can you please tell us what this is about?" said Jill.

"Walter, what's going on?" said Sarah. She listened to the phone for a
few seconds, and then said, "Oh my God." Her face suddenly lost all its
color.

"I can't find her anywhere," said Julie. "Jesus, Sarah, you look awful,
what's going on?"

"I'll call you right back," said Sarah into the phone. She looked at
Julie and the Maases. "We've got to go find the kids, Julie. Now. Jill, Peter,
please call us if you find Dot. In the meantime, you should consider her
dangerous. Please call the police."

"What the hell is going on?" said Jill.

"No time," said Sarah, heading out the door with Julie right behind.
"Just do it. Now."

—⟪⟫—

They burst through the door of Avery's Restaurant, where Adam
greeted them with a relaxed smile that turned into an expression of alarm
as soon as he saw Sarah and Julie's faces.

"Are you guys okay?" he said.

"Where are the kids?" said Sarah.

"They just left with Dot," said Adam. "She came over here and said
that you guys were done with your meeting and you'd asked her to bring
the kids back to the law office. You didn't see her on your way over here?"

Sarah clung to a chair for support while Julie raced outside. She returned only a few seconds later.

"They're gone," she said.

43

"**B**ERT, PLEASE BE CAREFUL," said Sarah, as Bert climbed out of his patrol car.

"Don't worry, I will. Just please stay in the car until I have a chance to find out what's going on in there."

"OK, just hurry."

They had driven two miles out of town to the tiny, ramshackle house that Dot Ferguson called home. Her yard had been kept tidy, but the effect had been ruined by the rusting doublewides on either side, each with a satellite dish on the roof, their yards strewn with old auto parts and discarded furniture.

Bert pulled his pistol out of its holster as he strode across the small yard, wishing like hell that his most recent request to load it with bullets hadn't once again been denied. He walked up to the front door and knocked.

"Police!" he called out. No answer. The place had that quiet feel of an empty house, and there was no car in the yard, but you can never be sure, he reminded himself.

"Police!" he called out again, knocking louder. Still no response.

The door looked flimsy, but he hesitated to put his shoulder to it and knock it in. His one previous attempt at that maneuver hadn't ended well, and he'd had to hold his fork in his left hand for a week afterward when he ate. So he decided to try the obvious. He turned the knob. The door opened. He stepped in and looked around, letting his eyes adjust to the dim light. At first glance the house looked empty. A copy of *People* magazine lay on an old sofa in the cramped living area. A small television sat on a table against the opposite wall. He turned the corner that led to a tiny kitchen and dinette area and peeked in.

He ran back to the front door.

"Sarah! Get in here! Quick!"

Sarah bolted from the car and ran inside the house, racing around the corner to where Bert was pointing.

On top of a small Formica table, perched in the baby seat that he was rapidly outgrowing, sat Daniel. He began to babble happily when he saw her.

Under the chair was a leaf of Maas & Maas stationery with a brief note scribbled on it.

I have no time to explain anything right now, but I think you already know what I want. I'll be in touch later and your daughters will be fine as long as you do exactly as I say.

Dot

———◦◦◦———

"SO WHAT HAVE WE GOT?" said Walter, ignoring the cup of coffee Adam had placed before him. He and Sarah were sitting in the restaurant along with Levi and Julie, the Maases, and Bert. Adam had put out snacks and drinks, but no one had any appetite.

Sergeant Mayhew had broadcast their car model and plates to the Massachusetts State Police patrolling the Mass Pike, so Levi and Walter had averaged close to 95 miles per hour driving across the state back to Dutch River, with Levi driving and Walter constantly on the phone. They were back in Dutch River in less than two hours and arrived at the restaurant about the same time as Bert, Sarah, and the baby.

"We have an APB out on Dot's car, along with a description of her and the kids," said Bert.

"What kind of car?" said Walter.

"It's a 2005 silver Honda Accord."

"Great, there are only about a million of them within a fifty-mile radius of here, and she's probably already changed the plates. How much of a head start do you think she got?"

"No more than half an hour," said Bert, "but that's a lot around here. There are so many small roads, and most of them run through wooded areas, so a cop can't see that far ahead. If the police spot her on the road it'll just be dumb luck unless she does something stupid like get on a main road."

"This damn letter doesn't tell us anything," said Walter, throwing the note Dot had left at the house on the table in front of him.

"What do you think she meant when she said that we already know what she wants?" said Adam.

"It's a long story, and we'll have to fill you in, but the short version is that Armin Jaeger had a storage room full of priceless art hidden on his farm, and she wants at least some of it," said Levi.

Walter turned a stony face to Jill Maas.

"And she's already killed for it. So it's now or never, Jill. What do you know about Dot Ferguson? And I'm warning you, don't fuck with me."

For once, Sarah didn't criticize him for his use of profanity as she sat beside him, expressionless.

"I will tell you everything I know, but I'm afraid it's not going to be very helpful."

"Why don't you let me be the judge of that," said Walter. "Come on, we're wasting time."

"We hired Dot in 2008," said Jill. "I got a call from an old friend from law school just after we'd received the first payment into the Rensselaer Partners account. We'd worked together on Law Review and she was also a native upstate New Yorker, so we'd been close. She had moved to Boston and become a partner in a highly respected firm out there, and we'd always stayed in touch. Anyway, she asked me if I could do her a favor. It seemed that one of the paralegals who'd once worked for the firm and was now working for an important client had just gone through a messy divorce and was anxious to get as far away from Boston as possible. She remembered that I'd stayed local, and she thought that upstate New York would be the ideal place for this woman to get her life and emotions back in order. Would I be willing to help out? Dad and I had wanted a paralegal for a long time, but we'd never been able to afford one. But now, with our subsidy from Rensselaer Partners, we could."

"So you hired her sight unseen?"

"No, we brought her out here for a visit. We wanted to meet her face-to-face, and we also wanted to make sure that she knew what she was getting into, moving here to the sticks from Boston."

"Did you learn much about her from the interview?"

"No, we didn't. Perhaps we should've dug deeper, but her credentials looked good, and she came highly recommended by someone I respected. We were mostly worried that she would take one look at Dutch River and run the other way, but she didn't, so we hired her on the spot."

"And she's never done anything that you would consider suspicious?"

"Not at all. You've met Dot. She's a little quirky, but nothing that would raise any suspicions. As you've noticed, we don't exactly have a lot of work at our firm, but the work that we gave her she did well, and she fit right into the town. Would you agree, Adam?"

"Absolutely. All I ever knew her as was a nice woman who liked my seafood dishes. She fit in right away and got along with everyone just fine."

"No disagreements?" said Walter.

"None to speak of," said Jill. "From time to time I'd try to encourage her to, you know, dress in clothes that were a little less provocative, but that was about it."

"And you never suspected that she may have had a connection with Rensselaer Partners?"

"Never."

"Who knew? Who knew?" said Peter Maas.

"Frankly," said Jill, "I'm still not sure how she fits into this whole scheme."

"We believe," said Levi, "that she was sent here to be the conduit between Armin Jaeger and Charles Martin Sewall, the person put in place to ensure that those two men never had to be seen together; to ensure that Armin Jaeger never had to be seen travelling to Boston or that Sewall never had to explain any trips to upstate New York. Once a year, she would make a late-night visit to Armin, who would have two or three paintings already pulled from the vault and ready to give to her. She would put them in a car, not her own, and drive them to Manhattan where she would hand them over to Sewall by exchanging identical cars with him."

"Well, that explains at least something," said Jill.

"What's that?" said Levi.

"Every year, usually late summer or early autumn, she would take a two-day trip to New York City. She said she loved Broadway shows and that she'd go down, take in a couple of shows, and treat herself to dinner at Sardi's. She said it was her one big indulgence every year, and she never got tired of it. It never occurred to us for a second that she wasn't telling us the truth. Why would it?"

"But what would turn her into a killer?" said Adam.

"We know for a fact," said Levi, "that Armin and Sewall had agreed to end their little arrangement, and that they were both eager to donate the remaining paintings to the world's museums."

"And you think that she didn't want that little arrangement to end," said Adam.

"But that doesn't make any sense," said Jill. "We paid her a modest salary, and you've been to her house, so you've seen how she lived. She wasn't exactly getting rich off this scheme."

"Maybe she had the money hidden away somewhere else," said Julie.

"Or maybe that's the point," said Levi, looking up. "Maybe she had never really profited from her participation in the deal, and she realized that now she never would."

"But how did she find out that the arrangement was coming to an end?" said Jill.

"Who knows?" said Walter. "Probably Armin or Sewall told her."

"But Armin was already dead by the time she made her last trip," said Levi, "and there was nothing in Martin Sewall's car when he died, even though he must have been expecting to make a pickup."

"I can't make any sense out of any of that," said Walter.

"Or," said Julie, her eyes widening, "maybe the people who had been buying the art all along found out that it was coming to an end, and they weren't happy about it either."

"That makes a lot of sense," said Walter, looking up. "Once they'd developed an appetite for all this rare art, they didn't want it to end. Remember, Armin said in his letter that they'd only sold about seventy-five out of over five hundred paintings. Maybe these guys thought they were just getting started."

"And you think they somehow got to Dot?" said Julie.

"We're getting way out ahead of ourselves, and I'm just guessing at this point, but that's what I'm starting to think."

"And I'm starting to think," said Sarah, her stony expression starting to crumble, "that all this talk hasn't gotten me one step closer to getting my kids back."

"You're right," said Levi.

"But what can we do?" said Adam. "It seems that unless the police get lucky, we just have to wait until Dot decides to communicate with us."

"I know what I'm going to do," said Levi, standing up. "Jill, Peter, I'd like to I borrow your office and use your Internet connection."

"Certainly," they both said in unison.

"Certainly," Peter Maas repeated by himself.

"What are you going to do, Levi?" said Walter.

"I can't log into the NYPD's most sensitive systems unless I'm back at headquarters in Manhattan on their secure lines, but I can access a lot of data just using my secure keycard from a remote site. I'm going to find out everything there is to know about Dot Ferguson."

"And maybe we can find her before she can get away," said Jill.

"It's worth a try," said Walter.

"Damn right," said Sarah.

"I know it's a stupid question," said Adam, looking at Sarah and Walter, "but how are you guys holding up?"

"We'll tell you when we get our kids back," said Sarah.

Just as they were all heading for the door, Bert's cell phone rang. They all froze as Bert held up his hand and said, "Hang on, guys." After only a couple of seconds he said, "OK" and hung up.

"What is it?" said Sarah, clinging to Walter's arm.

"It was a guy named Officer Pavlick from the state police."

"And?" said Walter.

"They found Dot's car."

"Was anybody in it?" said Sarah, gripping Walter's arm even tighter.

"No, it was empty. No people, no notes, nothing."

"Where did they find it?" said Walter.

"A few miles out of town in the garage of an old abandoned farm."

"Shit!" said Walter.

"What does that mean?" said Julie. "Where are Dot and the kids? Did they search the abandoned farmhouse? Maybe Dot's hiding out right there."

"They searched the house," said Bert, "and all the outbuildings. There wasn't anybody there."

"Of course there wasn't," said Walter. "God, how stupid could I be?"

"So where are they?" said Adam.

"They're in a black Mercedes Benz E-Class heading God knows where with a two-hour jump on us, that's where they are."

"I'll call the state police and change the APB right now," said Bert.

"Go ahead," said Walter, "but it's too late. She's gone."

44

"SO WHAT DID YOU FIND OUT?" said Sarah, before the door had even had a chance to close behind Leviticus. It was late and the cold night air blew into the farmhouse like a bad feeling.

"First," said Walter, "can we get you anything to eat or drink?"

"A cup of coffee would be nice. I'll eat in a little while. I've got a lot of talking to do first." He rubbed his eyes wearily while Julie poured him a cup from the pot they'd been keeping fresh all night. He had no notes in front of him and he didn't bother to open his laptop; his prodigious memory was all he needed. He took a sip of coffee. "This story goes back a long way, so please be patient."

"Take all the time you want," said Walter. "It's not like anyone around here is sleepy."

"Okay," he said, taking a couple of seconds to compose his thoughts. "Dot Ferguson was born Estralita Maria Flores in 1978, the youngest child and only daughter of Portuguese immigrants, in Gloucester, Massachusetts. Her father was a fisherman. Her mother was a maid at one of the local inns in nearby Rockport."

"Where's Gloucester?" said Walter.

"It's on Cape Ann, north of Boston. Fishing boats have been sailing out of Gloucester for more than two hundred years. Remember 'The Perfect Storm'?"

"Yeah?"

"Those ships sailed out of Gloucester. Anyway, fishing has been a way of life there forever, and the ship owners and the processing companies make out pretty well. But it's a hard and dangerous life for the fishermen, and their fortunes tend to fluctuate between bad in good times and worse in bad times. They tend to drink hard and die young, but they stick at it, generation after generation."

"But why?" said Julie.

"Because it's all they know. Anyway, Estralita's parents were both dead by the time she was seven. The oldest of her four brothers was a hard worker, and he did his best to raise her, but he drowned at sea when she was fifteen. Her other three brothers were drunk every minute they weren't out at sea and apparently, although they didn't throw her out, they did nothing to help her."

"My God," said Sarah. "So what did she do?"

"The impressive thing is what she didn't do," said Levi. "A lot of Gloucester girls in her situation see drugs and the sex trade as their only way out, and they wind up in Boston or New York, used up and old before their time if they don't die of an overdose first. But Estralita had a different idea. On her eighteenth birthday, she changed her name to Dorothea Ann Ferguson."

"Where did she get that name?" said Julie, her curiosity sparked by the fact that she, too, had changed her name when she was a young woman.

"No idea," said Levi. "For all I could figure out, she just found it in a phone book."

"I wonder why she changed it," said Sarah. "'Estralita' is such a beautiful name."

"I can tell you why," said Julie. "She was determined to leave her past behind, and become someone else."

"Makes sense," said Walter.

"And that's exactly what she did," said Levi. "She enrolled in the Wentworth School of Secretarial Science in Boston, and two years later, she graduated with a degree as a certified paralegal. While she was going to school full time, she worked sixty hours a week as a maid in a Boston hotel to pay the tuition and support herself."

"I hate to say it," said Walter, "but that's pretty impressive. So where did she go wrong?"

"I'm getting there," said Levi, pouring himself another cup of coffee. "Once she graduated, she got a job at a downtown Boston law firm, the law firm where Jill's old law school buddy is now a partner, and where by all reports she did excellent work. She did so well that when one of the firm's most prestigious clients, the Sewall Family Trust, was looking for reliable administrative help, the law firm offered up Dot."

"And the rest is history," said Walter.

"Except for I still don't get it," said Sarah. "She has such an impressive story. What would turn her into a murderer and a kidnapper?"

"Greed is a powerful motivator," said Walter.

"Actually, it's a lot more complicated than that," said Levi.

"What do you mean?" said Julie.

"Remember I told you about her three brothers who were such bums?"

"Yeah."

"As usual, being drunken bums didn't stop them from reproducing, and between them they managed to produce two boys and three girls."

"Who would have married guys like that?" said Sarah.

"As far as I can tell, all the children were born without benefit of matrimony. Whoever the two surviving brothers are with now, they're probably not the mothers of any of the kids."

"What happened to the third brother?" said Julie.

"Died in a fistfight outside a bar," said Levi. "The autopsy revealed that at the time of death he had a blood alcohol content of .35. If he hadn't died in the fight, he probably would have died that same night of alcohol poisoning."

"Jesus," said Walter.

"So, anyway," said Levi, "you'll probably find it unsurprising that Aunt Estralita, aka Dot Ferguson, decided to do what she could to help out her nieces and nephews."

"How could she do anything?" said Sarah. "She had nothing."

"She had her salary from Maas & Maas," said Levi.

"Which couldn't have been much," said Julie.

"Not much at all," said Levi, "but she managed to live on half of it."

"But still," said Sarah, "how much could she do for five kids with half of not so much?"

"It turns out that she was also paid $100,000 every year for her part in the operation."

"And she used every penny of that on her nieces and nephews," said Julie.

"Every penny," said Levi.

"How are they doing?" said Sarah.

"One of the boys fell by the wayside, but the others are doing well. They're all still in school and living in stable foster homes in a little town called Groveland, Massachusetts, which isn't far from Gloucester, but far enough. She went to court to make sure that her two brothers lost custody. They all plan to go to college."

"And suddenly the rug gets pulled out from under her," said Julie.

"Yes," said Levi, "and while she still has a lot of unfinished business with those kids."

"You can't blame Armin and Martin for wanting to do the right thing with the art," said Julie.

"No, you can't," said Walter, "and I'm willing to bet that they would have tried to help Dot out if she'd only gone to them."

"We'll never know now," said Levi, "but there's no reason to believe that they wouldn't have."

"So why?" said Sarah.

"I think she probably panicked," said Levi, "but I also think it goes deeper than that. I'm no psychologist, but there's nothing in her background that ever would have encouraged her to trust anyone but herself."

"Or maybe there's something we're still missing," said Walter, his eyes looking off in a middle distance, his mind turning inward.

"What do you mean?" said Julie.

"I'm not sure what I mean. Levi's done some incredible research, and what we know may be the whole story. But with everything we've learned about Dot, I also think it's possible that there had to be one more thing, one more chapter to the story, one that pushed her over the edge. But I also have to admit that I've seen plenty of people kill for less motivation than we already know Dot had."

"But we're not going to know anything until we find her," said Julie.

"And at the end of the day," said Sarah, "I can have only so much compassion for Dot, no matter what her story is. She's got my kids, and I'll kill her with my bare hands if that's what I have to do to get them back."

"You're right," said Julie. "So what do we do now?"

"We pay attention to human nature," said Levi.

"What does that mean?" said Sarah.

"It means that when people are in trouble, real trouble like Dot is, their first instinct is to go home."

"But where's home to Dot?" said Julie.

"Cape Ann," said Levi.

"But she knew nothing but misery there," said Sarah, "and she also left there at a young age."

"It doesn't matter," said Levi. "It's still home. It's where her family lived ever since they arrived in this country. She must be absolutely terrified right now, and she probably knows that she's made fatal errors, and there's no way out for her. This is the end for Dot, and she knows it. She's going home."

"Tomorrow's going to be a long day," said Walter, staring at his watch. It was close to midnight. "It's probably time we all got some rest."

"I'm not going to sleep, Walter, you know that," said Sarah.

"We at least have to try," said Walter. "We're not going to do the girls any good if we're so exhausted we can't think straight, and I have a long drive tomorrow."

"Are you going out to Cape Ann to look for Dot?" said Julie.

"Yes, I am, but first I'm going to Boston."

"Why Boston?" said Levi.

"Levi, I hear you about Dot being drawn back to Gloucester, and you may be right. But I've always been taught to follow the money, and I can't keep my conversation with Barclay Hollis out of my head. He was absolutely terrified of something or someone, and I need to follow up on that, because that same something or someone may be pulling Dot back to Boston with our kids as hostages."

"I can't argue with you, Walter. I guess it's a toss-up any way you look at it," said Levi.

"I don't know which one is right either, Levi, but I'm positive that we're going to find Dot in one of the two places. She's nowhere near New York anymore."

"And neither are the kids," said Sarah.

"Right," said Walter. His phone rang just as they were heading upstairs, making them all jump. "What the hell? Christ, it's Bert." He pushed the button to receive the call and said, "Hang on, Bert, while I put you on speaker."

"Can you hear me?" said Bert.

"Yeah, we can hear you just fine," said Walter. "So what's up?"

"I just thought I'd let you know, I went up to Loudonville tonight and chased down Boonesy and his buddies."

"Wasn't it kind of late?" said Julie.

"Nah, I got there just about the time those guys were scraping themselves off whatever floor they'd been sleeping on all day."

"What did you want to talk to them about?" said Walter.

"I thought it would be good police work to tie up a loose end and get a positive ID on Dot Ferguson as the one who bribed them to put the poison in Armin's bourbon."

"Good work, Bert. I should have thought of that myself."

"You've got a lot on your mind, sir. So anyway, I got a recent photo of her from the Maases and brought it with me."

"So did they give you a positive ID?"

"That's the funny thing, sir. No, they didn't. They said they'd never seen Dot in their lives."

45

"HOW MANY TIMES does my mother have to explain to you people that she's told you all she knows about this wretched situation before you decide to believe her, Lieutenant?" said Leverett Peabody Sewall, standing at the front door of the Beacon Hill town house.

Walter had left Dutch River before dawn after a few brief hours of desperately needed sleep, and it was just past seven o'clock when he'd knocked on the door of the town house. A shocked maid had answered the door and had refused him entry. She returned moments later with a disheveled-looking Leverett Sewall, dressed only in a pair of jeans and a gray tee shirt with "Harvard Law" printed in bold crimson letters across the front. He was tall and dark haired with an athletic build, though he was a couple of inches shorter and probably forty pounds lighter than Walter. He bore absolutely no resemblance to his mother.

"Please, Lev," said Abby, standing behind him, "it's all right. Please let him in."

"But, Mother . . ."

"I will speak to the lieutenant, Lev."

"Fine, but I insist on remaining with you during your discussion," he said as he reluctantly let Walter step past him into the foyer.

"You will do no such thing. I will speak to the lieutenant privately in my office. Please come with me, Lieutenant." She led Walter through the foyer as her son stood by helplessly, no more a match for his formidable mother than anyone else.

"Please excuse my son's behavior, Lieutenant," said Abby as they each settled into chairs in her office. She looked tiny in a tee shirt and jeans, and she wore no makeup. "He is a young man, and I assume you know how that can be. He is also taking on a great deal of responsibility far sooner than he had ever planned to do in the midst of grieving for his father, whom he loved very much."

"Ma'am, if anyone owes an apology it's me. I know our last meeting didn't go well, and I take responsibility for that. I know I can be a bull in a china shop, and I'm sorry."

"Please, Lieutenant, Sergeant Mayhew called me just a short while ago to explain what has happened, particularly concerning your daughters. Let's focus on that, shall we?"

"Thank you, ma'am. Just so you know, despite my behavior at our previous meeting, I take you at your word that you've told us all you can."

"Thank you, but, please, Lieutenant, let's move on."

"Ma'am, the last time I was in Boston I had a meeting with a man named Barclay Hollis."

"Oh, poor Barc. That must have put him all in a dither."

"I'm afraid it did, but not because of me, believe it or not."

"Oh dear. Was he at all helpful?"

"At first I didn't think so, but now I'm beginning to wonder."

"So why are you speaking to me instead of him?"

"Because I just don't think I'm going to get anything more out of him."

"You're confusing me, Lieutenant."

"Ma'am, when I spoke to him it was apparent to me that he was just as much in the dark as you were about the source of the money, at least initially. But when I pressed him, he seemed to admit that he knew that very wealthy people in this city probably owned private art collections that they obtained from, uh, questionable sources."

"I'm sure there are, Lieutenant. There are people like that all over the world, and I can't imagine that Boston is any exception. Was he able to give you any names?"

"No, he wasn't, but I'm convinced that he had certain people in mind."

"So why didn't he tell you? You are, let's say, a remarkably persuasive man when you choose to be. I'm surprised poor, timid Barclay was able to resist your questionable charms."

"I came on pretty strong, ma'am, I'll admit that. But it seemed that Barclay was a lot more afraid of other people than he was of me. A lot more. I thought of going back to him and pressing him some more, but I decided it would be useless."

"So you're coming to me instead because you somehow think I'm made of sterner stuff?" said Abby, giving him a beguiling smile that he was sure she'd used often to soften up wealthy potential donors who displayed any signs of reluctance.

"Well, yes, ma'am," said Walter, briefly breaking off eye contact to regain his composure. Jesus, he thought, what was it with this woman? "I know that you are in regular contact with most of the wealthiest people in this city. Can you think of anyone in that crowd who might be the type to own stolen art, and who would frighten Barclay Hollis like that?"

Abby picked up a small crystal bowl from the table in front of them and gazed at it silently. She turned it over in her hands, seemingly entranced by its exquisite beauty and the light that it refracted. She finally looked up at him, her eyes glittering as if they had absorbed the light of the crystal.

"You are correct, Lieutenant. I know people in this city, not many, but enough, with whom I would not be surprised were I to learn that they possessed stolen art, art they kept hidden for their own private pleasure. I do not approve of their behavior, and I am ashamed that my husband, for whatever reasons, played a role in satisfying their appetites. But they are not killers, and they are not kidnappers. They are merely greedy children who were never taught to control their appetites. It is apparently an unavoidable disease of the wealthy."

She turned the crystal bowl over in her hands and put it down.

"Except for one man. His name is Bruce Neville."

"What can you tell me about him?"

"The first thing I can tell you is that his name is not Bruce Neville; it is Boris Ilyich Nevsky. He makes no secret of that fact, especially since he still speaks with a heavy Russian accent. I think the name change was more for his children than for himself."

"Why? Does he want them to distance themselves from their Russian heritage?"

"No. I think he wants them to distance themselves from him."

"Why?"

"This all gets a little murky, and a lot of what I'm going to tell you is rumor and second-hand gossip, but Boston's rumor mill is generally on the mark, and I tend not to dismiss it."

"I understand."

"Apparently, Boris Nevsky was one of the oligarchs in Russia in the 1990s who accumulated immense wealth under the Boris Yeltsin regime. When I say 'wealth,' I mean billions, Lieutenant. But once Putin took power, people like Nevsky were in trouble. It wasn't that Putin was trying to right wrongs; he just wanted to get his own hands on all that money.

Nevsky was one of the oligarchs who saw the handwriting on the wall soon enough to get himself, his family, and his fortune out of Russia before the ax fell. So ten years ago, he arrived in Boston to establish a new life."

"But you can't teach an old dog new tricks, can you?" said Walter.

"Apparently not."

"I've dealt with the Russian mob in New York more than I ever wanted to. They are scary people."

"Mr. Nevsky, from what I have heard, fits that mold. He and his wife come to charity galas quite often. They appear to be charming people, and they are very, very generous. I will admit that I have gratefully accepted their donations on more than a few occasions. But still, the rumors persist: Drugs, extortion, teenage prostitution, assassinations so gruesome that they give me nightmares just thinking about them. In defense of his wife, who is a charming woman, I've heard that the marriage is a sham and that Boris has been engaged in a long-term affair with a woman named Kathryn Quincy, who is allegedly his business manager."

"But who's really nothing more than just another beautiful young Russian prostitute, right?"

"Not at all. That's why it's all so odd. Anastasia Nevsky, his wife, is a genuine beauty, but Kathryn is perhaps pretty, but not beautiful, and she possesses a rather vulgar figure one usually associates with exotic dancers. She's also American. So I guess there's no accounting for taste."

"I guess not," said Walter. "But you suspect that he has one of the 'private' art collections that we've been discussing?"

"I'm practically sure of it. I have friends who have friends who have been to the Nevsky mansion and who tell stories of being escorted to his private museum. I've heard it's breathtaking."

"But no one ever says a word to the authorities."

"People who speak to the authorities about Boris Nevsky turn up dead, Lieutenant, and so do their families."

"I am not surprised," said Walter, rising from his chair.

"I hope I've been helpful, Lieutenant. I will pray for the safe delivery of your children."

"Thank you so much, ma'am. You have been helpful, and you have been courageous." He turned to walk toward the door, then turned back. "Just one more thing, ma'am, if you don't mind."

Abby was standing, looking even smaller and more vulnerable than she had when he'd arrived. She seemed to know what was coming, but refused to flinch from it. "Yes, Lieutenant?"

"Ma'am, I'm way out of line to bring this up, and I apologize in advance if I offend you."

"Please, Lieutenant, what is it?"

"It's Sergeant Mayhew, ma'am."

"What about him?" said Abby, going pale. "Is he all right?"

"Yes, he's fine. It's just that he seems to have developed an infatuation with you. He's a happily married young man with a young family, and I'd hate to see any harm come to his marriage because of an infatuation. I was hoping that if you see him again you might talk to him and set him straight."

Abby Sewall didn't know just how much Walter Hudson knew or suspected, but knowing the man as she did, she assumed it was a lot. But now was not the time for confessions, dissembling, or denials. The man knew what the man knew, and she was in no position to try to change that. And in the end, she had too much pride to try.

"I will talk to him, Lieutenant, I promise you," was all she said.

"Thank you, ma'am," he said.

"And where are you going now?"

"I'm going to visit Boris Nevsky."

"I was afraid you were going to say that. Please be careful."

"Mrs. Sewall, Boris Nevsky either has my kids or knows where they are. I think he's the one who has to be careful."

Abby Sewall looked at Walter Hudson for a long time, her eyes taking the man in.

"I do not doubt you for a minute, Lieutenant."

46

"TO WHAT DO I OWE THIS PLEASURE, LIEUTENANT?" said Bruce Neville aka Boris Nevsky. They were sitting in his "office," which was really an entire wing of his mansion located down the street from the Boston Museum of Fine Arts. The mansion itself, a recent construction, was so large that Walter imagined tourists would have trouble deciding which building was the museum. The office wing reminded him of the West Wing of the White House, and the entire complex took up more than half of a city block.

Nevsky himself reminded Walter of Vladimir Putin: small and trim with carefully combed, thinning blond hair and small blue eyes that revealed no sign of life behind them. Walter guessed he was in his fifties. He was sitting behind a large desk in a room that looked like it belonged more in the Winter Palace in St. Petersburg than in Boston, Massachusetts.

Coffee had been laid out in a gold service with antique porcelain coffee cups that Walter had no doubt were genuine. Probably stolen from the Kremlin, he thought.

Sitting in a chair opposite his desk was a woman Walter guessed was his age, mid to late thirties. She wasn't plain, but she wasn't beautiful, her most striking feature being a remarkable pair of breasts that she did little to conceal. He presumed this was Kathryn Quincy.

Incongruously, a man uncannily resembling legendary Russian weightlifter Vasily Alekseyev stood behind Nevsky, giving Walter what he supposed was a menacing stare.

"Let's cut the crap, Mr. Nevsky," said Walter. "My two daughters have been kidnapped, and if you haven't kidnapped them yourself, you know who did and you know where they are."

"Does that mean you'll pass on the coffee?" said Nevsky, nodding toward the coffee service.

Walter said nothing.

"I apologize," said Nevsky, "I didn't mean to appear dismissive of a problem that I am sure is causing you great anxiety. But I am puzzled as to why you think I would have anything to do with it."

"Because two men have been murdered, I believe, because of their participation in a scheme to sell art stolen by the Nazis decades ago on the underground market."

"And what would that have to do with me, Lieutenant?"

"It is my understanding that you are one of the largest buyers of underground art sold in Boston, if not the country. I think you somehow got wind of the fact that the two murdered men, Armin Jaeger and Charles Martin Sewall, had decided to stop selling the art, instead, intending to donate it to the world's great museums. You, of course, didn't like that plan, so you had the two men poisoned with hemlock in their drinks, thinking that you could make a quick purchase of Armin Jaeger's farm, where you were sure the art was being hidden, find it, and take it for yourself. Unfortunately, my wife and I inadvertently got in the way of that plan. Even more unfortunately, I had become involved in the murder investigation of Mr. Sewall, and so I started connecting the dots."

"I have never heard of anything so preposterous in my life, Lieutenant," said Nevsky, carefully taking a sip of his coffee. "Where would you have gotten such strange ideas?"

"That doesn't really matter."

"Perhaps not to you, but it does to me," said Nevsky. "I like to know who's defaming my character."

"Assuming you have any," said Walter, trying to control his anger. "What I want to know, and I want to know it now, is where is Dot Ferguson, and where are my children."

"And why would I know where this 'Dot Ferguson' is, Lieutenant? Why would you think I've ever heard of her?"

"Because she was sent to Dutch River to be the conduit between Armin Jaeger and Charles Martin Sewall, and I believe you knew that and when your plan to buy the farm was ruined, you told her that she would either find the hidden art and deliver it to you, or there would be awful consequences for her. I think that she was so frightened and desperate that she kidnapped my kids, thinking that there might be some way she could use them as leverage."

"Lieutenant Hudson, I find your accusations not only absurd but insulting, and I am not sure I should sit here and listen to them any longer." He turned to the woman sitting opposite him and said, "Kathryn, perhaps you can leave now. I'd like to have a few words with Lieutenant Hudson in private."

"Sure, Mr. Neville," said Kathryn. Perhaps it was just Abby Sewall's description of her that lingered in his memory, but as she walked across the large room toward the door, she reminded him of a stripper strolling across a stage, leaving articles of clothing behind her as she went. She glared at him as if she knew what he was thinking. Perhaps she knew that was what many people thought of her.

The bodyguard, Walter noticed, stayed where he was.

"Perhaps I should make something clear to you now that we are alone," said Nevsky, in a quiet voice. "I do not take well to having my reputation and my business interests threatened, especially not by the likes of some shitty little detective from New York. Am I being clear, Detective Hudson?"

"Perfectly, Mr. Nevsky," said Walter, in an equally quiet voice. "And now let me be just as clear with you. I am going to find Dot Ferguson, and I am going to find my kids. And if they are harmed in any way I will hunt you down and tear you into little pieces. Is that clear enough for you?"

"Assuming you are in any condition to do so, Lieutenant," said Boris, staring at Walter with his dead eyes. "And let me remind you of one important fact: Everything you have heard about me is undoubtedly true. So if you think your children are in danger now, think again. And that goes for the rest of your family. If you continue this unwarranted persecution of me, no one you hold dear to you will ever be safe, and what will happen to them does not bear contemplation. I do not make threats, Lieutenant. I merely state facts. Now, I believe our meeting is at an end. Yuri, please show the good lieutenant out." Boris Nevsky looked down at his desk and began to shuffle papers, moving on to other business.

Yuri the bodyguard moved toward Walter with the confidence of an undefeated heavyweight champion facing an unranked challenger. "Let's go buddy," he said, reaching out a hand the size of a catcher's mitt to grab Walter.

"I'm not your buddy," said Walter, not budging.

Yuri stepped straight into Walter's perfect left jab. Walter felt and heard cartilage cracking and teeth breaking as his equally massive fist found home. Blood started spurting out of the man's nose and mouth immediately as his eyes widened in surprise. He hesitated, confused by a situation he had never confronted before. That moment gave Walter the chance he needed to unload a shattering left hook into the man's ribs, and Walter heard the satisfying sound of bones breaking. He dug his fist into the man again, this time just below the ribs, finding his liver. The man's stomach was rock hard, but a great liver shot is devastating, and the man let out a small groan as he slowly bent over. Walter struck the side of the man's head with a massive right cross, and he went down. With his large leather right shoe, Walter kicked him in the stomach, and then stomped on his left knee, the sounds of cartilage tearing and ligaments snapping, echoing off the walls.

"Enough!" said Boris, coming around from behind his desk.

"No, not enough," said Walter, breathing hard. "You so much as harm a hair on the head of any member of my family and I'll come after you, and what I'll do to you will make what I just did to this punk look like patty-cake. Do you understand?"

"I understand perfectly," said Boris, "now please leave."

Walter left quickly, knowing that a half-dozen Yuris would descend on him momentarily if he didn't. His pulse was still racing, but his mind was clear, and contained only one thought:

Either he or Boris Nevsky would now have to die.

47

IF CAPE COD is a great arm extending out from the mainland of Massachusetts, Cape Ann is more of a knuckle.

The ride from Boston is short, but the roads are narrow and crowded, and Walter's swollen hands made the drive painful and awkward. At least he hadn't broken any bones, he thought, knowing that his hands were going to come in for more rough use before this day was over.

Under different circumstances the drive would have been a scenic pleasure, but on this day Walter noticed none of it, the landscape going by in a blur as he focused on the traffic around him, trying not to cause an accident as he wove the BMW through the traffic at frightening speeds. It was only just past noon, but it had already been a full day for Walter, and he was functioning on nothing but adrenalin.

Luckily, he'd remembered to sync up his phone with the car's wireless system before he had left. He called Sergeant Mayhew and told him to meet him in Gloucester, and he called Levi to give him a quick update on his meetings with Abby Sewall and Boris Nevsky.

"Interesting," was all Levi had said.

"What does that mean?" said Walter.

"Look, Walter," said Levi, "you have enough on your plate right now. I'm going to look into a few things on this end and I'll get back to you. In the meantime, please be careful. I know how you can get at times like this, and I don't want you or anyone else getting hurt. Remember, at this point, it looks like Dot is just as much an innocent victim as your kids are."

Walter hung up and drove on.

Gloucester, he remembered thinking, looks good from a distance but doesn't stand up well to close inspection, at least the section he was in. He didn't know the town at all, and he didn't really know where he should start looking, but he knew the nice part of town wasn't it. He knew a bad neighborhood when he saw one, and when he found himself on a small block occupied by nothing but run-down, dangerous-looking bars with hard-looking men and harder-looking women hanging around outside the entrances with open beer bottles in their hands, he figured this was in as good a place as any to begin his search. He parked the car on a side street, leaving his detective's shield on the dash and hoping for the best. He remembered wondering if the auto insurance they'd bought covered days like this.

Walter was a big man who still bore the demeanor of someone who had decided at an early age that he wasn't going to take anybody's shit, but no one on that street, man or woman, seemed all that impressed.

"I'm looking for Dot Ferguson," he said to the first man he reached.

"Good for you, dickhead," said the man, his New England accent making "for" come out as "fuh." His eyes were slightly unfocused, his voice raspy and slurred. He had the gaunt, unhealthily ruddy complexion of an alcoholic who'd been smoking since he was ten, but Walter didn't doubt for a minute that the man was as dangerous as a cobra.

"Where is she?" said Walter.

"How th'fuck should we know?" said a woman standing behind the man wearing torn jeans and a stained tee shirt that said "Get Your Own Fucking Lobster" on the front.

"Look, I'm a detective with the NYPD, and I'm here investigating a murder. I need to find Dot Ferguson," said Walter. It must have been the exhaustion and stress that caused him to blurt out that rookie mistake. These people would rather beat an out-of-town cop half to death than get free tickets to a Patriots game.

"Th'fuck?" said the man. "You're a long way from home, man."

"Yeah, probably a mistake, y'know?" said another man, sidling up to the first one, "bein' this far from home." His flat New England vowels made "far" sound like "fah." A crowd was gathering, and Walter realized too late that he was in trouble, that these people had been expecting him. Somewhere in the crowd he heard a beer bottle smash.

"I'm not looking for trouble," said Walter.

"Not looking for trouble?" said the first man with a chuckle that rattled, "then what th'fuck you doin' here? All we got here is trouble, y'know?"

Walter sensed more than heard someone coming up behind him. He turned around just in time to block a man's right arm. The hand held a broken beer bottle. It was now or never, he thought. He kicked out viciously at the man's groin and followed up with a kick to the head, and the man went down like a sack of cement. He spun around quickly and lashed out wildly with a roundhouse kick that broke the ringleader's jaw and put him on his knees. The woman at the front came after him with a beer bottle, and he threw a right to her abdomen while he blocked the bottle with his left. There's no sexism in a fistfight. He was hoping that the crowd would break up once they saw some of their companions injured, but he should have known better. These men faced death every time they went to sea, and a couple of busted heads weren't about to intimidate them. Three more men came after him. He fended two off, but the third landed a blow to his head. It was a glancing blow, but it hurt, and while he was trying to recover, a woman hit him with a hard kick to his thigh that caused his right leg to buckle. He felt another fist strike his head as he tried to roll away and give himself some room to regroup. But the mob was relentless.

"Aw, shit," he heard himself say, feeling no fear but only shame that he had failed his wife and daughters at the moment they needed him most. He stood up but was immediately shoved back to the ground. A heavy boot struck his ribs and took his breath away. He heard heavy footsteps rushing at him from behind, but he didn't care; more assailants couldn't possibly make this any worse. He tried to cover up, waiting for the inevitable blows.

But the footsteps went running by him, and he heard a sound he hadn't heard in many years: the sound of hard wood on human bones. There were four men, all big and none in uniform. He hazily recognized one of them as David Mayhew. They were all carrying old-fashioned nightsticks made of heavy oak, the kind that had long since fallen out of use as Tasers took their place, the Tasers being far less lethal.

Walter heard bones breaking and cries of pain, but the fearless mob did not retreat, nor did the cops back off a single step. Blood was now flowing freely. This was not going to end well for anybody.

"Stop it! Stop it now!" shrieked a voice from directly behind him. It was a woman's voice, and suddenly both the mob and the cops froze. Walter turned in the direction of the voice.

It was Dot Ferguson, and she looked like hell.

48

"YOU SURE YOU WANT THE KIDS TO HEAR THIS?" said Dot. She was no longer the gum-popping young woman with the big hair and the small clothes that Walter had come to know. The gum was gone, the hair was flat and hastily combed, and the skimpy skirt and tight blouse had been replaced by a pair of oversized jeans and a bulky knitted sweater.

"I don't see where we have much choice," said Walter, holding a cold towel to the side of his head that hurt the most. "I'm not letting the kids out of my sight until my wife gets here in a couple of hours, and we have to talk." Beer is the official medicine of Gloucester, and Walter Hudson was holding one in his free hand as his two daughters sat in his lap. Sergeant Mayhew stood nearby gazing out a window, looking like he'd just scratched an itch. The Gloucester police had generously offered to stay out of the whole mess.

They were in the living room of a third-floor apartment normally occupied by Dot's two surviving brothers, who were both currently on a fishing trawler somewhere off the shores of Newfoundland. The furniture was broken down and the place stank of stale beer, tobacco, and weed.

"I know it's a stupid thing to say, but I'm sorry," said Dot.

"I guess I'm confused," said Walter. "I still don't understand what you expected to accomplish by kidnapping my kids."

"That makes two of us," said Dot. "I was scared, and I panicked. I was sitting there in the Maases' conference room listening to how close you guys were to unraveling the whole thing, and I didn't know what to do. One minute I was sitting there, and it seemed like the next minute I was driving away with your kids in the backseat."

"But what were you so panicked about?"

"I didn't know if you guys were going to suspect me of murdering Armin and Marty."

"But you didn't, and we know that now," said Walter.

"But it was more than that."

"What do you mean, Dot?" said Walter.

"Do you mind if I just start at the beginning? Maybe it'll make sense to all of us, including me, if I do that."

"I think that's a good idea," said Walter. "David, why don't you take a seat, this may take a while." Mayhew came over and plopped on a sofa that made a cracking noise as he landed on it.

"I was doing all right, you know?" said Dot, looking out the window. "I'd gotten out of this town. I'd left everything behind, even my name, which I'm sure you know by now, and I'd started a new life. I was the youngest and the best paralegal at Dunston & Burns, which was one of the top law firms in Boston; still is.

"Then they came to me one day and said that I'd been selected to work for one of their most important clients, the Sewall family, as a personal secretary, at double what the law firm was paying me. I wasn't going to turn that down, so off I went to Beacon Hill."

"Did you like your work with the Sewalls?" said Walter.

"I loved it. They were such a wonderful family, especially Mrs. Sewall. Always so considerate and generous."

Walter couldn't help noticing David Mayhew turning bright red at the mention of Abby Sewall. He was still mystified at what exactly had gone on between the two, but he hoped that Abby would honor his request and have a conversation with the man.

"Were you having an affair with Mr. Sewall?"

Dot hesitated, looking down at her hands. "Not while I was in Boston, no. Marty was always a perfect gentleman, except I caught him staring at me a lot. I think he really loved Mrs. Sewall, I mean, who wouldn't? And I think she really loved him back, but, well . . ."

"'Well' what?" said Walter, as Mayhew turned an even deeper shade of red.

"Look," said Dot, "it was none of my business, but there didn't seem to be much of a spark between them, you know? I mean, I know they loved each other, and I never saw anything that would make me suspect that either of them was being unfaithful . . . but I don't know. You know how you can always tell when there's a spark between two people? It just wasn't there, at least not as far as I could tell."

"You said you didn't have an affair with him while you were living in Boston," said Walter. "I guess that means you had one with him at some point."

"I'll get to that, okay?"

"Okay. I'm sorry. Keep going."

"So, anyway, one day Marty, you know, Mr. Sewall, came to me and told me he had an exciting opportunity for me. That's what he said, 'exciting opportunity.' He told me that he and an old friend who lived in this place called Dutch River, New York, were going to start dealing in rare art. It was all going to be done on very confidential terms, and they needed someone with 'discretion' to coordinate the effort. He asked me if I'd be interested."

"And you said 'yes.'"

"Not right away. I mean, I didn't even know where Dutch River was, and I wasn't sure how I felt about this rare art business they were talking about."

"Why not?" said Walter.

"I don't know, it just seemed kind of not right, you know?"

"So what changed your mind?"

"Marty paid for me to take a trip to Dutch River. The second I drove into town I just loved the place."

"I know the feeling," said Walter.

"And then I met the Maases, and they were really nice."

"Did they know why you were moving to Dutch River?"

"No, they didn't know a thing about it, and Marty had told me not to discuss it with them. All they knew was that they were doing a favor for one of Jill's old law school friends and getting a really good paralegal in the deal. I think they'd made up some tale about me being in a messy divorce or something."

"Kind of what I thought," said Walter.

"And then I met Mr. Jaeger, and he was so nice. And he convinced me that the art transactions that I was going to be assisting him and Marty with were for a good purpose. He was such an easy guy to believe, you know? And, of course, I really wanted to believe him."

"Because of the money, right?"

Dot looked up at Walter, surprised. "So you know about the money, huh? I guess I should have known."

"We also know what you were using the money for, Dot," said Walter, "so nobody's blaming you, okay?"

"Thanks."

"So when did you start having the affair with Mr. Sewall?" said Mayhew, blushing once more as soon as he asked the question.

"It was on my first trip to New York."

"But why?" said Mayhew. Walter suspected that David Mayhew had his own personal reasons for asking Dot about the affair, but now wasn't the time to question him about it.

"I don't know," said Dot. "Why does anybody have an affair? I loved my life in Dutch River, but I guess I was lonely. New York City was a scary place to me, and Marty was, you know, someone familiar, someone safe. It wasn't like I had the hots for him or anything, you know? If he hadn't wanted it, I don't think I ever would have considered it. Honestly, I don't think either of us was ever very enthused about it. In the end, having sex with him once a year was easier for me than saying no, and I think it was easier for him than telling me that he was ending it. I did feel shitty about Mrs. Sewall, though. I looked up to her so much, and I know she never would have even considered such a thing."

David Mayhew was starting to look flustered, and Walter knew that, for everyone's sake, he had to change the subject. "Okay, let's move on," he said. "When did things start going bad for you?"

"I was sad when old Mr. Jaeger died, but he was a really old guy, you know? And I figured these things just happen. They happen to all of us, right? It's just a matter of time. But then I started getting the phone calls."

"Phone calls?" said Walter.

"Yeah. I started getting these calls telling me that certain very influential people were going to be very disappointed if the art sales stopped. The caller said that I was going to be held responsible for making sure they didn't. They also told me the transactions wouldn't be going through Marty anymore."

"Then why did you make that last trip, and what happened to the art you were supposed to be delivering?"

"There was no art."

"What do you mean?"

"I mean, they told me to make the trip, because it was already scheduled, and they didn't want to make Marty suspicious; but I wasn't supposed to bring any art with me. They said Marty wouldn't notice right away, because he never checked, and they'd deal with him after that. Jesus," she said with a shudder, "I should have known what they were up to."

"Just so you know, it seems that Marty knew that the arrangement was over, too. Apparently he didn't want to have to be the one to tell you. So there was a little dishonesty going on on both sides of that final visit."

"Huh," said Dot, a hint of a smile briefly lighting up her face,

"But, anyway, we know you stopped off at Armin Jaeger's farm before you left for New York. Why?"

"Because I wanted to see if I could find any of the art they were expecting me to deliver to them, but I couldn't. I couldn't even get past the front door. When I told them that, that's when the threats started."

"So they threatened you?" said Walter.

"Yeah, they did," said Dot, "but that wasn't the worst part. The caller said that bad things were going to happen to my nieces and nephews. That's when I panicked. And now here we are. I am so sorry, Lieutenant. I never meant to harm anyone, but when they threatened my nieces and nephews, I lost my mind. That's no excuse, I know."

"Sure it is," said Walter. "I don't know if I would have behaved any differently if it were my kids."

"That's awfully kind of you, Lieutenant," said Dot. "I'm . . . I'm really sorry about hitting Bert. Is he okay?"

"So that was you?"

"That was me. I'd gotten another call, this time saying that I had until the end of week to find the paintings or else, so I followed him to the house that night. I felt awful."

"Well, Bert's got a hard head, so I wouldn't worry about it."

"Thank God for that."

"So I'm willing to bet," said Walter, "that this mysterious man who was making these threatening phone calls had a heavy Russian accent."

Dot looked puzzled. "It wasn't a man, Lieutenant, it was a woman, the same voice every time, and she didn't have a Russian accent. She didn't have any accent. She just sounded, you know, like an American."

A dozen questions popped into Walter's mind, but they were all interrupted by the sound of his phone ringing. He looked at the caller ID, frowned, and then picked up the call.

"Levi? What's up?" There was a long pause as he listened, his eyes widening. He finally said, "Okay, thanks," and hung up.

"What was that all about?" said Mayhew.

"Sergeant Mayhew," said Walter, "I need you to get back to Boston right now."

"And do what?" said Mayhew.

"Go directly to the Sewall mansion, keep Abby in your line of sight, and make sure that no one—and I mean no one—is allowed to see her."

"Lieutenant, I'm confused," said Mayhew.

"Please, Sergeant, just go, now. My wife will be here in just a few minutes and as soon as she gets here I'll follow you down. I'll try to call you on the way."

"What should I do?" said Dot.

"Please go with Sergeant Mayhew," said Walter. "We can't let you out of our sight."

"But why?"

"Because I was wrong again, that's why. Every time I think I'm right on this case, I'm wrong, and I'm getting sick of it."

49

"I SEE YOU BROUGHT REINFORCEMENTS THIS TIME," said Boris Nevsky. "May I assume you've come here to put a couple more of my employees in the hospital?" Nevsky was sitting at a small table in a corner of his office with his business manager, Kathryn Quincy, whose expression remained inscrutable at the sight of Walter and the two Massachusetts State Police he had brought with him, though Walter thought he noticed her body tense up. Nevsky himself appeared outwardly calm, but there was no missing the anger in his voice. A maid came in from a side entrance and put a tray down on the table before quietly exiting. The tray seemed to hold some snacks and a pitcher of martinis.

"This visit is for business, not pleasure, I'm afraid," said Walter. "I've come to make an arrest." It was only six o'clock, but he couldn't keep the weariness out of his voice. He had always prided himself on his stamina, but after getting up before dawn after only a few hours' sleep, driving across Massachusetts and getting into two fistfights, he'd just about had it.

"You seem to losing your mind, Lieutenant," said Nevsky. "On whose authority are you going to arrest me? And on what ridiculous, trumped-up charges?"

"I'm not here to arrest you," said Walter.

The look of confusion on Nevsky's face was no act. He said, "I believe you have taken leave of your senses, Lieutenant. Officers," he said, looking at the two state policemen, "are you just going to stand by and allow this man to harass me? He may be an NYPD detective, but this, may I remind you, is Boston, Massachusetts."

"That's why we're here, sir," said the officer who appeared to be the senior of the two. The nameplate on his shirt said "Sweeney." Like most Massachusetts State Police Officers, they both looked like they'd played linebacker for a Division I football team.

"You are going to have to explain yourselves, Officers. I am now completely at a loss."

"Kathryn Quincy," said Sweeney, "you are under arrest for the murders of Armin August Jaeger and Charles Martin Sewall. You have the right to remain silent, and anything you say can and will be used against you in a court of law. You have the right to an attorney, and if you can't afford one, one will be provided for you. Do you understand these rights?"

There was no fear on her face, only anger and defiance as she stood up and faced the policemen.

"On what grounds are you arresting me?" she said. "You can't possibly have any probable cause."

"Yes or no, Ms. Quincy."

"Yes, of course, I understand my rights. I'm not an idiot."

"Ms. Quincy," said Walter, "on a hunch, my colleague, Captain Leviticus Welles of the NYPD Intelligence Division, downloaded a recent photo of you from the Internet. He sent a copy to Officer Bertram Steffus of the Dutch River, New York, Police Department, who brought it to the liquor store employee whom you bribed to poison Armin Jaeger's bourbon. He also sent a copy to the Vernon, Connecticut, Police Department, who paid a visit to the waitress whom you bribed to poison Charles Martin Sewall's iced tea. They both immediately picked your photo out of an array of photos they were shown. Neither of them had any doubt whatsoever."

"George Boone," said Kathryn, "whose nickname as I recall is 'Boonesy,' is a chronic cocaine user if not an addict; and Iris Stanton is a compulsive gambler who would say anything to anybody to get another crack at the blackjack tables at Mohegan Sun Casino. Their testimony will never stand up in court, and you know it."

"You understand that you just admitted that you know these people," said Walter. "We never mentioned their names to you."

"And since we Mirandized you," said Officer Sweeney, "your statement is on the record."

"Kathryn?" said Nevsky, looking like he'd been slapped in the face. "Please tell me what's going on."

Kathryn Quincy's defiant expression suddenly melted into one of resignation. She sat down and poured herself a drink from the martini pitcher, took a large gulp, and refilled the glass. She glanced up at Nevsky with an expression of raw contempt.

"Look at me, Boris," she said. "For once, just look at me. How long did you think I'd be able to put up with pretending I was grateful for the crummy salary you paid me while I watched you raking in your billions?

How long did you think I could stand fucking you and pretending I liked it while I stood back and watched you escort your glamorous wife to every elite social event in this city while I stayed in my crummy condo watching reruns of *Friends*?"

"But, Kathryn, I thought . . ."

"You thought what, Boris—that I really believed all those things you said? That I actually believed all those promises you made to marry me someday? That I at least once didn't have to fake an orgasm? For God's sake, I had better sex with my high school prom date in the backseat of a car. So I made it my business to find out just where all that precious art of yours was coming from, and when I found out that the whole scheme was going to come to a stop, I said, 'no,' this was going to be *my* chance to make a killing."

"Probably a bad choice of words," said Walter, "but I get your gist. What I don't understand is how you found out who was involved. My understanding was that this was all done through blind intermediaries so that no one on either end could know who they were dealing with."

"I can answer that for you," said Boris. "I think you know enough about me, Lieutenant, to understand that I don't like being kept in the dark. I can't afford surprises."

Kathryn made a derisive noise as she took another drink from her martini glass. Nevsky stared at her, but continued.

"It wasn't that difficult to find out who the conduit was," he said. "It was no great secret in Boston that Charles Martin Sewall had lost the family fortune. The man was always a bit of a dolt and no one was all that surprised. And then, out of the blue, he was suddenly rich again, richer than he'd ever been before. At about the same time, I began to receive informal, confidential feelers asking me if I would be interested in acquiring some very rare art on the private market. Putting two and two together after that wasn't all that difficult, at least not with the intelligence resources I have at my disposal."

"And, of course, you couldn't stop yourself from bragging to me about it, could you?" said Kathryn. "You thought it would get me all excited in bed, right?"

"I thought you were my confidante, Kathryn, the one person I could trust."

"Oops," said Kathryn, with a derisive chuckle.

"I must compliment you on your ruthlessness, my dear Kathryn," said Nevsky. "I honestly didn't think you had it in you. A rare misjudgment on my part."

"I think it's time you came with us now, Ms. Quincy," said Officer Sweeney.

"Almost, but not quite," said Kathryn as she drained her glass and set it down carefully on the table. "First, you have to give me the chance to explain to Mr. Nevsky the one last favor I did for him as a kind of final farewell."

"We'll give you a couple more minutes, ma'am," said Sweeney, "and then we have to take you into custody."

"I always hated the way you made martinis, Boris," she said, looking contemplatively at her empty glass. "You damn Russians with your vodka. Don't you know that the only way to make a proper martini is with London dry gin?"

"You always seemed to like them well enough," he said.

"I hope by now you're starting to realize how good I am at pretending, Boris."

"Fine, but what does this have to do with anything?"

"He's right, ma'am," said Sweeney, "you need to stop stalling. Tell him what you have to say."

"There was one more person I had to eliminate to complete my plan," said Kathryn, staring at Nevsky. "I know how nosy you can be, and I couldn't risk having you find out what I was up to, now, could I?"

"And how were you planning to accomplish that? People far more cunning than you have tried and failed to get rid of me. The bottom of Boston Harbor is littered with their bodies."

"Cocktail hour," said Kathryn, picking up her glass and tilting it back and forth, "our nightly ritual."

"You were planning to poison me?" said Nevsky, a look of genuine surprise on his face, "with our cocktails?"

"Nothing is sacred anymore, is it?" said Kathryn.

"And when were you planning to do this?" said Boris.

"Well, thanks to our intrepid Lieutenant Hudson and his colleague Captain Welles, I was running out of time, so it was going to have to be soon."

"Okay, okay," said Officer Sweeney, "enough of the true confessions. Please stand up, ma'am. We need to cuff you and bring you in for an arraignment."

"I'm afraid that won't be possible," said Kathryn.

"Why?" said Sweeney.

"Because I can no longer stand up, that's why."

"Jesus!" said Walter. "You were going to poison him tonight! You poisoned that pitcher of martinis with poison hemlock!"

"Straight-A's for you, Lieutenant. And I just drank enough of it to kill ten people. And I added a couple of kickers to speed up the process."

"Somebody call 911!" said Sweeney, panicked.

"Don't bother," said Kathryn, "there is no antidote." She took a deep sigh and looked at Nevsky. "Oh, Boris, I so much wanted to be just like you. I took one look at you all those years ago when you came into that strip club where I was working and said to myself, 'There he is. There's my ticket.' I decided I was going do whatever I had to do to get close to you, and I was going to learn just how you did it. I didn't care how; I was willing to do anything, anything to be as rich and powerful as you."

"I don't share, Kathryn, not even with you," said Boris, staring at her now with an almost clinical detachment.

"And now, Lieutenant Hudson, I have one last dying request," said Kathryn, her breath now becoming labored.

"What would that be?"

"Tell me: Where are the fucking paintings? I had Dot Ferguson search that farmhouse from top to bottom, and she never came up with a single clue."

"She should have looked harder in the basement."

"But she did look! She swore to me that she did!"

"Not hard enough. There was a secret tunnel that led to a vault. Just think: you were so close. But don't worry, you never would have gotten into the vault anyway."

"Why not?" said Kathryn, now only barely audible.

"Because you didn't know the code, Kathryn. It's a code you should have learned a long time ago. You would have saved yourself a lot of trouble if you had."

"Code? What? What was it?" she said, her head starting to nod.

"It was 'A Mighty Fortress Is Our God.'"

She stared at him, but was no longer able to say anything.

"You're passing now, Kathryn. 'A Mighty Fortress Is Our God.' Please try to hold on to the thought."

She made no reply.

Walter crossed the room and stood over Kathryn Quincy. He reached out with one hand and gently closed her eyes.

"Somebody call an ambulance," he said.

He turned and left the room without saying good-bye to the living or the dead.

50

"I GUESS that at least gives me some closure, Lieutenant, thank you," said Abby Sewall.

Walter was out on his feet by the time he'd arrived at the Sewall's Beacon Hill town house, and he wasn't sure how much was left in his emotional gas tank. He'd seen and done a lot of things in his years as a cop, but he'd never talked a person from this world into the next before, and no matter what he thought of Kathryn Quincy, the experience had left him shattered. But he'd felt an obligation to visit Abby Sewall as soon as he could. She deserved to know who had murdered her husband and why before it was plastered all over the news.

He'd at least been able to get in touch with Sarah and make sure his family was now safe. Sarah had suggested that they book a suite at the Marriott Long Wharf and Walter had said, "Why not?" What was all their newfound wealth good for if not for easing situations like this?

And now he was sitting in Abby's third-floor office along with David Mayhew and Dot Ferguson. As usual, there were coffee and pastries laid out before them and, as usual, they remained untouched.

Sergeant Mayhew was sitting at the far end of a love seat, as far away from Abby as he could possibly get without stepping out of the room, his head hanging almost to his knees. He looked like Lassie waiting for Timmy to come home, thought Walter.

Abby sat in a chair on the other side of the room looking composed, perhaps a little pale, but Walter could have sworn he detected a faintly amused expression on her face that lit her eyes as she glanced at Mayhew. She was wearing slacks and a modest blouse, her hair was carelessly brushed back from her face, and she wore little or no makeup; but there was something breathtaking about this outwardly plain, fiftyish woman. There were many things, Walter knew, that he would never understand.

"It's the least I could do, ma'am," said Walter.

"And now," said Abby, "I believe it is time for you to go to your family. You look exhausted, and they must be as well."

"I have to admit it's been a long day," he said, rising to leave, his legs feeling leaden. Mayhew and Dot stood up at the same time.

"Dorothea," said Abby, "I suggest that you stay with us tonight. I'll have a room made up for you. In the meantime, why don't you go downstairs. I'll meet you in just a few minutes, and we'll have a light supper together."

"Thank you, ma'am," said Dot, too tired to resist. She quietly left the room after giving Walter a grateful hug.

"Now, David," said Abby in the soft, compelling voice that David Mayhew had found irresistible from the first time he heard it, "I'd like you to stay a moment, please. I believe we need to talk."

David stood mute and still, as if his boots were nailed to the floor.

"David?" said Abby.

"I . . . I'd like Lieutenant Hudson to stay here," said David.

"But, David, whatever for?" said Abby.

"Abby . . . Mrs. Sewall, please," the big man stammered. Walter stared at him, hardly able to believe that this frightened boy quailing in the presence of a tiny woman was the same fearless man who had beaten back an angry mob by sheer physical, brute force just a few short hours ago. "I'm just not sure I trust myself is all, I guess."

"Oh, David," she said, "I'm not frightened to be alone with you, if that's your concern."

"No, ma'am, that's not it."

"Then what is it?"

"I don't know. I'm sorry. I'd just feel better if he stayed, that's all."

Abby looked at Walter, her luminescent eyes silently imploring him for help.

"I'm sorry, Lieutenant," she said, "I know you need to get back to your family."

This is why we have priests and pastors, thought Walter. This is why we have counselors. This is not why we have NYPD cops.

But he heard himself say, "I intend to, ma'am, but it seems there may be some unfinished business here that's bothering Sergeant Mayhew. He probably saved my life today up in Gloucester, so if I can be of any help, I'm more than willing to try."

"Thank you, Lieutenant," said Abby, looking relieved. "It's really quite a private matter, but perhaps we need your help."

"I do not wish to intrude upon your privacy, Mrs. Sewall."

"That's perfectly all right, Lieutenant. I'm not quite sure who I am anymore or what I'm becoming, but I'm not ashamed, and my only desire is to help David."

Walter sat back down, and so did Mayhew.

"Now, first things first," said Walter. "David, eat a pastry. Eat two. You probably haven't had a bite to eat since breakfast."

"I'm not hungry."

"Did that sound like a request? Eat." Walter noticed that Abby couldn't resist a smile at the exchange.

"Okay," said Walter after observing Mayhew wolf down a pastry, "I'm a cop, not a pastor. Who goes first?"

"Let me start," said Abby. She rose from her chair and went to sit beside David on the love seat.

"David, look at me," she said. She waited until he slowly raised his head and made eye contact. "David, what we did was wrong. I think you understand that."

Mayhew silently nodded his head and looked away, but Abby wouldn't let him.

"Look at me, David. It was wrong. It was a sin. We should both be ashamed of ourselves, and it will never happen again. Do you understand? Never."

"I understand," mumbled the big man.

"Good. Now, listen to me carefully. It was wrong, but it was also the greatest sexual thrill of my lifetime. It was one of the most joyous moments I have ever experienced, and I will treasure the memory forever. Can you possibly understand that, Sergeant?"

"I don't know," said Mayhew.

"Perhaps someday you will."

"Maybe."

"And now, there is one final thing that you need to understand. Are you still listening to me carefully, David?"

"Yes, ma'am."

"You are guilty of the sin of adultery, and no one can absolve you of that sin but God, and you must beg Him for forgiveness. I'm a religious woman, and I believe that in my heart. But I will also tell you that on that day you were absolutely helpless. I knew what I wanted the moment you first walked in my door, and nothing was going to keep me from getting it. It was my doing. It was my fault. That doesn't absolve you of your sin, but it is the simple truth. Are you capable of understanding that?"

"I don't know. I guess so," said Mayhew after a moment's hesitation. "But, Abby?"

"Yes, David?"

"Now what do I do?"

"Here's what you will do, dear David. You will go home to your wife and children. And you will spend the rest of your life loving your wife with all your heart, with all your soul, and with all your mind. And you will not make the same mistake that I made with my marriage, David. Marty and I loved each other, but we let the passion die. Don't let that happen. It's just too sad. And, David?"

"Yes, Abby?"

"You must take what we did with you to your grave. Not for my sake, and not for your sake, but for your wife's sake. What we did was bad enough. Please don't compound it by burdening the rest of her life with our sin. You have no right to change her life like that. You must understand that, David. Do you?"

"Yes, ma'am. I think so."

"Good. Now, it's time for both you and Lieutenant Hudson to get back to your families before you both fall over." She looked up at Walter, who looked back with an expression of open admiration.

"You are quite a woman, Mrs. Sewall."

"Well, we'll see about that. But the least you can do, Walter Hudson, on the odd chance that we ever meet again, is to call me 'Abby.'"

"Done," said Walter, smiling.

She gave them each a brief hug, and they were gone.

After the door had closed behind them, she poured herself a cup of coffee and took a pastry, an indulgence she resolutely never allowed herself. Then she sat down in the silence and privacy of her own home and wept quietly, but not for long.

After all, she was a Sewall.

51

"JESUS," said Walter, scanning the suite with a stunning view of Boston Harbor, "this place is bigger than our house."

"Daddy, you're not supposed to swear," said Robin.

"Thank you, Robin," said Sarah, "sometimes Daddy has to be reminded, doesn't he?"

Walter plopped himself in the enormous sofa in the main living area of the suite and let the girls climb all over him while Daniel sat happily on the floor with what smelled like an epic load in his diaper.

"Have the kids been fed?" he said.

"Long ago," said Sarah, picking up Daniel. "C'mon, girls, let's get to bed. It's been a long day for everyone."

"I'd like to take a shower," said Walter, between yawns, "but I don't have anything clean to change into."

"I bought you some stuff from the men's store downstairs, but I strongly recommend the hotel bathrobes. Why don't you take a shower and get comfortable. I'll call room service as soon as I get the kids to bed."

Walter took a long, hot shower and got himself into one of the hotel's bathrobes, which was, indeed, soft and comfortable. He decided to lie back on the bed for a few minutes and turn on the television while Sarah finished getting the kids to bed. When the room service trolley arrived Sarah went to the bedroom door and knocked softly, not wanting to disturb the kids by calling out from the living room.

"Honey," she said, opening the door when she heard no response from the knock, "dinner's here; let's eat it while it's hot." But it was too late. Walter was already sound asleep, and she knew that nothing would wake him, even if she tried, which she didn't.

She ate alone, enjoying the quiet and the comfort, and the knowledge that her family was safe. It was before dawn when the two of them, sharing the silent signals that pass between loving couples, awakened and wordlessly came together in a passionate embrace, falling soundly back to sleep when their lovemaking was done without uttering a word.

EPILOGUE

WINTER COMES EARLY to upstate New York, and Thanksgiving at the farm was a snowy affair, but the warmth generated by the occasion more than overcame the winter chill.

Sarah had bundled up the kids, and Fred Benecke had harnessed a horse to the sleigh and taken them for long rides in the countryside.

"I think that's the first time I've ever seen him smile," said Sarah as the sleigh finally pulled back into the yard.

"Who," said Walter, "Fred or the horse?"

Sarah hooted. "Probably both. And look at the kids. I've never seen their cheeks so red. They'll be sound asleep early tonight."

"Good," said Walter, giving his wife a lingering pat on the behind.

"Hey," she said, swatting his hand away as they walked into the house, "let's not forget that we have company here."

"That's only temporary," said Walter, giving her another pat.

It was going to be a large gathering, but the old farmhouse never felt crowded.

They had initially planned to eat in the formal dining room, but by an unspoken consensus they wound up settling down around the huge Shaker table in the middle of the kitchen. As Walter looked around, he was astonished to realize that, other than Leviticus Welles and Julie Remy, he had known none of these people, people who had come to mean so much to him and his family, only a few short months before. What a shame, he thought, that the deaths of two fine men were the cause of this happy gathering.

Fred Benecke had brought a cornucopia of autumn vegetables with him and was accompanied by his son, Arthur, and his wife. Arthur had decided to move back to Dutch River and help his father out with the farmwork, and his wife, Bridget, was opening an arts and crafts shop in town. Adam Avery and his wife Sally were busily chatting with Margie and Mike Hunter, who had resolutely kept himself sober for almost a month now, while Adam carved the first of two fresh turkeys that he had brought from the restaurant. Adam had prepared a stuffing for the birds and had worked his customary magic with the vegetables that Fred had brought, and the aromas were overwhelming.

Officer Bert Steffus, drinking diet soda and looking like he'd lost a couple of pounds, had arrived with a date, a plump farm girl from Kinderhook named Maura.

At the far end of the table, Peter and Jill Maas were involved in an intense discussion with Dr. Mel Williams and his wife Evelyn. Peter had recently announced that he would not be running for reelection as mayor of Dutch River, and Evelyn had announced that she would be running, unopposed as it turned out, to fill the office.

They had a lot to talk about.

"I guess Dutch River will never be the same," said Julie, looking around the table.

"No, I guess not," said Sarah, "but I can't help being happy for everyone."

"And besides," said Levi, "towns like this never change all that much. I think the biggest change for Dutch River is that all the businesses that have been propped up by subsidies for so long will finally be able to stand on their own."

"So you're telling me I should stop being angry at Captain Amato?" said Walter.

"I'd never say that," said Sarah, "but you've got to admit, all that publicity has really helped this little town."

Walter and Sarah had been packing to leave the Marriott Long Wharf when the florid countenance of New York City Police Commissioner Sean Michael Patrick Donahue had suddenly filled the screen under a red CNN *"Breaking News"* banner. He was announcing, he said, that the NYPD, under the direction of Captain Eugene Amato of the Midtown South Precinct, had solved the murders of both Armin August Jaeger of Dutch River, New York, and Charles Martin Sewall of Boston, Massachusetts. During the course of the investigation, he announced, "a magnificent trove of stolen Nazi art" had been discovered. Walter could see Amato, standing just behind Donahue's left shoulder, grinning like a supporting cast member in a grammar school play. Walter's name was never mentioned.

The story had made Page One of the *New York Times* and was followed up by a lengthy piece in the Sunday edition titled, *"Dutch, Reformed: How Murder and Scandal Transformed a Small Town."*

Curious travelers to Saratoga, Lake George, and Lake Placid started getting off the highway to take a look at the little town, and it wasn't long before reports started to trickle back to New York City about the incredible cuisine at Avery's Restaurant. The *Times* restaurant critic declared it to be the "culinary discovery of the year," comparing it to the unearthing of King Tut's tomb. Adam had to hire two sous-chefs and a waitstaff, and it was now harder to get a table at Avery's than at Rao's.

Adam was conflicted about his newfound success, but he couldn't help being proud of the fact that his restaurant's notoriety and prosperity had trickled down rapidly to the rest of the village. "Margie's Essentials" was now stocking the latest designer fashions from New York City, and she could barely keep her shelves stocked. The law firm of Maas & Maas was thriving as long empty buildings along Main Street were snapped up and new businesses opened. Sarah and Walter had received multiple unsolicited offers to buy the farm, all of which they had firmly rejected.

"Have you heard the news from Boston?" said Levi.

"What's that?" said Sarah.

"After what was a reportedly 'lengthy but cordial' meeting with the 'doyenne of Boston's philanthropic community,' Abby Peabody Sewall, Boris Nevsky has announced that he is donating the money for a new wing to be built onto the Museum of Fine Arts to house half of the art collection recovered from Armin Jaeger's vault, to which he is adding numerous pieces from his own private collection."

"Wow," said Julie, "and what about the other half?"

"Abby has been appointed by a judicial conservator to oversee its distribution to the major museums of the world," said Levi.

"That's going to be quite a project, considering the egos involved in the art world," said Julie.

"They won't stand a chance against Abby, trust me," said Walter.

"And guess who she hired as an administrative assistant to help her out?" said Levi.

"No, really?" said Walter.

"Yes, really," said Levi. "Dot Ferguson, except she is now going by 'Dorothea.'"

"Well, despite everything," said Sarah, "I guess I can't wish the woman any ill. We're too lucky to do that, aren't we, Walter?"

"You've got that right," he said.

"Have you heard anything from Sergeant Mayhew, Walter?" said Levi.

"As a matter of fact, I just talked to him yesterday."

"How's he doing?" said Bert, from the far end of the table.

"He's doing well," said Walter. "After threatening to fire him if he didn't take himself off the case, the Massachusetts State Police tried to turn him into an unsung hero in order to garner a share of the credit for themselves. But David wasn't having any of it, and he quit."

"So what's he going to do now?" said Sarah.

"He was offered the job of chief of security at Old Sturbridge Village. The guy who'd had the job for the past thirty years just retired, and David, being a local kid, was the first person they thought of to replace him. They even offered him a raise from his cop's salary. He accepted on the spot."

"I'm happy for him," said Levi.

"So am I," said Walter. "I think it's all he ever wanted. And to top it all off, he and his wife are expecting a baby."

There was the sound of tinkling crystal as Bert Steffus gently tapped his fork against his water glass. He rose from his chair, wincing only slightly as his weak ankle gave him a twinge.

"Adam and I have been rehearsing you folks all week," he said, "and now it's time."

They all rose, and as their way of saying grace, this unlikely collection of good people gathered around a wooden table in an old farmhouse still haunted by the ghost of its former owner sang "A Mighty Fortress Is Our God," in the original German, of course. All except Detective Lieutenant Walter Hudson, who was tone-deaf.

As his wife would tell anyone, the man was a cop, not a singer.

THE END